Cook
En

~~Michelle Connell~~

http://Michelleconnellwrites.net

Cookie Encounter
Copyright © 2015 Michelle Connell

All rights reserved.

ISBN: 978-0-9968570-1-7 (pbk), ISBN: 978-0-9968570-0-0 (e-bk)

Http://Michelleconnellwrites.net
Illinois, USA

Cover design © Lucy Burton

Cookie Encounter is a work of fiction; all characters are a figment of the author's imagination.

THE HOLY BIBLE, NEW INTERNATIONAL VERSION®, NIV® Copyright © 1973, 1978, 1984, 2011 by Biblica, Inc.® Used by permission. All rights reserved worldwide.

To Darlene ~
Thanks for reading!

For Mike, and our children, Madelyn, Molly, Michael and Mariah; I love you all

Acknowledgements

This book would not be possible without the support of my loving husband, Mike, and my four children. They have put up with my zoning out episodes (listening to characters arguing in my head), our messy house and less than stellar dinners. Thank you for not giving me too hard of a time. I love you all.

To my parents for taking me to the library each week to get new books that continually grew my love for words and stories and for keeping me stocked with notebooks and pens. I love you both.

And I have to thank my friends from Paddle Creek Writers: Susan Korich, Beverly Lindbo, and Patricia Meyers, for pushing me to try National Novel Writing Month (NaNoWriMo) several years ago. Without them, this novel would never have come to pass. Thank you, ladies. It has been a grand adventure writing with you and I thank God for each of you!

A big kudos to my first readers for your input. I also thank Ruby Walker for the medical and hospital issues. Thanks to Al Fennewald for answering my questions about illnesses.

Thanks to Sgt. Kathy Kelsheimer (Ret) for her police procedure help. Thank you all for answering my questions and helping me out! Any mistakes are mine alone.

Cookie Encounter: a Chance Encounter Inspirational Romance by Michelle Connell

Chapter 1

"Finally, something besides a casserole," a tall, clean shaven man with dark hair said in a husky voice.

Startled by his appearance at the door caused a spike in my heart rate. I, Natalie Alexander, nearly gasped for breath as I stared at a familiar face, yet one I'd never seen before.

After ringing the doorbell of what I thought was Mr. Norton's house, I wondered if I was at the right address. This man with warm chocolate eyes, strong jaw line, and darker hair than the elderly Mr. Norton I expected, could be a younger version of him.

A much taller version.

A more leaner and muscular version.

And definitely a more handsome version.

There must be a God after all.

If only. But I refused to let my mind go there. This was not the time. All of these thoughts swirled through my brain while waiting for this guy to say something a little more normal. Like "hello".

This Mr. Norton look-alike stared at me through the glass door looking confident in his crisp oxford and navy slacks. What a strange greeting. I stared back, wondering if he was serious. Perhaps a round foil wrapped plate gave it away. Intelligent, too. A little slow on the manners, perhaps, but otherwise the Richard Castle look-alike seemed intelligent and looked yummy without being overly aware of the fact. My feet shifted awkwardly, my mouth not working. I shivered, waiting.

He finally noticed my plight. "Oh, forgive me. Come in from the cold. My manners completely left me. And I was joking about the casserole. Though anything sure beats another one of those!" He smiled at me.

Maybe he's normal after all. I stepped into the foyer, gingerly knocking the snow off my boots onto the rug. I looked at my plate of cookies, wondering if he would ever take it.

My surprise host leaned down and whispered, "But seriously, how many casseroles can four people eat in a day?"

I couldn't help smiling. I've seen the amount of food that can accumulate for grieving families and knew what he meant.

"I'm Jim's nephew by the way. Nick, last name also Norton. And you are?"

I'm glad I had a moment to digest his comments as it gave me a chance to find my voice. "Natalie. Natalie Alexander from down the street."

We were still standing in the foyer as if Nick kept me there on purpose. We were like new comrades, if that made sense. I shook Nick's offered hand with my mittened one, the other still holding the cookies.

"Come on in, Natalie." Nick backed up and shut the door. "Nice to meet you. Everyone is in the living room." He finally took the plate almost as an afterthought and motioned for me to follow. Slipping off my mittens, I snuck a peek at his left ring finger. Bare. Hmmm.

We walked down a short hall, the walls displaying family photos in varying sizes. In the living room several people sat on plush chairs and overstuffed sofas. This room was considerably warmer than the hallway since a blazing fire radiated welcome heat. The elder Mr. Norton sat in a crimson chair near the fireplace. His crumpled navy cardigan and striped shirt hung limply on his frame as he leaned forward with his head in his hands, his hair flopped over them.

"Uncle," Nick whispered, "this is Natalie from down the street. You've never mentioned your pretty neighbor." Nick softly rested his hand on his uncle's shoulder.

Upon hearing his comments—though Nick whispered them—my internal thermostat rose ten degrees at least. I fingered the mittens in my coat pockets, wondering why Nick wasn't attached. Not that I was interested. Nope.

Then he added, "And she brought cookies. Homemade oatmeal chocolate chip looks like," he said, in a normal tone after peeking under the foil.

Mr. Norton looked up and smiled briefly. "Thank you," he said in a hoarse voice. The poor man looked lost as he flipped his hair back in place. I could see why Nick answered the door.

"I'm so sorry about your wife. If there's anything I can do, let me know."

Mr. Norton nodded and stared at the fireplace. I glanced around the room and saw only white or gray heads except for Nick's. No wonder he had kept me at the door!

I looked back at Nick and he motioned his head toward the kitchen. "He's not doing too well, he's still in shock. She was in fairly good health for 83. I'll miss her though." Bits of conversation trailed behind us as we headed to the kitchen near the front door. Nick gestured toward an empty chair.

"I can't stay, sorry. Mrs. John is waiting for me." I noticed a two-inch stack of envelopes and three plants on the round dining table. I glimpsed a counter lined with square and rectangular dishes covered in foil before we moved closer to the front door. Scents of pastas mingled with brownies and cakes made my mouth water.

"What happened? Was your aunt sick?" I started for the front door, Nick following my lead.

There was a silent pause as he tasted one of my cookies. "Very good, these won't sit around long." He brushed crumbs off his shirt and answered my question. "No, not really. She seemed to have some sort of mild episode with her heart or something and Uncle Nick called for an ambulance. Uncle Nick thinks something happened to her on the way to the hospital, we aren't sure."

"That's too bad. I'd only met your aunt and uncle once at Mr. John's birthday party back in November. It's hard to believe something happened to her."

"Everybody's surprised by it." Nick slid his hands into his pockets, not moving to open the door. He looked directly into my eyes. "I don't recall seeing you before. I think—no, I *know* I would have remembered."

My heart beat faster. "I've only lived here since August."

"Ah. The metro-east is a great place to live," and I thought I heard him say, "and it just got better."

His startling statement nearly caught me off guard. "I didn't know you lived here. Were you at Mr. John's birthday party?" I think— no, I *know* I would have remembered.

"I was invited, but it was teacher conference night."

"What do you do? Er, I mean, what do you teach?" Work, brain. Now I'm butchering the English language with a teacher of all things.

Nick tried not to smile, but went on, "Freshmen and Junior English."

"Wow, that's great. I'm a writer. Do you happen to know anyone interested in starting a writer's club? Students or coworkers perhaps?" If I believed in fate, this would be a great example. I hadn't had any great ideas of starting a new group after moving to the area.

"I do."

I glanced back at his face taking in his grin and tilted my head waiting for him to share whom he was talking about.

After a few seconds of silence, he announced, "Me."

"Oh!" Suddenly the lint in my mittens seemed important. This was too much. I'd been surprised too often in such a short time; I didn't think I could take any more. I tried not to let his good looks distract me and tuned into the words coming from his mouth.

"...I've always wanted to get around to writing more."

From the kitchen, I could hear a clock ding the quarter hour. I sucked in my breath. "I forgot about Mrs. John. She's got water boiling for hot cocoa. Sorry, but I better go." I pulled out my mittens and slid them onto my hands, not that my hands needed any additional warmth.

"Would you like to get together sometime and continue this conversation?" Nick asked, opening the door. "I'd like to talk more about writing."

"Uh,...I work at home most of the time, but occasionally go to the coffee shop on Main Street. I'll be there in the morning." I didn't expect him to come, under the circumstances.

"Some cousins and other relatives are coming in later today, making it easier for me to escape. What time?"

"Not before nine. I try to exercise and clear my head before writing." Did I just say that out loud?

"I'll stop by then. I enjoyed talking shop with you." He grinned at me before opening the glass door.

"Same here. Perhaps I'll see you tomorrow. Oh, and tell your uncle he's in my thoughts. I don't want to bother him again." The reason for coming almost escaped me, with Nick's presence throwing me for a loop.

"I'll let him know. Thanks for stopping by with your delicious cookies. See you tomorrow."

He seemed positive about tomorrow, but I wasn't so sure with his family grieving. I walked through the January cold and retraced my steps to Mrs. John's. Oh, dear. What was I getting myself into now? I didn't have the time or desire to start dating. Not Nick or anyone. I couldn't. Who was I kidding?

Snow started to fall again as I walked. Our neighborhood was an eclectic mix of older, stately homes with smaller bungalows here and there. Mascoutah (pronounced mu-scoot-uh) is not quite two-hundred years old, with some original buildings still standing on Main Street. The town is quite charming, which is partly what drew me here in the first place. The people are super friendly and willing to help in any way.

The air was silent as I trudged through the snow, bending with the increasing wind. I thought back to the party in November where I met Nick's aunt and uncle. There had been a crowd gathered at the John's house, to celebrate Mr. John's 65th birthday.

    The party was a few weeks before the Giving Thanks holiday. I'd mingled among the guests, some older, some young. Mrs. John invited me saying it would be a good opportunity to get to know some of the neighbors. I thought, why not? I'm usually holed up in my home office, so this was an excuse to get out and meet people.

    That day Mrs. John's kitchen table had displayed three delectable desserts. These were not your run-of-the-mill birthday cakes. One was a creampuff concoction with layers of pudding, whipped topping and drizzled chocolate syrup. The second was a pumpkin and nut cake. And the third was a chocolate and cherry creation, also with whipped topping. How could I possibly choose only one from such an array? I didn't! I followed suit of a couple of other guests and asked for a small sliver of each. The chocolate and cherry dessert turned out to be my favorite.

    Mr. and Mrs. John were great hosts, making sure I felt welcome and introducing me to everyone there. I vaguely remember Nick's aunt and uncle among the crowd.

    I shook the memory from my mind before knocking on Mrs. John's door and letting myself in since she was expecting me. I'd stopped by earlier to get Mr. Norton's house number so I could deliver the cookies.

    "Hello again, dear. Did you meet Mr. Norton, Nick Norton, that is?" Her knowing smile was wide and expectant. Perhaps that's why she declined to go with me.

    How did she know? "I did. He seems very sure of himself." I sat down at her kitchen table and slipped out of my coat, hanging it on the back of the chair. Her table though, was uncluttered with only a doily in the center displaying a purple-flowered African violet.

"Ah, I suspected so. He's handsome isn't he?" Her wrinkled hands poured water into two mugs and stirred the cocoa with a spoon. She pushed a steaming mug toward me. The cup said, 'Greatest Grandma'. I smiled. "He's also very available," she said, raising her eyebrows slightly before returning the kettle to the stove.

I carefully sipped the steaming cocoa. I had to tread carefully here. "Well, who knows? He certainly seems nice, but a little confident." I didn't know what else to say. I hadn't fully digested the encounter with Nick yet. And I certainly wasn't expecting to meet him or anyone else that made my heart gallop like a winning race horse. But this was ridiculous; we just met. And I wasn't sure if I could handle a romantic relationship.

"How is your book coming along, dear? Are you still working on the one you told us about at the party? The one about the crazy writers?" She pushed a loose gray curl behind her ear and sat at the table across from me.

"Yes. It's coming along slowly. All of the characters write different kinds of stories from westerns to science fiction. And those genres are so different from what I usually write. I don't know much about either one, but all my characters belong in a writing group and someone challenged them to write a book in their genre in one month, so they took it."

"I don't write much of anything except letters and email. When the computer doesn't have a virus or something else wrong with it." She blew on her cocoa. "My kids have talked to me about texting, but I don't see the need."

I took another sip of my beverage. It was finally cool enough to drink without burning my tongue. I helped myself to a slice of pumpkin bread she had on a platter. "Good bread."

"Thank you, it's left from Christmas. Every year I bake too much, but I can't help it. I love to bake."

"Me, too. I just made cookies this morning, so that's what I took to Mr. Norton's." I giggled.

"What's so funny?"

I told her what Nick had said about the cookies when I got there.

Mrs. John chuckled too. "Yes, I suppose if you just met and that's the first thing he said, it would rattle you. But he really is a nice young man."

"Maybe he doesn't like casseroles," I said.

"Oh, he eats anything other people make. I understand he's a horrible cook according to his mother. But she tried."

"Most men aren't good in the kitchen. My dad's cooking was terrible. Whenever mom went out of town, my brother and I always tried to eat at a friend's house or pick up fast food when we could drive."

"I suppose that's true. But there are a few good men who know their way around in the kitchen—like that Bobby guy on television. You're right though, I don't know too many myself."

"I don't either. My brother is as bad as my dad, if not worse. One time, he tried to make some sort of pasta dish for dinner when he had a girl over and made the biggest mess I've ever seen. When mom came home and saw it, she banned him from the kitchen for life."

Mrs. John laughed. "What would men do without us?" She reached over and patted my hand. Hers was wrinkled and soft from lotion, mine smooth and slender.

"Starve, I guess."

"Well, if you and Nick get together, I'm sure it will be a done deal if you ever make dinner for him." She winked.

I blushed. And not for the first time today. I finished my piece of pumpkin bread and the last sip of my cocoa. "Thank you for the delicious snack. I better get back to my office and get some work done before supper." I got up from the table and slipped into my coat.

Mrs. John walked me to the door. "Thank you for keeping an old lady company and for the laughs."

I gave her a hug and thanked her again for the cocoa. I didn't notice the frigid air as I walked home thinking about the conversations with Nick and Mrs. John. Would Nick show up tomorrow? Could we get a writer's group going? That would be great.

Though I had lived here several months now, I still didn't know many people and didn't know where to plug into a writer's group. There were many online, but I would like to find one that met in person somewhere around here.

I checked my mailbox beside the front door before going in. Though Mr. Norton's and Mrs. John's houses were similar bungalows, my house was a huge Victorian with a wrap-around porch. I loved houses with character and this one definitely qualified. The white paint peeled in some places and the gingerbread trim could use some touching up, otherwise the house was certainly in great shape for its age.

I'd always loved older homes, especially the house my grandparents had. When I was a child, I enjoyed exploring in the attic and playing on the upstairs landing with my brother and cousins. The landing alone was big enough for three billiard tables.

The landing in mine wasn't as big as grandma's, but it was large enough for me and Felix, my mischievous cat. I even had a dumbwaiter that worked, which I didn't use of course. Although there was a back staircase off the kitchen, I preferred the wide wooden staircase off the hall. I loved the sound of the tap-tap-tap echo as I went up or down the stairs.

My upstairs office looked out over the flower garden and served a perfect retreat to observe and think when I couldn't write. It was now snow-covered, but I knew from my first viewing of the house that in the spring and summer the garden would again display a splendor of color from the dianthus, snapdragons, petunias, and impatiens planted there.

When I decided to move south to Illinois from Wisconsin, my brother Ashton thought I was crazy. "You don't know what you're doing," he argued. "You've never owned a house before and now you're going to buy one over four hundred miles from home?"

Well, so far things had worked out. The house was sound as far as I could tell. Except for the occasional weird buzzing I heard from the top floor somewhere. But since it passed inspection, it has been a good first house. When I moved in, the overgrown lawn needed mowing right away. I quickly found a service that promised they wouldn't use those obnoxious leaf blowers. There's nothing worse than being in the middle of a good writing spell and having that awful cacophony jar me out of my concentration. Those machines should be outlawed as disturbing the peace violators.

I tossed my coat on the coat tree after going inside, leaving the mail on the small hall table to deal with later. I worked for a couple hours on a new pamphlet for an electric company before realizing Felix was rubbing against my leg. I rescued him from the local animal shelter shortly after moving in so I'd have some company. "Ok, Ok, I'll get your chow, settle down." I rubbed his back for a minute, before heading downstairs. Felix continued to meow until I had enough food in his dish to satisfy him. He wasn't a finicky eater, but when he was ready to eat, he was hungry *now*.

At bedtime, Felix raced me up the stairs. It was his nightly ritual. He knows when I'm going to bed, no matter what time it is. He always races to the top of the stairs and turns around to wait for me. Then he tries to trip me when I'm going into the bathroom. "Oh, Felix! If I didn't know any better, I'd think you did this on purpose every night."

"Meow," he replied innocently.

"I don't buy it," I told him.

Felix normally slept at the foot of the bed on a folded towel to keep the fur he sheds to one spot, but occasionally he managed his way up to my pillow. More than once I've woken with a feeling that I was being watched only to find him staring at me. The first time he did that it spooked me, but I'm used to it now.

As I readied for bed, I wondered again if Nick would show up at the coffee shop in the morning. I didn't want to come across like a love-sick teenager, but I secretly hoped he would. Then I thought, could I even cope with a guy right now? Perhaps the better question was would he even want me?

Chapter 2

The next morning, a Saturday, I exercised to the nerdy music on my DVD. And after a quick shower, gathered my laptop, a couple writing magazines, a pen and notebook for a writing session at the coffee shop. During breaks from writing, I'd read and take notes from the magazines.

I gave Felix fresh water and added his lunch portion to his dish before pulling on my coat and stuffing my feet into boots for the six-block walk. Pale sunlight barely made a dent through yesterday's clouds and the temperature held below freezing. Yesterday's snow fall only amounted to an inch or so, but it was messy and slick. Though the calendar said January, some houses still wore Christmas lights and wreaths.

At the end of my street, I took a right and headed for downtown, if you could call it that. I wondered for a town with less than ten thousand people, if it could be considered a 'downtown'?

Mascoutah was a great family town, with fall festivals, ice cream days and a homecoming in the summer with a popular parade where children happily collected candy thrown into the street by those in the passing floats. I had just missed the homecoming parade by a week or two, but had seen the pictures in the local paper. So far, I'd been to the chili cook-off with the Johns' in October and the Christmas parade in December. It looked like a lot of work went into the floats for the parade. I shivered, remembering how cold it had been that Friday night and how lonely I'd been, even in a crowd of people.

Anyway, today I headed for The Common Grounds Coffee Shop on Main Street between a bank and a flower shop. Talk about heavenly scents to work by: fragrant roses and carnations and fresh-brewed coffee. I love the aroma of coffee, but can't bring myself to drink the stuff. After trying several brands, different flavors with or without sugar and cream, I still can't stand it. Instead, I have a cup of cocoa along with a cinnamon roll or muffin.

I entered the small café and stood in front of the display case with cake platters lined with paper doilies. Today the muffin choices made it difficult to decide: chocolate chip, pumpkin, or morning glory. Since I had pumpkin bread yesterday with Mrs. John, I chose the chocolate chip. You can never go wrong with chocolate. I carried my tray to a table by the window and plugged in the laptop. Though the window provided appreciated light, it was the outlet underneath that made my seat a prime location. As the machine booted up, I savored the muffin and cocoa.

Several tables were occupied, but the noise level was such it shouldn't bother my concentration. And the light jazz music playing shouldn't interfere either, since there weren't any words to the music.

At least winter had its redeeming qualities: eating and baking cakes, muffins and cookies; and consuming lots of delicious hot cocoa. I didn't care for snow, but didn't have to drive in it much since I worked at home most days. Though I grew up in Wisconsin, I never got used to winter driving.

While eating, I wondered if Nick would show up. It seemed to me that if there were a death in the family, he would be occupied. But every family is different and I had no idea how large of an extended family he had or what his role would be.

Finished with my muffin, I turned to my work in progress or WIP, and wrote about my character, Joe, who was writing a western. Besides the typical cowboy riding off into the sunset, I knew little about the western genre, having not read any. A trip to the library for research was in order. I set the laptop aside and read my magazines instead. The library could wait.

I was engrossed in an article on writing more efficiently when a slightly familiar male voice asked, "May I join you?" I looked up to see Nick smiling down at me. It hurt my neck to look up that far, so I nodded yes. The magazine dropped to the floor. We both reached for it. He picked it up, glanced at the title and handed it back. "Thanks. Let me make some room." The magazines slid too far and fell off the table, making a smacking sound. I scooped them up and shoved them into my computer bag and closed the laptop, not daring to move it.

"Hi. How's your uncle doing this morning?" I noticed the beginning of a smile on Nick's face. I ignored it, trying to keep my own face from flushing.

"Good morning." Nick slid out of his coat, resting it on the chair next to him. Even in a navy sweatshirt and jeans, he looked good. Yesterday he must have been in work clothes. Nick continued, and I tried to pay attention. "His doctor gave him something to help him sleep. He managed to eat some toast and have a cup of coffee this morning, but that was all. He's in good hands though with my aunts and cousins."

"It must be tough. How long were they married?" I traced the rim of the mug with my finger while I listened.

"Forty-three years, I think. They were both a little older when they married. The Norton's seem to take longer than the average bear to find their mate." Nick sipped his coffee.

"Wow. I hope whoever I marry, we're married that long. I don't know though, not many couples stay together anymore." I sighed.

"Unfortunately that can be true. Doesn't have to be though."

Just then my phone beeped. "Excuse me for a minute," I said before answering it.

"Hello?" I turned away from the table, trying to concentrate. I heard a voice I knew, but couldn't place it right away. "Oh, hi, Luke. How have you been?" I glanced at Nick, who was looking out the window.

I listened to Luke for a minute, snatching a sip of my cooling cocoa. "Sure, I have plenty of room. For how long?"

I nodded. "Yes, I can text it to you later." I turned back to the table and flipped open my notebook to a blank page and jotted some notes. "Sounds good." I disconnected.

"An old friend is coming to visit. He's searching for a new job in St. Louis and the metro area."

Nick nodded.

I sipped my cocoa not sure what to say.

Then Nick mentioned writing together. "Would you like to meet at the library one day a week to write?"

"I would. What day is best for you?" Since my schedule was flexible, it didn't matter to me.

"How does Wednesday afternoon sound? Four o'clock?"

"Sounds great."

He looked pleased and added, "By the grandfather clock?"

I nodded.

He smiled at me, as if he knew something I didn't. He wrote his number on a napkin in case I had to cancel. I put it in my purse.

"I'll see you Wednesday afternoon, then."

"Sounds good. Thanks for stopping by."

"My pleasure." He got up from the table. "I better get back to the house and see what funeral plans are being made. I need to know for sure if I need a day off. I'll have to call a sub this afternoon."

"Oh, joy. Your poor students."

"Oh, no. It's poor sub, believe me!"

I watched him take his coffee cup to the counter and he waved before going out the door. I waved back.

After he left, I read through the magazines, taking note of four articles I wanted to save. Then I gathered my laptop and reading materials and headed for the library. My brain certainly wasn't in work mode anymore. Go figure it would be a man to blame.

The library was fairly new and modern and had all the items most people were interested in. The granite and stone building had two pillars on a small porch. The doors were of heavy wood and took some strength to open.

The library was equipped with Wi-Fi, several computers, DVDs and CDs and of course, books.

I walked in and headed for the computerized card catalog. I looked up westerns and found a few on the shelves. Another great thing about this small town library was that it was connected to a whole slew of libraries. You could check out a book on almost anything if it was in their system. It certainly came in handy.

"Hi, Natalie. How are you today?" Fran, the head librarian asked.

"Doing great, thanks."

"Good. I'm catching up on some backlog since it's been slow today. You reading westerns now?" She slid down her glasses to peer at me.

I laughed. "Not really. One of my characters is writing a western and I don't think I've ever read one in my life. So, I guess you could say it was research."

Fran nodded. "Well, you picked some winners. Louis L'Amour wrote some of the best. You might actually like them."

"I might. I'm not opposed to reading one, just never have. Don't be alarmed if in a few weeks, I check out some fantasy or sci-fi books."

After smiling she said, "We'll be here. We have those too."

I thanked her, adding the books to my bag and walked home. I started a fire in the fireplace since I would be staying put the rest of the day. I put the computer on the coffee table and turned it on. If I read parts of the books, I could get enough of an idea of what to write in my own book.

I took a lunch break and started some chili in the crock-pot. I would reheat it tomorrow since Luke was arriving mid to late afternoon. Then I started some dough for cinnamon rolls since I was in the baking mood.

While they baked, I cleaned the house. Felix acted excited, not quite knowing what was going on. From the bathroom and the guestroom, I could hear that strange faint buzzing sound again. I'd heard it a few times when moving in, but now it seemed a little bit louder. Maybe when Luke was here, he could help me figure it out.

That night I went to bed wondering why Nick was yet unattached. After what happened to me six years ago, I've not been close to any guy. Most likely Nick was looking for someone who was sweet, pure, intelligent, loving, and thoughtful. Some might say I was most of those things.

Except one.

Chapter 3

I took too long upstairs, putting clean sheets on the guest bed and making sure it was dusted and aired out a few minutes before Luke's visit. Felix demanded his breakfast, yowling at me from the just made bed. He begged and meowed like he hadn't eaten in weeks. I didn't believe his antics.

Right after breakfast—his and mine—the phone rang. It was Ashton. "Hi, big brother. What's up?"

"Not much, just checking to see if you're still there and your house is still standing."

"Very funny. Yes, we are both standing. Tall. Straight. Stable."

"Ok, already. Are you sure you won't talk to mom and dad? They worry about you being so far away."

"Are you kidding? After the way they treated me and everything?" I puffed out air, lifting my bangs off my forehead.

"I know they didn't handle it the best, but they're only human."

"Anything else?" I was done with this sore topic.

"Nope, guess not. How's the weather down there?"

"Cold and colder. Some snow, but not much."

"Here, it's a lot of snow and cold. Take care of yourself."

"Thanks for checking in. Bye." I hung up, frustrated. On to other things. Like preparing for company.

At four-thirty I answered the doorbell.

"Hi, Natalie. Thanks for letting me come."

"Hi, Luke, come on in." I gave him a quick hug. Luke was good looking, and a friendly guy, but I always got a hint of something not quite right about him whenever I had been around him in our former writers group. He didn't scare me or anything, but I remained cautious. "You can bring your bags up and I'll show you to your room."

"This is a nice place, Nat." He looked around, admiring the crown molding on the ceiling and the woodwork of the staircase.

"Thanks. It was a steal. And didn't need a lot of work, either. I think the owner died and the son just wanted it off his hands."

"Good timing, then."

I nodded, entering his room. "Here you go, and the bathroom is across the hall. We have to share it."

"Not a problem. I'll just put my things in here." He opened the closet and hung what I assumed were his interview clothes.

"Need any help?"

"No, I just have the two bags. Thanks."

"I'll be downstairs."

He nodded, and continued to hang his clothes. A faint buzzing surrounded me, and I looked for a fly, but didn't see anything. It sounded bigger than that, but I didn't know what it was. After giving Luke the nickel tour, we sat in the living room and caught up with each other's news.

"So how have you been? Life been treating you well?" Luke sat down at the opposite end of the sofa. I had gotten us some tea, his iced, mine hot.

"Pretty well, yes. Writing has kept me busy, plus meeting new people and getting to know the area. So what happened at TK Foods?"

"Oh, they decided I didn't know what I was doing after three bosses and getting conflicting orders. They let me go. I've been on unemployment for a month now. But, there are a lot of companies in this area where I could find work. I really appreciate your putting me up, Nat."

"Not a problem. Come and go as you need. I usually work in my office, or at the coffee shop on Main Street. I'll show you around town if you want."

"That would be nice. I brought my laptop, too." He swigged the last of his tea and set his glass on the table.

"My first interview is in a suburb of St. Louis, and I already have the directions in my phone. It's at ten tomorrow."

"Ok. We can breakfast beforehand."

"Oh, I wasn't expecting that."

"But you have to eat, Luke."

"I know, but I don't want you to go to any trouble."

"It's not any trouble. I'll take two plates out of the cabinet instead of one. It's really no big deal." Felix sat on my lap, and I rubbed his back. He seemed a little leery of Luke for some reason. Probably just being a scaredy-cat.

Luke finally agreed to breakfast after I told him I'd just baked some cinnamon rolls from scratch.

Luke was one of the regulars from the writers group I missed. We discussed our writing, and he filled me in on what had been happening with the group. We each had a bowl of chili and some crackers and after dinner I gave Luke a quick tour of Mascoutah, pointing out the café where I wrote, the library, and the essentials like the gas station, banks and an ATM in case Luke needed them while in town.

It had been a cloudy day, with wind blowing from the north. The white snow on the ground together with the glow of streetlights helped illuminate our short tour; otherwise it would have been difficult to see anything.

"Nice town," he said.

"Believe it or not, small town living suits me."

In his seat, Luke turned to me. "I've missed you at the writers group. It hasn't been the same." He rested his hand on my forearm.

I reached to adjust the heater, making it necessary for Luke to remove his hand. His touch threw me off guard. I wasn't used to being around guys after my trauma. Nobody in my former writing group knew about what happened, and I wasn't about to share it with Luke. He was a great guy and a good writer, but I wasn't interested in him as boyfriend material.

"Anybody in your life?" he asked.

I shook my head. "Nope, and that's just fine with me."

Luke grinned, but I wasn't sure why. I didn't want to know.

"Well, you still have time. Of course, I don't know what you're looking for."

"I'm not looking."

Luke's eyes grew round and his jaw dropped. "I-uh-not that it's any of my business, but why not?" he sputtered.

"Personal reasons." That was enough of this conversation.

Luke dropped it, but I could tell he was curious. I pulled back into the driveway and into the garage. We walked across the yard to the front door. My garage was unattached, the only thing I didn't like about the house. But only in winter was it a problem.

We removed our coats and shoes by the door. "I'm going to study some notes, before turning in. Good night," Luke said, walking up the stairs.

"Good night. See you in the morning."

I sat in the living room, trying to read. I couldn't focus. I hoped Luke didn't think I would be interested. He was good-looking enough, with broad shoulders and a ready smile. But he didn't quite have that GQ caliber like Nick had. Not that I was looking.

I wondered what Nick was doing right now. Maybe I would see him on Wednesday. If he showed up.

In the meantime, I had Luke as a guest for a while and that was enough to keep me occupied. I wasn't used to having anyone around, since having a college roommate. I hope I didn't come to regret it.

The wind whipped around the north side of the house and I made sure everything was secure for the night. Felix and I went up to bed. Luke's light was still on. I quietly used the bathroom and went to my room, leaving the hall light on as usual. A few minutes later I heard Luke in the bathroom and then all was quiet. He turned the hall light off, and I got up to turn it back on.

A few minutes later, it was off. I turned it back on. Luke opened his door. "Natalie, do you leave the hall light on?"

"Yeah." I looked at the floor.

"Sorry. Good night."

I nodded and went to bed. It wasn't long before I fell into a deep sleep.

"You're never going to compete against me in debate and make a spectacle of me again!" the menacing voice breathed in my ear, sending chills down my spine. I swallowed hard and fought to get away.

I kicked his legs off me and tried to run. I couldn't move. Sweat and tears ran into my eyes and down my face. I scratched them away. A few minutes later it was too late. After the attack I ran to the car and drove home, my interior light on the whole way. I took the longest hot shower of my life. "Never! Never, can I forgive you!"

Suddenly I sat straight up, gasping for air. It had been months since I'd had a nightmare. I looked at the clock. The glowing red numbers told me it was only a few minutes past two. I plopped back onto my pillow and cried for the umpteenth time. Felix jumped back on the bed, curling up at my feet. My screaming and kicking no doubt freaked him out. I wondered if Luke being here had triggered the nightmare. If so, I would have to live with it. Hopefully my cries didn't wake him.

A few hours later, I awoke to the aroma of coffee. Again, I couldn't figure out where I was. Why did I smell coffee in my house? It took my brain a few minutes to recall Luke was here. Though I didn't drink coffee, I owned a simple coffeemaker and kept a small bag of grounds in the freezer for guests.

I quickly dressed and went down to see what he was up to. I entered the kitchen to see a well-dressed Luke cooking eggs and bacon on my stove. I hadn't even cooked bacon and eggs on it myself yet. Seeing Luke dressed up was another first. It made a difference in his appearance. He used to come to writer's group in jeans and a t-shirt or a polo.

"Good morning, Natalie."

"Morning," I rubbed sleep from my eyes.

"Did you sleep well? I thought I heard you cry out." Luckily Luke turned back to his cooking.

My face flushed. "Oh, sorry."

"Not a problem." He stopped stirring the eggs. A look of concern crossed his face. He put down the fork. "Are you Ok?"

"It was just a nightmare."

He nodded and took a plate, serving up his aromatic breakfast. "I hope you don't mind me helping out in the kitchen."

"You didn't have to—"

"It's the least I could do. I don't expect you to cater to me. I just a need a 'home base' to speak of for a few days until I figure out where I'm settling."

I nodded and sat at the island. "Smells good. Looks good." I took a bite. "Tastes good."

Luke smiled, taking a seat next to me. "Good." He removed an apron that kept bacon grease from splattering his clothes. His slate blue oxford matched his tan slacks perfectly. A blue and silver tie draped over the bar stool.

He left for his interview and I cleaned up the kitchen before heading to my office to work. Embarrassment over my nightmare clogged my brain. I hoped I didn't have one again while Luke was here. Every so often I would have them for a few days and then they would go away again.

I turned on the computer in the office and stared out the window. This was my first winter here, and the trees all lost their leaves ages ago, looking naked against a bleak sky. I wondered if I would ever stop having these nightmares and if I could find someone who would love me. Putting these thoughts behind me, I got to work. I had a pamphlet to finish for a corporation in Indiana.

The net proceeds from this job would boost my checking account considerably. Extra cushion was always a good thing. Luckily I wasn't high maintenance and didn't have any bills except the mortgage and living expenses. At least my parents did one thing right. They taught me the value of a dollar and how to avoid debt if at all possible.

Luke got back around one. "How did it go?" I went downstairs for a break.

"I think it went well. We talked quite a while and then I drove around the area. I should hear something by Thursday."

"That's good. So what's next?"

"An interview here in Illinois, for a state job. Most likely won't get it, but it's another interview for the unemployment. That one's Wednesday morning at eleven."

"Make yourself at home. I was thinking of making pasta for dinner, how does that sound?"

"Would you mind if I took you out?"

"You don't have to do that, your funds are limited and—"

"Nat, I'm not in the poor house. Besides, I have savings and investments. I'm not homeless."

"I don't want to—"

"Where would you like to go?" He took my elbow and led me to the sofa.

I paused before speaking. Apparently I didn't have a choice. "Um, there's a nice Italian place down the street," I suggested.

"Great. Six?"

"That's fine. If you're sure."

"I'm sure. I'm going up to get out of this monkey suit. Do you have a place I can iron out my clothes?"

I set up the ironing board for him in the laundry room in the basement. When he came back up, he asked if I had work to do. I shook my head.

"Can we look at some writing?"

"Sure. I'll get my laptop." I went upstairs to get the novel in rough draft on the machine.

He was booting his up when I rejoined him. I sat next to him on the sofa and we discussed his work in progress until it was dinner time. He insisted on driving. I almost felt like a prisoner of my guest. Luke was just being a gentleman, but slightly over-bearing. I had known him pretty well from up north. He had had a girl friend once, but it didn't last. I never found out why and never asked. I wondered if he was a little too pushy.

We sat in a booth and looked over menus. The glowing candles on each table made the room warm and inviting. Briefly I wondered if I would ever eat here with Nick. Luke was updating me on the group members and their current projects. A new member had joined after I left and Luke said he didn't really like him or his writing. "He seems a little pompous," he finished.

"Maybe he's nervous about being the newest guy and is trying to be macho about it."

"Could be, I suppose. I didn't think of that." Luke sat back. "You've always been positive and give people the benefit of the doubt. I think that's why I liked you."

"Luke, I'm just an ordinary person. That's all." I rested my chin on my hand. My stomach was telling me food better come soon.

"I'm not so sure about that." He reached to put his hand on mine.

Just then a husky voice said, "Hi, Natalie."

I yanked my hand back, feeling caught. "Oh, hi, Nick. Nick, this is Luke Powers who's staying with me for a few days."

I gathered my composure and slowed my heart back to normal while they exchanged hellos and shook hands. "Will I be seeing you both Wednesday afternoon?"

"Yes, looking forward to it," Luke answered. Earlier while working on our books, I had told him about our writer's meeting.

"See you later then, enjoy your dinner." Nick left, holding a takeout box.

"You like him?" Luke asked, watching his back.

"Hard to say, we just met a couple days ago." I told Luke about the encounter, leaving out my personal thoughts regarding Nick. "He teaches English at the high school."

"What does he write?" Luke sipped his root beer.

I told him what Nick told me the day I met him. "He doesn't write as much as he'd like. That's why we're thinking of starting a group."

"That would be great for you. In your forum emails you said you hoped to find one."

"Yeah, I hope we can get something going. I don't know who else is interested in the area, but we'll put a notice in the library."

The rest of the evening went fine and I fell into bed, tired. I hoped the nightmares stayed away.

****

Tuesday was cold and gray so I slept in. Luke said he was going to the library to check on emails and job ads. When he got back, we were going to a movie and dinner. I was looking forward to it, but hoped Luke didn't think anything of it.

During the movie, Luke put his arm around the back of my seat, and I kept waiting for him to rub my neck or shoulder, making me lose concentration on the movie. Since Luke knew I wasn't looking for a relationship, I hoped he wouldn't push the issue. I tried to keep my hand on my drink and the other on the arm of the seat. It was a big relief when we left. I was so stressed out; I hardly paid attention to the movie.

"Did you like it?" Luke asked as we walked to his car.

"It was okay," I lied. I didn't know if it was or not.

"Yeah, it could have been better."

I went to bed, relieved the night was over.

****

Wednesday morning started out bright and sunny and grew gradually cloudy throughout the day. Luke left for his interview after breakfast and I showered and cleaned the bathroom and vacuumed the house. I put beef stew in the crock pot since both Luke and Nick would be here for dinner. I had to change our plans slightly since I now had a house guest. Nick didn't hesitate to come to dinner when I asked. I also started another batch of cinnamon rolls for a snack. The pan from the other day was long gone, with Luke around.

In between cooking and cleaning tasks I worked on the novel and played with Felix. He was quite spoiled.

By the time Luke got back, it had started to snow. I was glad I had a hot dinner cooking for us.

I had called Nick yesterday asking if we could meet at my place since Luke was staying with me. When I offered to make dinner, he readily agreed.

"How did it go?" I asked after Luke changed and settled on the sofa.

"I'm not sure. It was hard to read the guy. I answered all his questions, but we didn't really connect, know what I mean?"

I nodded.

"Anyway, probably won't get that one. But that's all right. I still have resumes out I haven't heard on yet."

By the time Nick arrived, the stew smelled divine and made our mouths water. We sat in the living room, Luke and I at opposite ends of the sofa, Nick in the wing chair. I kept plenty of space between us. Nick and I discussed what we wanted most out of our group while Luke listened and made suggestions.

"Let's recap and then eat. I'm starved." I figured if the aromas from the kitchen were making my stomach growl, surely it was making theirs.

"Sounds good," they said in unison.

"We're going to meet Wednesday afternoons, write for a while and send in something for critiquing by Friday night and have it ready by the following Wednesday. And occasional meetings on Saturday mornings as our schedule allows. Right?"

Both of them nodded.

"Good. Let's eat. Luke, you can set the table, Nick will you put a quick salad together and I'll get the biscuits in the oven and get the stew on the table."

"Yes, ma'am." Luke saluted.

Nick found salad ingredients in the fridge and I gave him a bowl. We sat down a few minutes later and before Nick took a bite he bowed his head.

We ate in silence a few minutes before Nick said, "This is delicious, Natalie. Thanks for feeding us."

Luke seconded his statement. I watched both of them eat like they hadn't eaten for days. I didn't have to worry about what to do with any leftovers. There weren't going to be any. Nick was on his third biscuit and Luke on his fourth while I sat in a daze.

"Can we have writer's group every day?" Nick asked while scraping his plate.

We chuckled and cleared the table, and then I loaded the dishwasher. Nick followed me to the kitchen. "Thanks for a great evening, and dinner. Both were wonderful," Nick said.

"You're welcome. I'll think about what to make next week."

"If tonight was any indication, it'll be tasty. What should I bring?"

"How about a salad?"

"Salad is doable." Nick leaned on the island, rubbing his finger on the surface. "I really did enjoy the dinner with you both." We walked back to the living room. "Good luck with your job search, Luke," Nick said.

"Hey, thanks."

"Good night," Nick said.

"Good night." I shut the door.

"He seems all right," Luke said. We sat in the living room, a roaring fire going thanks to the two pyros in the house. They had been like little kids, adding kindling and logs like they were in a fire-building contest.

Luke and I sat in companionable silence, digesting our dinner. It was comical watching the two of them, as if they were in a secret game of tug-of-war for my attention. They made me smile, at least for the moment. But there was no use in either of them playing for my affections.

****

The next morning Luke got a call and was offered a position from one of his interviews. "Care to go apartment hunting with me?" he asked after hanging up.

"Congratulations! When do you start?"

"They're giving me a few weeks to find a place and get moved."

"Great. Give me an hour?"

He nodded. "I'll pack my bags."

I went upstairs and finished a rough draft of my project. I turned everything off and fed Felix his lunch. I slipped off my slippers and put on my boots since two more inches of snow fell yesterday.

Luke cleared the new snow off his car with a long-handled brush and we headed across the river. "What kinds of amenities are you looking for?" I asked as I pulled a notepad from my purse.

"Let's see. The job is in St. Charles, a fairly large city. Don't have to have a pool or gym, but laundry facilities would be nice. Definitely a garage. Balcony for the grill. Two bedrooms, for guests/ office space. No pets."

"Shouldn't be too hard. I don't know much about St. Charles but it's a nice town."

"I think so. I drove around some the other day."

"Maybe you can drive down occasionally and meet Nick and me on Saturdays."

"That would be great. Thanks. I might have to do that until I get into another group. I'm sure St. Louis has some."

"Most likely. Definitely gotta be some writers in a city that big."

We pulled into the outskirts of St. Charles and stopped at a gas station. Luke picked up some apartment books and hot chocolates.

"Thanks. This hits the spot." I set it in the cup holder and flipped through one of the booklets he handed me.

"The least I could do. See what you can find in your book and I'll look at mine."

I nodded, already flipping pages. We both circled possibilities and then compared them. With his GPS, he punched in four complexes and we followed the directions to the first one.

"Very upscale. I like the brick/ siding combination. Balconies, check."

Luke parked in a visitor slot and we entered the office. I sipped my cocoa while we waited for assistance.

Two hours later, we sat at a pizza joint discussing pros and cons of each one. "Which one would you pick?" Luke asked after we placed our order.

"I liked them all, but that's no help to you. As a single female, I like the gated one. But I doubt that matters to you. Do all of them have garages available?"

We munched on salads, while waiting for a small supreme pizza.

"Three of the four do. So that reduces the list to three." He crossed off the one without garages available. "They're all relatively close to the office, so that doesn't matter. I think I like the buildings of the second complex better. They seemed a little more solid."

"I thought they were very nice, too. And the rooms were spacious."

"I think I'll go with that one." He put down his fork and called the rental office. He made an appointment for the next morning to put down a deposit.

"Thanks for helping me, Natalie. I appreciate it."

"No problem. I enjoyed it, actually. I haven't seen any apartments around here and it was fun."

Our pizza came and we devoured it. Afterwards we drove around town so Luke could locate important places near the new apartment. On the way home, I rested my head against the headrest with my eyes closed.

"Tired?"

"A little. Do you mind?"

"Not at all. You've been gracious to put me up and helping me find a place. I know it's put your routine out of whack. I really appreciate it."

I looked at him. "Not a problem at all. I'm glad it worked out."

"Me too."

I put my head back and "snoozed" the rest of the way home. What I was actually doing was thinking. About how some guys and girls in our situation would have been in the same bedroom for the time Luke was here. I just wasn't the type. Maybe he was; I had no idea. Even though I was already tainted in my own eyes, through no fault of my own, I wanted the first time to be extra special. Worth waiting for. And I had my dignity after all. That was worth something.

When we got back to my house, Luke finished packing his suitcase and laptop. He would head home after getting his apartment key in the morning.

I went to bed, happy he got a new job and that I was able to help in some small way. He said he would invite me over after he got settled.

The next morning I woke up to fresh coffee and Luke cooking again. "You didn't have to do that," I protested.

"I know, but I didn't mind at all. I appreciate you putting me up. Now, eat your breakfast while it's hot and then I'll get going." He sat down next to me at the bar and we talked about what his next two weeks would be like.

"I have to set up the utilities, cancel the old ones, all that kind of stuff. It's a hassle, but at least I have a job."

"That's right. With the job market and the economy the way they are, I'd say you got lucky."

"Perhaps so. Well, I better get going," he set his plate in the sink. "Do you want me to—"

"Goodness, no. You cooked, I'll clean. Not a problem."

He nodded and ran upstairs for his bags. I held Felix in the living room. Luke came down a minute later. "Thanks again, Natalie. I hope you know how much I appreciate this. It was a huge help to be able to stay here and eat your great cooking. And it was helpful to get your input on finding an apartment." He held out a small bunch of yellow roses with a card attached.

I let Felix down and reached for the flowers. "Hey, how did you manage that?" I asked.

"I have my ways," he handed them to me and gave me a hug. "Thanks and take care of yourself."

"You, too. Thanks for the flowers; they're lovely." I laid them on the table before opening the door for him. He kissed me on the cheek and left. After waving from the glass door until his car disappeared around the block, I shut it, sighing with relief. I opened his card and something fell to the floor. I picked up a gift card for the local café. How sweet of him. I wouldn't have to buy my hot cocoa for some time.

Now life would return back to normal, for what that was worth.

I put Luke's flowers in a vase of water then washed our breakfast dishes and worked for a couple hours. The library called letting me know that they had books I ordered, so I decided to walk over and get some fresh air.

I walked briskly in the cold, my mind whirling. I considered Luke a friend, but got the feeling he was looking for something more. I liked Nick. A lot. Probably more than I should like any man. I was at the library in no time, walking on autopilot.

"Hi, Fran. I hear you have some books for me."

"Sure do. Is it still snowing?" she asked, pulling off a few books from the hold section behind her.

"No, it's just cold."

She nodded before scanning my offered library card.

"Here you go."

"Thanks. I think I'll warm up before I go back out."

"I don't blame you." As she turned to assist another patron, I went in search of a quiet corner to lose myself in one of the novels I'd just checked out. I found a seat in one of my favorite areas of the library, an inviting nook where two plush chairs covered in fabric with a book motif were arranged around a large glass-topped coffee table. Soft chimes from a handcrafted grandfather clock in the corner reminded me of sitting in a cozy living room minus the roaring fire.

    As I slid out of my coat, I caught movement out of my peripheral vision. A gentleman resembling Nick was reading a newspaper at a nearby table. But was it him? What if it was? What do I do now? I slowly and quietly sat down and started reading, ignoring the guy who may or not be Nick. After a few minutes of torturing myself, wondering if it was or not, I got up and walked around the end of the bookshelf, peaking through books on drug enforcement. I spied Nick looking at some papers, perhaps grading some essays.

    Now that my curiosity was satisfied, I went back to my seat and got lost in my book. But half an hour later, he spied me. "Natalie! How are you?"

    I looked up from my book, forcing myself not to be too anxious. "Hi, Nick. I'm good. How are you?"

    "Very well, thank you. I'm grading some papers. I don't see Luke, is he here?" I watched his eyes roam around the library and tried not to smile.

    "He left this morning. He got a job offer, so yesterday we found him an apartment in St. Charles. He found an apartment that had almost everything he was looking for."

    "That's great. Glad to hear it."

    "He's pretty excited. He starts his new job in two weeks."

    "Mind if I sit for a minute?"

How could I refuse? "Be my guest." I closed my book and set it on my lap, trying to keep my jiggling knee still.

He whispered, "Since you had your house guest, I didn't know if you'd have something ready to critique yet this week, so perhaps we can meet next week?"

"Uhh." Good grief. Why does my brain always freeze around this guy? "Uhh, yeah, good idea. I don't have anything ready, no." What was I getting into? Letting Nick read and critique my stuff, when I could hardly think around him? What if he thought my writing was boring? Terrible? It made me feel a bit uncomfortable, but I was looking forward to reading his writing. After all, that was the point of a critique group. Yet that was part of the problem, we were a group of two. Nick and me.

"No school today?" I asked, matching his whispered tone. I realized it was only two o'clock, too early for him to be off work. I noticed his navy slacks and striped shirt, which was open at the neck, but no tie.

"Half day," he answered. "It's an in-service day. I've been here catching up on paperwork and chatting with the librarians, and getting details of the upcoming town events. I didn't feel like working at home."

"What are you reading? Anything good?" He tried to read the title of the book I was holding.

"Yes, it's a mystery by Mary Jane Clark. She writes about television personalities who solve mysteries using their journalistic methods."

"Sounds interesting. It's been a while since I've read a good book."

The moment became awkward with silence. Then Nick asked if I had any plans for Sunday.

I said I didn't. Because I didn't.

"Care to go to brunch with me?"

I thought about it briefly. "I'd like that, sure."

"Great! I'll pick you up after church, around 11:30."

I wasn't sure how far this relationship would go, but for now I didn't mind Nick's friendship. Especially after Luke's departure. It would make me feel less lonely.

****

On Sunday morning I woke up with a headache. I'd had another nightmare and tossed and turned the rest of the night. It didn't help that I wasn't sure what to wear. I assumed that if Nick came straight from church, he would be in business casual. I dressed accordingly and had a small breakfast of a yogurt and banana so I wouldn't be too hungry before Nick arrived.

Nick came to the door in a long black wool coat which was unbuttoned, and I glimpsed a navy shirt and red tie. GQ, watch out! I wondered why he was so interested in me. We hardly knew each other and didn't meet under the best of circumstances. And most intriguing, I wondered why he was single.

"Good morning, Natalie. Are you ready?"

"Good morning. Come on in. I'm almost ready." I invited him in where it was warmer and so I could put on my coat and get my purse. I asked about his uncle while I bundled up.

Nick looked right into my eyes before answering. "Thanks for asking. You're a caring person." He jingled his keys before answering my question. "Better. I stopped by there just now. But he still didn't eat much breakfast this morning. Of course, it's not the cooked breakfast he's used to having, either. One day at a time, I guess."

"So how did the funeral go, I never got to ask you since Luke was here." We walked out to his car and Nick opened the door for me. I slid in.

He answered after sitting behind the wheel. "It went well, as far as funerals go. I was a pall bearer, so that was a bit tough. It will take Uncle Norton some time to get used to being alone though."

Nick's car was immaculate. As I listened, I didn't see a speck of dust or lint anywhere. The interior still smelled new. I didn't know cars at all, but knew enough to know his was a Mustang, so maybe it was the latest model. It sure looked like it. Did he clean it just for me, or was he always this neat?

My stomach felt like it was doing summersaults for an invisible audience. My hands were cold, despite my mittens. My headache was starting to come back. I really wasn't looking forward to this. How did I get myself into this mess? What if he wanted to really date? What will I do then?

We made small talk until we got settled at our table. We were shown to a booth at the Italian bistro that served a brunch buffet. Aromas of breakfast meat, eggs, and fresh fruit made my stomach growl.

A few minutes later I fiddled with my straw wrapper while looking at the menu. Nick mentioned he would order the buffet, and I could order whatever I liked. I wasn't big on breakfast, because I was never that hungry in the morning, so I ordered a Belgian waffle and fresh fruit.

After our server took our orders, Nick said, "I'll wait for your meal to come. I don't want to eat until you have your food."

"You don't have to do that. Go ahead," I offered.

"No, that won't do." He sat back in his seat as if nothing could change his mind. I didn't want to argue, so let it go.

"What brought you to this area?" Nick asked.

Our server brought our drinks before I could answer. He asked if we needed anything else and we said no. Before I could figure out how to answer his question, another server brought my plate. Nick bowed his head again like he had at my house. Then he reached for a plate and asked to be excused.

He came back with a plate loaded with three large pancakes, scrambled eggs, sausage, bacon, and fresh strawberries. Nick took a bite of pancakes, drizzled with strawberry syrup.

I wasn't going to answer Nick's earlier question unless he repeated it. Instead I asked where I could get a new office chair.

"What kind are you looking for?"

I swallowed a bite of cantaloupe before I could answer. "Ah, that's a good question. I need one with a high back that supports my back and shoulders. Preferably in burgundy, black or gray. Oh, and one with arms, so I can think on my elbows."

"Think on your elbows?" Nick asked.

"Yeah, like this," I showed him what I meant. "I do a lot of thinking sometimes when I'm trying to figure out my character's names, plot lines or what conflict to throw at my characters. That sort of thing."

"You know, I've never thought much about what writers go through to put a book on paper. I read a lot and teach English, but now that I think about it, writing a book is a whole different ball game. How long does it take for you to write a book?"

"It depends. Sometimes the story just 'comes' and you're able to get it done in a few months. Other times, it's like yanking on a rusty nail, and you feel like nothing is working right. And then there's the editing process, which can take a few months as well."

"I didn't realize that. So how many books have you written?" Nick's eyes were on me with an intent gaze.

Now that we were on a safer topic, and one about my passion, I spoke with more confidence. "Three; they're part of a series." I took a sip of my juice before continuing. "I'm thinking about self-publishing any others. I'm reading up on the software and mechanics of e-books. I haven't quite decided."

"What are your books about? Knights and rebels? Steamy love stories?"

I almost choked on my waffle. "I should hope not! They're fictionalized stories about families who adopt internationally and the hoops they go through to adopt each child."

Nick didn't say anything for a minute. He seemed to be absorbing what I said. "What?" I asked.

"They just sound interesting. Did you have to do a lot of research?"

"Oh, sure. I have some friends back home who adopted from China and Korea. Their experiences gave me the idea for my books and they shared a lot of insider information most people don't have until they actually try to adopt themselves. You wouldn't believe some of the things they went through or the ridiculous amount of red tape involved in international adoption."

"I can only imagine, considering two governments are involved."

"Exactly. Dealing with just one is nightmare enough." I finished my fruit and pushed my plate back. Nick was leaning back against the seat looking at me thoughtfully.

"What are you thinking about?"

"Nothing in particular," Nick answered.

I squirmed in my seat, fiddling with my napkin.

"Are you sufficiently fortified for shopping?"

I laughed. "I think so. Everything was delicious. Thank you."

"You're welcome. I'll go pay up front."

"I'll use the restroom and meet you by the door." I watched Nick walk away, wondering what he had been thinking about.

Moments later, we were back in the car. Though the sun was shining, it was still cold enough to see your breath. I shivered on the now cold seat. I asked where we should go to look at chairs.

Nick turned the heater up full blast. "If you want better quality, we can skip the office supply stores. So let's see what Carlton's has. It's not quite Ethan Allen, but better than some."

"Sounds good to me. Do you drive into St. Louis very often?"

"Occasionally, if I'm looking for something the smaller communities don't have. Sometimes I have to for school-related seminars or field trips;

that kind of thing." He turned the heat down some.

"Do you teach summer school or take the summer off?"

"It depends on how many students sign up for English. If I don't want to teach, I work on home projects, travel, or read. If I teach, I do the other stuff too, just less of it."

"Where have you traveled?"

"Mostly to places I haven't been before, either on one coast or the other. Last year I flew to Maine and rented a car. I enjoyed exploring the state, stopping at random sites and enjoying things like lobster lasagna. I even toured L.L. Bean and a place called Portland Jet Port. It's a fun way to travel, but not for everyone."

"I've never been to Maine. The furthest east I've been is Boston. I have a goal to get a photo of every state sign, but since I flew in to Boston, I didn't get one of Massachusetts."

"You'll just have to go back again."

"Someday."

"How many photos do you have so far?"

We were pulling into the parking lot of Carlton's as I rattled off the ones I had. "Minnesota, North and South Dakota, Wisconsin, Iowa, Nebraska, Kansas, Colorado, and a few others. Oh and Illinois and Missouri of course."

"You've got a ways to go, then."

"True, but I like to travel, so it makes for a fun challenge. I've been to other states for book signings, but since I usually fly, I don't have those. It's kind of a bummer."

"You'll just have to find a travel companion and drive next time," Nick said.

"That would be fun. If I could afford it, I'd travel to the popular places around the country, like Niagara Falls, the Grand Canyon, Yosemite, places like that. And then there's the international places like Italy, France, England and Australia—those are on my dream list, too."

"Is that all?"

I chuckled before answering. "I think so."

"Well, how about we tackle some chair shopping first?"

"Sure." I opened my door out of habit as he came around to open it. I wasn't used to someone getting the door for me. Nick was quite the gentleman.

We were barely in the door when two salespeople quickly approached us. "Just looking," we said in unison. We shared a smile and acted like we knew where the office furniture was even though we didn't. "Why do they always do that?" I asked.

"I don't know. It's annoying, isn't it? Kind of makes you feel like they're pirates going after gold."

"I suppose when you think about it, in order to get a sale, you have to get the customers coming in the door."

"True."

We spent a couple hours looking at several chairs in a few stores and then headed back home. The afternoon was still chilly and clouds had gathered turning the sky to a soft gray. I saw a chair or two that I liked, but not enough to buy.

Nick offered to stop for some hot chocolate at a café near the last store we went to, and being the hot chocolate lover I am, I couldn't refuse. When we got settled at a table, we talked more about traveling and writing.

I mentioned the book signings I had scheduled for the year so far. "I have one in

Oklahoma in June. But I'll be flying, so I won't get that state photo, either."

"What if you collected post cards, instead?" Nick suggested.

"That's an idea, I suppose. I guess I can collect those from the states I visit but don't get the state sign. I'll have to seriously consider that, thanks."

"You're welcome. Are you ready to head home?" He wiped a narrow whipped cream mustache from his lip with his napkin. He had ordered a sugar cookie with his drink. My brownie was long gone.

"Thanks for the snack. It hit the spot."

"My pleasure." He beat me to car door and opened it for me. I slid in, shivering against the cold.

"Let's hope there's not much traffic on the way home." He adjusted the heat and we were on our way. The drive seemed to be over in no time. We chatted easily all the way back to town and in what seemed like seconds, he was pulling in front of my house.

"Here you are, Natalie." He got out and opened my door and walked me to my front door. "Thank you for joining me for brunch. I had a wonderful time."

"You're welcome; I had a good time too."

Nick smiled. "You're welcome. See you Wednesday?"

I nodded, and dug out my keys.

"See you then."

I unlocked my door and heard Felix come running. "Hi, boy, did you miss me?"

I heard Nick pull away. Whew! What a day. The emotional roller coaster had worn me out. First, I was nervous about going on a date, then was relieved at his gentlemanly manner and was able to enjoy myself. I relaxed for the rest of the day with my library book wondering if I was entangling myself with a man too good to be true.

Chapter 4

On Wednesday morning, my phone rang. I had the thought maybe Nick had to cancel our writing meeting that afternoon, but it was my college roommate.

"Hi, Ellie! How are you?" Ellie was a blond, outgoing and fun. Why we became friends still puzzles us and others that know us both. I guess you could say in our case, opposites attract.

"Great. We haven't talked lately and I thought I'd see how you're doing after the holidays. Did you go home?"

"Nope. Stayed here by myself. I did go see the town parade though. It was freezing that night. What did you do?"

"I went home, stayed with mom and dad. Went for a sleigh ride, all that. Have you met anyone there yet?"

I thought for a minute about what to say. "Well, sort of."

"What do you mean sort of? Isn't that a yes or no question?"

"Yes...usually. But I don't know about him. Don't get me wrong, he's well-mannered and gorgeous. He's tall, has dark hair and brown eyes and just handsome."

"But?"

"Well, he might be a religious nut. That's what I mean."

"You mean David Koresh nutty, or Billy Graham serious?"

"Not Koresh, but not quite Graham, either. It's like he *knows* God. It puzzles me."

"Well, have you been out together? Is he nice?"

"We had brunch on Sunday after he went to church and he's coming over later to write. And yes, he's very nice."

"He writes? For a living?"

"No, he's an English teacher." I took the phone off the base and sat down on the sofa. Felix joined me and I rubbed his back.

"Oh. What grade?"

"High school."

"Cool. Never married?"

"Don't know. I don't think so though."

"Interesting. How are...other things?" Ellie asked hesitantly. I knew what she was referring to.

"Fine mostly. Had some nightmares recently when Luke came to visit."

"Luke was there??" Ellie never met him, but knew of him from conversations we've had about my former writing group.

"Yeah, for a couple days. He had interviews in the area after losing his job."

"How'd that go?"

"Fine, for me, awkward maybe for Luke. He seemed to be more interested in me than I was in him."

"He didn't do anything, did he?!"

"Gosh, no." I sighed.

"Whew! You scared me for a sec."

Ellie knew about my past and why I moved here. She was a great friend during that crisis. She now worked in the business office for a hotel in Ohio. We chatted a few more minutes before we hung up.

Then I started preparations for Nick coming over for our second writing meeting. Luke declined my invitation, saying he was still in the middle of moving and didn't think he could make it. Somehow, we changed our writing location to my house that mysteriously included dinner.

I didn't want to work on my novel or have Nick read anything too personal yet, so I planned on revising a brochure I was writing on for an electric company.

I preheated the oven for the lasagna I made earlier and took out a loaf of French bread and wrapped it in foil. Peach pie cooled on the island.

After Nick arrived, we worked as the lasagna baked. The table in the dining room was already set with a pale turquoise tablecloth and white cloth napkins. A clear vase displayed a fresh bouquet of white and yellow daisies in the center of the table, adding a spring element to the room. Luke's dying roses were in the kitchen, which Nick commented on after putting his salad on the counter. I explained why Luke had given them to me and Nick seemed to visibly relax which made me smile. He just nodded, with a thoughtful look on his face.

We then sat down with our laptops and worked in silence. I occasionally peeked over at Nick, which caused a spurt in my heartbeat. Felix came wandering in, rubbed against Nick's pants and then settled next to me on the sofa. Except for Felix's purring and the clock ticking, it was quiet. The oregano and basil from the lasagna was getting stronger, making my stomach grumble, which I hoped Nick didn't hear. The oven beeped, bringing our writing session to an abrupt end. I closed my laptop. I waited for Nick to stop typing.

"Hungry?"

Nick nodded, still looking at his laptop. "Starved. The aroma made it hard to concentrate." He shut his machine and leaned back.

I gave him a smile before going to the kitchen. Men and their food.

During dinner Nick asked me questions about Luke. I explained we knew each other only from the writer's group back home and had never dated.

"He's friendly enough." Nick paused his eating and looked at me.

Hmm, heard that before. I swallowed my water, thinking how to respond. Was he fishing for information on our non-relationship? Or just making conversation? "He is. I'm glad he found a job. After he got the call, he asked me to help him search for an apartment. He invited us over after he gets settled in."

Nick nodded. "That's cool, just let me know when."

I got up and took our plates to the kitchen. We planned to write and then have dessert as an incentive to get more work done.

At the end of our work session, I cut the pie, giving Nick a generous slice. I'd have to store the rest in the freezer for another time. We made small talk, enjoying our dessert. "Thanks for another excellent dinner and the delicious pie."

"You're welcome. Have you made notices for the library about our group, or would you like me to?"

"I haven't had a chance. If you want to, that would be fine."

"I'll think about making one and show it to you before putting it up." For some reason I had a feeling Nick preferred I forget about it.

Nick left, saying he had papers to grade before morning. I enjoyed his company and having someone to write with. Wednesdays were becoming my favorite day of the week.

****

A couple weeks later I had errands to run. Snowflakes drifted from the sky, dusting the grass and sidewalks with white powder.

When I walked outside, the frigid air took my breath away. I secured my hood under my chin and pulled my mittens over my wrists. Thank goodness the post office was only a few blocks away.

After mailing a package and buying stamps, I headed back into the snow, now swirling in miniature whirlwinds. It measured almost an inch on top of the previous three. When I got home, I pulled the car out of the garage and drove the mile to the store. Parking spots were sparse. The store was probably filled with paranoid shoppers buying all the milk and bread.

There were only a couple grocery carts left. I pushed mine toward the aisle of cat food and found the bag I needed, put it in the cart and headed for the tea and cocoa aisle. Both items were at the top of the list. After I chose my favorite flavors of tea, I turned toward the next aisle, but my foot hit a slick spot and I slid down to the floor while the cart shot out into the main aisle.

"Aah!" I had tried to hold onto the cart, but it went flying away from me, and I went straight down. An elderly gentleman ran over from the meat aisle, "Here, let me help you." He was strong and about six feet tall. "Are you ok?"

"I'm not sure. My ankle hurts." I looked at it and saw that it was twisted behind me. He helped me up and a sharp pain shot through my ankle. "Ow!"

"Here, dear, let me help you." Another customer offered me her hand. She was about the size and age of Mrs. John, but with a head full of white hair. She looked slightly familiar. She let me lean on her cart. The tall stranger left to get the store manager so the floor could be mopped.

"Thank you. That was a quick unplanned trip on my part," I tried to joke. I winced as I tried to stand on my foot.

"Do you need to sit down?" she asked.

I nodded, biting my lower lip.

"I'm Mrs. White, by the way."

"Nice to meet you," I grimaced. "Natalie." My ankle was starting to throb. I wasn't sure where my cart ended up. We half hobbled, half stumbled over to the pharmacy counter where there was thankfully a bench in front of a blood pressure monitor. "I'll get your cart and I'll be right back." Mrs. White stood about five-foot-eleven, wore an ugly green wool coat, polyester slacks and thick-soled shoes. She reminded me of someone from TV, the strong, bossy type. But she seemed nice enough. She left her own cart at my side. I peeked over the side of her cart and saw spinach, bananas, grapefruit, milk, butter, bread and Bran Flakes in it.

Yuck. Getting old must be the pits. And boring.

She came back and announced, "I brought a bag of frozen peas for your ankle until we figure out what to do. I'm not sure what's done in this situation." She held onto her own cart, a determined look on her face. Somehow she thought it was now her dilemma.

I smiled. "That makes two of us." I tried to hold my ankle up on the bench, but the bench was too short to be comfortable. I leaned down with the peas pressed to my ankle. It was really starting to throb now.

"Here comes the manager. I'm sure he'll know what to do." Mrs. White tapped her leather gloves into her hands. She looked like a woman of purpose and confidence.

"I'm so sorry, ma'am. I'll get your name and information and fill out the insurance forms. Can I get you anything in the meantime? Do you want me to call an ambulance?" His lean face held an anxious look, his eyes shifting from my ankle to the floor.

"I think I can get home ok. Luckily it's my left ankle and a short drive. It could have happened to anybody on a day like today."

"You can at least let her have the bag of peas, young man." Mrs. White interrupted.

"Oh, of course." The clerk's face reddened. He turned back to me, "We still have to fill out an incident form to cover our liability. I'll get one in a minute. Can I get you anything to eat or drink?"

"No thanks." I tried to remember to breathe. In and out.

The manager left and Mrs. White spoke. "I'll finish my shopping and I'll be back in a jiffy. I can take you home if you live here in town," she offered.

"I do, over on Railway. Thank you, but I'll be fine. I only need a few more items." Breathe in, out, in, out.

"Are you sure? I could at least get the rest of your list for you. What do you need, Natalie?" She dug out a pen and paper from her large purse. "Tell me what you need, and I'll get it."

I gave in rather readily. "A loaf of whole wheat bread, a small bag of green grapes, three bananas, two cans of tuna and a carton of eggs." I paused between items so she could write them down.

"All right dear, I'll be back in a jiffy. I'll finish my shopping and yours at the same time. Just hang tight." Jiffy must be one of her favorite words.

"Here we are," the manager said. His nametag read Jake Thompson. "If you'll fill out the top part of this page and the next one, and sign here, I think that should do it. Again, I'm so sorry. The floor has been mopped up and checked for other puddles."

"Here you go," I handed him back the forms after a few minutes. I filled them out as quickly as he gave them to me. I wanted nothing more than to get out of there. Though the peas were melting, my hand was freezing. I put my mitten back on and readjusted the plastic bag around my ankle. My throbbing ankle was giving me a headache, making me one big throb from head to toe.

Jake said, "Your bill is on the house today, Natalie. Again, I'm so sorry. If you need anything else, just have the pharmacist ring for me."

I nodded, glad when he left. I was trying to keep the tears back. Mrs. White returned with my cart. "Ok, Natalie, here you go. Anything else I can get for you?" Mrs. White asked.

"I'll need some Tylenol and a bag of frozen corn. Jake, the manager said my bill was on the house. Could you also throw in some Peanut M&Ms? But that's all. I just want to get out of here." I winced trying to get comfortable on the short bench.

Mrs. White nodded. "I'll get those items and I'll be right back after I check out. I'll get you the biggest bag of M&Ms I can find." She winked.

I smiled.

"I'll have someone help load your groceries and I'll follow you home, to make sure you get there ok. Is that all right with you?"

"Sure. Thank you very much, Mrs. White."

After she left, the friendly male customer came back to see if I needed help to the car. "Oh, what a relief! Mrs. White is following me home after she pays for her groceries."

"All right. Can you take a hold of my arm?"

I slowly stood up and turned around on my good foot, barely putting weight on my ankle. I took a hold of the gentleman's arm. I didn't even know his name.

He must have read my mind, for he said, "By the way, my name is Olsen, Charlie, if you like."

"You've been very kind, Mr. Olsen. I appreciate it very much."

"Oh, now Mr. Olsen makes me feel old. Just call me Charlie."

I smiled. "You win, Charlie. Thank you very much." We slowly made our way down the pharmacy aisle. I leaned on Charlie, hobbling down the lane like a dog missing a leg.

We met Mrs. White by the check-out. Charlie told her he'd help me into the car. I took out my keys and Mrs. White followed us with her cart. Somehow my items were processed and bagged separately from hers. I unlocked my car trunk and Charlie helped me to the door. "You sure you're going to make it, Natalie?" he asked.

I grimaced. "I'll make it. Tylenol and a nap are in short order." He nodded and left. Mrs. White came over and told me she was in a silver Buick. I nodded and waited for her to drive over. I started the car and warmed it up for a minute. The snow was coming down fast and thick. She drove down the parking lot row where I waited and I backed out cautiously. I thought my ankle was going to throb right off my leg.

I pulled into the driveway five minutes later with no incident. Mrs. White pulled up the driveway and parked. I managed to get out of the car and hobbled around to the trunk, popping it open. Mrs. White grabbed one of the bags and headed to the door. I hobbled to the door and unlocked it. "You can just put them on the table there, Mrs. White." I slid off my coat and tossed it onto the sofa. Felix came running and stopped when he saw my guest.

"Now, now, I can at least take them to the kitchen for you. I'll get the other bag and I'll be right back." She took the first bag and set it on the counter and I stumbled my way to the kitchen and put the cold stuff away. I left the rest on the counter. Mrs. White brought in the other bag and set it down.

"What do I owe you?" I asked, reaching for my purse.

"Oh, goodness. Nothing at all, dear. I was glad to help." She seemed upset at my offer of money. "Now, can I get you anything before I go?"

"No, thank you. You've done plenty already. I just need a few pain tablets, some ice, and a few pillows and I think I'll be set. Thank you so much." I hobbled after her to the door.

"Do you have anyone to help you until your ankle gets better?" she asked, turning back to me.

Her concern caught me off guard. "No, not really. But I'll be fine," I added quickly.

"Here, let me at least give you my phone number. I don't think you're going to rob me blind, are you?"

"I sure hope not!" I leaned on the doorframe while she wrote down her name and number.

"Here you go, don't hesitate to call. I might check on you myself if I don't hear from you."

"Thank you, Mrs. White. You've done more than enough already. Be careful going home."

"You're most welcome. You take it easy now." After she left, I hobbled back to the kitchen as fast as my throbbing ankle allowed to get the pills and ice. Then back to the living room, where I placed toss pillows under my ankle, ice over it, and fell asleep as the painkillers did their job.

Felix's cold wet nose on my chin woke me up. At first I didn't realize where I was or why I was in the living room, which was now dark. I woke up cold, and found a wet puddle on the floor from my now melted bag of ice. I sat up and tried to walk on my ankle. No good. I took my bag to the kitchen, refilled it with fresh ice and fed Felix. It was now after five. I ate a ham sandwich with a chaser of Peanut M&Ms. A warm bath was in order. Before going upstairs, I took two more pills. I hobbled slowly up the stairs, and started the bath water. I got out clean pajamas and slid into the warm water. Usually Felix avoids the bathroom, but maybe because he knew I didn't feel well, he perched on the toilet seat. Now I'll have to wash the cover, as it's now covered in white fur. My bathroom is decorated in mauve and green. And now a little white. Oh, well.

After getting out of the tub and into my robe and slippers, I grabbed a book from the office and curled into bed with it. This book was about how to write dialogue and gave examples from classics by Jane Austen, Charles Dickens, Louisa Alcott and other famous authors.

It was a well-written book, but I couldn't keep my eyes open. Felix kept coming in and out of my room. He wasn't ready to call it a night yet, but he didn't quite know what to do. I got out of bed, hobbled downstairs and adjusted the thermostat for the night, and made sure the front door was locked.

It was only eight o'clock, so I grabbed the candy, pills, and more ice and went back up and read some more. At half past nine, I turned the light out. It was hard to get comfortable, as I kept bumping my ankle on the mattress. I finally settled on my right side, with my left leg way over. I finally fell asleep dreaming about ice-skating on grocery store floors.

The next morning, I didn't feel any better. My ankle was killing me. I slipped into my robe and hobbled back downstairs, the Tylenol in my hand. After taking some with a sip of water there was a knock at the door. Who in the world could it be at 8:30?

I opened the door to Mrs. John. "Good morning, Natalie."

"Good morning. What brings you here?" I opened the door to let her in.

"Mrs. White told me what happened. I'm going to fix you a nice breakfast and get you situated for the day." She was already heading to the kitchen. "How is your ankle this morning?"

"It's killing me, to be honest. I just took some pain killers." I sat down at the counter. "But how? Why—"

"Oh, don't worry about a thing." She waved her hand as if shooing away a fly. "Mrs. White's in my Sunday school class and she asked if I knew you since we live so close. I said, yes. And when she told me what happened, I told her I'd look in on you this morning. She's coming by this afternoon."

I leaned on my elbow, waiting for the pain to ease up. That's why she looked familiar. I must have seen her with Mrs. John somewhere. "But—"

"No buts. We'll have you taken care of and back to normal if we can help it. Now sit yourself down," she turned back to me, "oh, good you already are. Now, I'll fix you a few eggs and some toast. How does that sound? And would you like cocoa or tea this morning?" She was already filling up my kettle that sits on the stove.

"Uh, tea, I guess. But why are you doing this?" I was still trying to figure out why she was here. Didn't Mrs. White do enough yesterday?

"Why? What kind of a question is that?" She seemed miffed at my question.

"Don't you have other things to do?" I tried again. I couldn't quite fathom their concern and kindness. To me.

She adjusted the knob for the water and replied, "When there's someone in need, it's our job to do what we can. Now, I'm going to cook you breakfast and get you settled with your computer or whatever you need this morning, and Mrs. White said she'd be by this afternoon. And I think she said someone was coming around five, but she didn't tell me who. But don't worry, it will be somebody trustworthy." She turned back to the eggs in the small pan. "Scrambled or over easy?"

"Uh, scrambled." I took out the tea and cocoa from the bag still sitting on the counter. I fiddled with the nearly childproof plastic wrap on the packages.

"Scrambled it is. I'll get your toast started and get out the butter and jam." I watched her take over my kitchen as if she'd been in it her whole life. I still didn't understand why she was here and why two strangers were coming later. But I was getting hungry and decided to deal with that first.

"I'm going to get dressed. Be back in a minute."

Mrs. John nodded, stirring my eggs.

I put on navy sweat pants and a red and white sweatshirt. I combed my hair, pulling it in a simple ponytail and put my slippers back on. No need to dress up for old ladies. I hobbled back down to the kitchen. My breakfast was on the counter in front of the stool I vacated. I sat back down. "It smells great."

"Eat up and I'll wash the dishes for you. Then we'll get you set up for the day. Do you need any errands run?" She leaned on the island, her grayish brown curls bouncing as she talked and gestured with her hands.

"But you can just put the dishes in the dishwasher," I protested. "And I don't have any errands, no."

"Dishwasher? You don't dirty enough dishes in a week to use a dishwasher." She opened the machine and shook her head. "I'll just wash these while you eat." She filled up the sink and wiped down the counter and stove. She reminded me of my mother.

I ate my eggs and toast with strawberry jam in silence. I didn't really know what to say. Until I remembered Mrs. Norton's funeral. "Did you go to Mrs. Norton's funeral, Mrs. John?"

She turned to me. "Yes, and it was lovely. I met some of her family and there was a nice lunch afterward. Of course, most of us from Sunday school brought the food, so it was bound to be good." She smiled. "She'll be missed, but she's in heaven and has no more pain." Mrs. John turned back to the sink and rinsed the plate from my dinner last night.

"And you should have seen Nick, all dressed up in a suit and everything. Mhmm, he sure looked handsome. If I weren't married and fifty years younger."

I chuckled and listened to her ramblings while I finished my breakfast and sipped my tea. I could envision Nick myself, and he did look fine in my mind's eye. But now wasn't the time. "Can you stay for tea, then?"

She turned back around and took my dishes. "Yes, I'd love to. Would you like me to put these away for you?" She pointed at the grocery sack.

"That's alright. They're all dry goods, they can wait."

She reheated water for her own cup of tea.

"Mrs. White was so kind to follow me home and everything." We took our tea into the living room where I propped my ankle up with ice. Mrs. John took the wing chair across from me.

"Yes, she's a dear. Her husband just passed a little over a year ago. But she keeps herself busy with this and that. Mostly with serving others."

"I still don't understand why you're doing this. I didn't expect her to do anything about my problem. It wasn't even her fault."

Mrs. John rested her cup on her saucer. Her curls shook again as she put it down. She looked straight at me as if to explain to a slow child. "It doesn't matter. She now has the opportunity and the responsibility to do what she can or to enlist others to help. She was there Johnny-on-the-spot and that's that."

"But, it wasn't her problem. Why are you both helping me?" I still didn't understand why Mrs. John was here.

Mrs. John frowned.

"I don't mean I don't appreciate it, I'm just not used to anyone helping me with anything, especially strangers as in Mrs. White's and Mr. Olsen's case. I'm a little bewildered."

Mrs. John nodded. "I think, Natalie, that you and I are from two different worlds. And in today's world of rush, rush, people don't take the time to help others as much as we did in my generation. There's too much fear and crime these days, unfortunately. Have you heard the story of the Good Samaritan?"

"Is it a brand name?" I set my empty cup on the coffee table.

She chuckled. "It could very well be. But the one I'm referring to is a story in the Bible. Jesus tells the story in the New Testament. It's about a man who is on a journey and gets robbed and left for dead. One man sees him and crosses the road. Another man walks by and ignores him. The third man stops, puts him on his donkey, and takes him to an inn where he leaves money for the innkeepers to care for him. The point is, if you come across someone in need, or someone who is ill, you do what you can to help him. In this case, though the Good Samaritan couldn't stop and stay with the man, he left money at the inn for them to care for him. He did his part.

"Mrs. White is simply doing her part and has asked a few friends to help out. It's a simple concept really, and one we need more of in this day and age. Most of the time, it doesn't even take that much time or money to help others, it's just seeing the opportunity and jumping in with both feet."

I felt awkward that they were doing this, but at least now I understood why. Their thoughtfulness touched me. "I don't know what to say," I said softly. I wasn't used to this kind of treatment, especially from near strangers.

"You don't have to say anything Natalie, but a simple thank you and you already have. Are you finished with your tea?" she asked getting up.

"Yes, thank you."

She took the cups to the kitchen and washed them up. "Now, how can I help you get settled for the day?"

I looked around and sighed. Everything I needed was upstairs. "Well, I guess you could bring the laptop down from the office. There's also a western book on the desk and one about dialogue on my bed. I think that will do. The laptop is plugged in, so you'll have to unplug it first. I'll need the cord also."

"All right, then. Which room is the office?" she asked heading up the stairs.

"Second door on the left and my room is the first on the left." I sat up further on the sofa and readjusted the pillows under my ankle. I still wasn't used to this idea. But I was more grateful than I realized. There were definitely benefits to small town living.

A minute later, she carried everything over to me. She stacked the books and cord on top of the closed laptop and presented it to me like a tray. "Thank you, Mrs. John, I really appreciate it."

"You're welcome, Natalie. How about some water?"

"That would be great," I answered. Before she got too far, I asked, "Could you feed Felix and give him fresh water, please?"

I saw her nod before she went into the kitchen. I could hear cat food falling into his dish and the water running. It sure saved me from hobbling around.

"Your kitchen is cleaned up and your cat is fed. "Felix, huh?"

I nodded.

"I'll be going now. I'll close the door behind me. You give a holler if you need anything, ok? You have my number." She put on her coat.

"Thank you, Mrs. John."

"My pleasure. I'll see you later." I felt alone after she left. Except for Luke's short visit and a couple of writer's meetings, I've never really had anyone over since I moved in. I didn't know anyone well enough or very many people my age to have over to watch a movie or play a game. I hadn't noticed till now how lonely I sometimes was. How sad is that?

Felix jumped up on my lap and started purring. I chuckled. "You always know how I feel, don't you?" I rubbed his back before he curled up beside me. I picked up the western and read more of the story about a man looking for his missing wife. Some Indians had kidnapped her and the husband was on their trail. I read for an hour or so, and then turned the computer on. Mrs. John had plugged it in under the end table for me.

I wrote some western style paragraphs for Joe, my western character. I guess it sounded good enough. But it definitely will need work later on during editing. Right now, I just wanted to get the story down.

Next, I wrote some paragraphs for my historical romance writer. She was writing about a woman who grew up next door to a friendly male neighbor and they hadn't realized they were a perfect match for each other until the girl went away on a journey with her parents. When she got home, she found her neighbor had missed her horribly and wanted to marry her. Corny maybe, but for now it was all I had.

After writing for an hour, I dozed off. I woke up when the laptop hit the floor and nearly knocked me senseless. I was disoriented again, and my ankle was throbbing. I took more Tylenol and picked up my story where I left off. I worked for another couple hours before I heard a knock at the door. It must be Mrs. White.

"Come in," I hollered. I was taking a risk of it being somebody ready to attack, but since it was just past noon, I didn't think so. And they most likely wouldn't knock first anyway.

"Good afternoon, Natalie. How is our little patient doing?"

"Hi, Mrs. White." I looked at my ankle. "It still hurts and I'm getting kind of stiff and bored."

"Well, let's move you around a bit. As far as the bored part, I don't know how I can help, but I'll try." She gave me a grandmotherly smile, her wrinkles dancing.

She helped me around so I was sitting straight up. We moved the pillows to the coffee table and moved it closer to the sofa.

"Now, I brought you some turkey and cheese for a sandwich. I assume you have mayo and mustard?"

"Yes, ma'am, in the refrigerator. Light on the mayo with a little more mustard. And could you get me a glass of milk please, and help yourself to whatever you find?"

"Of course, dear. I'll just be a jiffy." She unbuttoned her coat—I caught a whiff of moth balls—and she marched for the kitchen.

There's that word again. I could hear her in the kitchen, looking for silverware and opening the fridge. I moved the laptop over to a cushion next to me. My ice long ago melted. I wondered if I still needed it or if I should use heat now. I searched for the answer on Google while she made our sandwiches.

"Here you go. I added some chips and a pickle. I love the little dills, too." She handed me a plate and put the milk on the table. "I'll get my plate and we'll say grace before we eat."

Grace? Again?

Mrs. White sat in the same chair that Mrs. John sat in this morning. She put her milk on the table, sat down and bowed her head. I did, too.

"Dear Lord, we thank you for this day and for this food. Please bless it to our bodies for your use and please heal Natalie's ankle quickly. Thank you for family and friends and all the blessings you bestow on us. Amen."

She prayed for me! That's the second time in less than a week somebody has prayed for me. I didn't know quite what to make of it. I was hungry though, and took a large bite of my sandwich. "Perfect. Just the right amount of everything."

"Good. Eat up and I'll get some cookies in a minute."

"Wow, I'm getting spoiled. Why does a sandwich taste so much better when someone else makes it?"

"That's a good question, Natalie. I've often wondered that myself. I think maybe it's because we're grateful somebody else made it."

"That could be." We ate in silence for a few minutes. Felix wandered back in and rubbed against Mrs. White's leg. "Hmm, I think he might be begging."

"Well, it wouldn't be the first time someone begged from me, although it's been a long time." She dropped a small piece of turkey on the floor. Felix gobbled it right up.

"Now you have a friend for life."

"I was afraid of that," she chuckled.

"How long have you lived in Mascoutah?" I asked before popping the last bite of crunchy pickle in my mouth.

"Oh, my. Let me think. Over forty years. Frank and I moved here a year or so after we married. He had a job at the wood mill east of town. How he loved the smell of that wood! That seems like centuries ago, and at the same time seems like yesterday."

"How long were you married?"

"Forty-two years. And for the most part, they were wonderful. We had our little share of ups and downs as most couples are fit to do, but got through them one a time."

After a minute, she asked, "Are you ready for some snickerdoodles?"

"That's one of my favorites. How did you know? I still have some milk left, too." Except for the Bible lessons, it wasn't too bad getting all this special treatment.

"Here you are." Mrs. White held a platter out. I don't remember her having it when she arrived, but I didn't let her in.

I took two and thanked her. She sat down and put the platter on the table. "I'll leave the plate with you and get it in a few days."

"Wonderful, but I'm sure it won't take that long to eat them. Especially since they'll be in easy reach."

She smiled. "That's fine. I'll get the plate one way or another. Now, what can I do for you while I'm here? Do you have any laundry or cleaning needing done?" She looked around the room.

I shook my head. "No, I'm all caught up on that."

She looked around. "How about a game?"

"Sure. What do you like to play?"

She looked at my stack on the bottom bookshelf by the fireplace. Sorry!, Connect Four, Clue, Skip-Bo and a few others were stacked there. "Oh, I haven't played Skip-Bo in years. How about it?" She almost seemed excited.

"That's one of my favorites."

She got up and brought the game over to the coffee table. "I'll take these dishes to the sink and wash them up quick while you shuffle. Deal?"

"You bet." We laughed at our joke.

I dusted the lid off with my hand and took out the cards. I shuffled them and dealt. It had been a while since I played myself; I hoped I remembered how.

Mrs. White came back in and pulled her chair up to the table. "Are you going to be comfortable like that?"

"I'll make do. I certainly can't sit on the floor."

"Oh, no, I don't expect you to."

I looked around for a better chair or a better table. What to do? "What if we move to the dining room and I put my ankle up on an extra chair?"

"Will you be comfortable that way?" She seemed doubtful.

"Sure, besides I'd like to get off this darn couch for a while." I got up and took the pillows with me. She brought the game board. And the cookies. I liked this woman!

"Ah, this will work."

She sat down next to me so we could both reach the board. Someone had given me the deluxe version that comes with a blue board to play on. "Guests go first," I said.

"So, I flip this card over and try to use up this stack of cards first, right?" she pointed to her stock pile.

"Yes. And stack each of these piles one through twelve in the middle and then move it off the board."

"That's right. I remember now. I used to play with the grandkids when they came to stay. They're too old for that now although we sometimes play games at Christmas."

"How many grandkids do you have?" I readjusted the pillow under my ankle and grabbed another cookie.

"Sixteen. An even eight girls and eight boys. Isn't that unusual?"

"That's kind of neat. Do they all get along?" I took my turn while she answered. I was able to use four of my cards, and then drew more from the draw pile.

"Most of the time. We've had to wrestle siblings away from each other a time or two, but it seems like when cousins are around, they get along better. They can separate from their own brothers and sisters and play well together."

"I have only two cousins in Minnesota. I hardly see them."

"That's too bad." She took her turn.

I played all my cards and drew five more and put most of them down as well. Then it was her turn.

We played two games before she had to leave. We each won a game. "Now, I'll put this away and get you settled wherever you like." She took the board back into the living room.

"I think I'm ready to work upstairs in my office. If I take these pillows up and put them on the extra chair up there, that should work."

"Can I carry the computer up for you?"

"Please. And those two books and the pain tablets." Oh, yeah, definitely those.

I hobbled behind Mrs. White and showed her my office. "Very nice, dear. I like your decorating tastes. Oh, these are your books?" she pointed to the side table.

I nodded.

She picked one up and read the back cover. "I hate to say it, but I've never heard of you before. But it's the truth."

"That's ok. I don't write to be famous, anyway. I just can't quit."

"A passion, then?" She looked back at me.

"Of sorts. I can't seem to get it out of my system."

"God gives us all our talents and it's great to see you using yours. Keep it up." She started to put it back, when I said, "Take it, if you'll read it."

"Thank you, I'd love to! Will you sign it for me?"

"Sure." I took a pen from the cup on the desk and signed my name on the inside flap. "Here you go."

After she left a few minutes later, I had to think about where my talent came from. Nobody in my family had any writing ability that I knew of. Did it really come from God? I never considered him in the equation of my life. I only knew I couldn't quit.

I continued working in my fictional world for several hours, and then hobbled to my bed for a nap. My slippers fell off as I got under the covers and got comfortable. After an hour's rest I went downstairs and fed Felix. It was just starting to get dark. I closed the curtains and blinds around the first floor and flipped the porch light on for whoever was coming next. Perhaps it was another elderly woman from their class. Mrs. White simply said I'd be taken care of.

Chapter 5

The house started getting chilly, so I gathered junk mail and old newspapers in the grate and started a fire. I struck a match and dropped it on the small pile of paper and kindling. The house had central heating of course, but I loved the sounds and warmth from a fire. As I waited for whoever was coming, I stared at the flames, wondering which nice grandma was on her way.

The wood supply was running low in the house, but I wouldn't be able to restock it myself. An ample supply of wood sat stacked next to the garage alongside a barrel of kindling. Though the stock was near depleted inside, I had plenty available. I wanted to sit closer to the fire, so half pulled, half dragged the chair closer to the fireplace. Before I could get it where I wanted it, the doorbell rang. "Come in," I hollered toward the door.

"Natalie?" A distinctively non-female voice asked. Whoever it was, they weren't old or female.

"I'm in the living room." Who on earth could it be? It couldn't be, but the voice I barely heard trailing from the foyer sounded like Nick. If it was him, it was too late to do anything about it now. Soon a tall form with dark hair rounded the corner into the living room.

I almost fell into the chair I was trying to move. "Nick! What are you doing here?" He definitely did not fall into the senior lady category.

"What are you doing, up and around? A little birdie told me you had an accident." His frown almost made me feel caught. But not quite. He held a couple paper sacks.

"Uh, well..." Oh, dear. Nick was the last person I expected in my living room today. A gray-haired lady he was not. My hands grasped the chair for support, to prevent fainting from seeing my unexpected but welcome guest. Why didn't Mrs. John or Mrs. White warn me? Did they do this to me on purpose? Were they trying their hardest to set us up, not having a clue why I couldn't date Nick or any guy for that matter? Oh, how I wished I could!

Nick put the sacks on the coffee table and then led me to the sofa. "Are you ok? You look like I caught you with your hand in the cookie jar. You shouldn't be moving furniture around," he admonished.

"I was just moving it closer to the fire."

"Here, let me do it." He moved it over and faced it toward the flames. "Is this what you had in mind?"

"Yes, thanks." I hobbled around the chair and plopped down.

Nick looked satisfied. "I'll get some plates. You like Chinese, right?"

"You remembered from our conversation the other day?"

"Yep. Sit tight, and I'll be right back. I'll get the silverware." I heard him rummaging through drawers. I've heard that a lot lately. It seemed awkward, others searching through my cabinets and drawers, cooking even. But I so appreciated the kindness. And the great food.

I wasn't the least bit prepared for Nick, though. I'm sure my clothes were wrinkled and I knew my hair was a mess. I pulled a ponytail holder from my pocket and finger-combed my hair, putting it back up. Not much I could do about it now.

Nick came back with several white and red containers on a tray and two Styrofoam cups. "I've got some beef and broccoli, and some cashew chicken. And some egg rolls. I took the liberty of getting sweet tea; is that ok?"

"It sounds wonderful. Just the aromas are making me hungry."

"Good, here's your tea." He handed me a cup with a straw already in it.

I took a sip before setting it down on the hearth. "So, who told you about my trip to the grocery store? Or rather both of them?"

"Just a minute." He set the tray down near the fireplace and asked if he could move the coffee table over since I was in the furniture moving mood.

"Be my guest," I gestured.

Then he sat on the floor at the end of the table. "This is the perfect way to eat Chinese, you know."

"On the floor?" I smiled.

"Well, closer to the floor anyway. I think they use pillows or short stools. Anyway, I'll say a quick prayer and then answer your question." He waited for me to bow my head. I did. "Dear Lord, thank you for this wonderful day, and for no incidents in class today. Thank you for the beautiful snow and for friends and family and taking care of our every need. Thank you for Natalie and please heal her ankle with no complications. We thank you for this food. Amen."

"Amen." I was going to have to get used to praying before eating with this crowd.

"Now, which do you want, the beef or chicken?"

"A little of both please. They're both favorites."

"Wise choice. I think I'll do the same. Egg roll?"

"Absolutely. It smells savory. I don't know why I'm so hungry from hardly doing anything all day."

"Here you go. Maybe you haven't done much, but your body is still healing and that takes energy."

"Good point—I'll go with that." I quickly took a bite. I hadn't tried the local Chinese joint yet. I'd been missing out. "This is good. Thank you." I watched Nick a little longer and he caught me so I quickly took another bite. I couldn't believe how comfortable I was getting with Nick, whom I barely knew. Something drew me to him, besides his looks and excellent manners, but I couldn't figure it out.

"You're welcome. So, back to your earlier question, Mrs. White told me about your ankle when I saw her at the post office on my lunch break. I offered to take the evening shift tonight."

"Mighty gallant of you. Just how many shifts are there and who's taking them and for how long?" My voice rose slightly and then I plopped back against the chair with a big sigh. I had a right to know these things after all. The situation was both overwhelming and wonderful at the same time.

"I'm not sure. I don't run these kinds of things. But Mrs. White is very efficient and I'm sure she has it all organized." He took another bite before asking, "You don't mind do you? I'm sorry if you thought we were invading or anything."

I took a minute before replying. "I'm sorry. I didn't mean to be ungrateful. But to answer your question, yes and no. I like the company, and the food has been great. I just don't deserve it and wasn't prepared for you coming." Not that I didn't want him to come or anything. The complete opposite, actually.

Nick gave me a look like he was going to argue and then changed his mind. He pointed to his plate. "You're right; this is good." We ate in silence for a few minutes before he asked, "So how is your ankle?"

"It doesn't throb as much. I'm mostly bored, stuck at home. Which is so silly since I work at home most of the time anyway. But since I can't get out, it makes me feel worse."

Nick rested his fork on his plate and looked at me. "I understand perfectly. You don't miss something until it's taken away from you."

"Exactly. After Mrs. John left this morning, I felt lonely. It was strange to be alone again."

Nick nodded, a big bite of egg roll in his mouth. He gulped a swallow of tea. "I know what you mean. And sometimes in a room full of people you can still feel lonely."

"Yeah. Have you ever felt like that?" Surely, someone as confident and gorgeous as Nick wouldn't ever feel that way.

"At most school functions. Usually the students are with their friends or their parents. I'm usually with just one or two other single teachers or by myself. It's awkward, but I'm trying to get used to it."

I watched him take a bite, absorbing this mild shock. "I'm sorry. I feel the same way sometimes at writer's conferences or book signings. Especially when not very many people show up at a signing. It's embarrassing."

"I bet. What do you do if that happens?"

"I sit there and doodle or write in long hand in a notebook I carry around. That way, I have something to do and sometimes I get some writing done."

"Well, at least it's not a total waste."

"True." I took my last bite and after swallowing asked him, "So how was your day today?"

"Not too bad. I didn't have to send any students to detention or anything. We discussed Romeo and Juliet in my freshman classes and did some essay writing in my junior ones." He shook his head before adding, "Sometimes I wonder where they learned their grammar. Most of their papers are atrocious."

"Do you have them with you?" It would be interesting to see some of his student's writing.

"They're in my briefcase in the car. I haven't been home yet."

I almost choked on my tea. "Nick! You could have gone home first; I didn't even know it was you that was coming." Now I felt bad. And embarrassed.

"Oh, I didn't mind. It gave me something to look forward to this afternoon. And my evening was free, so it's no problem." Nick pushed his plate back and stretched out his legs. Today he wore a long sleeve navy oxford, a muted red and white tie, and tan slacks. His shoes must be at the door; his socks were navy. He looked very fine as he watched the fire. He belonged here. Didn't he?

I wish there was a way I could get used to this.

He asked me a question, bringing me out of my thoughts. "It's not very big, is it?" Nick turned back to me.

I glanced at the fire. "No, I'm running out of wood in the house. I have stacks next to the garage, but I can't bring it in." I threw up my hands, helplessly. Oh, the damsel in distress. What to do?

Nick jumped to his feet. "Say no more. Just point the way, and I'll get some for you." He stood up and picked up our plates.

"It's on this side of the garage, closest to the house. And the kindling is in a barrel next to it." I knew he would volunteer to get some, but I was still grateful.

"I'll take the trash to the kitchen and go get some. I'll be right back."

"Thanks." I sure was saying that a lot these days. I heard Nick zip up his coat in the hall and go back out. I readjusted my ankle on the sofa and stretched out. I could get used to all this pampering if it lasted much longer. A minute later, Nick came back in with his arms full of wood. "I'll get another load and then you should be set for a day or two."

"Thanks, Nick. I appreciate it."

Nick nodded and went back out. He came back in with another pile and stacked the wood on the hearth. He added two logs to the small blaze and stoked it up. It sparked into a bright orange. The crackling sounds and the good company made me feel quite cozy. "That should do for a while."

"I love listening to a good fire crackle and pop."

"Me, too." Nick sat down again by the table, stretching his legs toward the fire. I felt a strong urge to run my fingers through his dark hair, but didn't dare. I tuned into what he was saying.

"Though I don't get to much. My flue is clogged and the last time I made one, smoke filled my living room faster than a New England fog rolling in. I haven't gotten around to having it checked."

We enjoyed the fire a few minutes before I spoke again. "Luke wants to know if we can come up one Saturday morning and write."

"Oh, yeah. How's he doing?"

"He's settled in and likes his job. But he hasn't made it to the local library yet or searched for writer's groups in the area."

"I'm free the next two Saturdays but have a workshop to attend the following week."

I nodded. "I'll let him know and we can go from there."

"He's kind enough to include me."

"He's a good guy," I agreed, "though not my type." I noticed Nick's face looked relieved.

We sat a moment, staring at the fire in companionable silence. I was glad to have the company on this chilly night. Felix came in from somewhere and started pawing Nick's feet.

"Well, hello there. I wondered where you might be, Felix." Nick started rubbing the cat's back, much to Felix's satisfaction. He sat down at Nick's feet. Felix enjoyed all the company as much as I did.

I wondered if married life was ever this peaceful. I dated some when I was in high school and college, but it never got serious. I never felt I was with the right guy. Nick seems kind and thoughtful, but he's into church and all that praying stuff I know nothing about. I doubted we'd ever get serious, anyway. But for now, I enjoyed the company and didn't mind the praying stuff too much. I just didn't know if it was for me.

"I see your games on the shelf over there," he nodded with his head. "Are you up for a game of Scrabble? I bet us wordsmiths could play, couldn't we?" He turned back to me. Felix had moved over by the fireplace.

"I could try. I don't know how well my mental faculties are functioning right now." I was quite content daydreaming and staring at Nick, but I couldn't tell him that.

"Oh, I'm sure you'll be fine." He walked over to the shelf and brought the game to the table. He plopped back down and took the lid off. He was so near, and now his familiar musk scent was tantalizing. I had to resist thinking about being in those strong arms. He must work out some. I tried concentrating on helping him turn the pieces over in the lid. We each drew our seven letters. Oh, boy. I had six vowels and one consonant. This was going to be fun.

"Guests go first," I said for the second time today.

"Great. How about glove?" he put his letters across the middle of the board. He wrote down his points on the score pad.

"Well, you didn't leave me much to work with, considering my choices here." I sat thinking for a minute. I added the word 'give' using his g and my letters. "How many points is that, four?"

"Closer to ten."

I drew three more letters. Two consonants and one vowel. At least now I had some decent letters to work with.

We played our game for about an hour. Nick won of course, since my heart really wasn't in it. I just enjoyed the company and conversation. We also enjoyed some of Mrs. White's snickerdoodles.

"Whoever my future wife is, I hope she can bake like Mrs. White. These cookies of hers are one of my favorites."

"Mine, too."

"Your oatmeal cookies and cinnamon rolls are worth millions."

I laughed. "I wouldn't say that, but I do enjoy baking. I make a mean chocolate zucchini cake and you can't tell there's zucchini in it at all."

"I might have to try that some time. Think you could bake one when you're up and around?"

"Maybe. If someone came over and helped me eat it."

"Feeling better yet?"

I laughed. "Not quite, but I'm working on it."

"Maybe for our meeting next week?"

"Perhaps. I think I need some chocolate chips though." I tried remembering what was in my pantry.

"I'll get some and bring them tomorrow. How many bags would you need?"

"Just one."

"Ok. I better call it a night; it's getting late. Same time tomorrow? What would you like for dinner?"

"I get a choice?"

Nick looked at me straight in the eye, with a serious expression on his face. "Of course. All my patients do."

"Really? Just how many patients do you have?" Two could play this game.

"One. But she gets the royal treatment." Nick's playful eyes sparkled.

"Oh, how come?"

"Because she's special. And kind. And writes wonderful stories which I've not had the opportunity to read. I can't believe you haven't given me a copy of one of your books yet."

"Well, you can go get one from my office if you really want one."

He was already on his feet. "Really? Will you sign it for me?"

My cheeks felt hot. "Oh, come on...I was only joking." Surely he wasn't serious.

"Seriously, will you? I want one." He was heading for the stairs.

"I guess. Hand me the pen from the game." He came back to hand me a ball point pen from our game, and then took the stairs two at a time. "Second door on the left," I hollered after him. I was saying that a lot this week. If this kept up, the whole town will know my house in and out.

I could hear him say, "Found it." It was a minute or two before he returned. What was he doing? Choosing which title, I guess.

He came back down, handing me a book with a flourish and a wide grin.

I wasn't sure what to write in it. I ended up with, 'For Nick, A newfound friend. Best Wishes, Natalie Alexander'. I closed it and handed it back. He took it without reading my inscription and put on his coat and shoes. "Tomorrow then, same time, same place?"

I nodded. "I'll be here. How about Italian?"

"Sounds good to me." He squeezed my shoulder and started for the door. He turned back and asked, "Are you going to be up for writing tomorrow?"

I leaned back and thought about it. I glanced at Nick's face, which was a mistake. His puppy dog look was so eager. I tried not to laugh at his obvious concern about not coming back the next day. "How about we play the writing part by ear?" I finally answered.

"So I should still come?" His voice was so full of hope; I had to stifle a giggle.

"Oh, definitely. You wouldn't want me to starve after all."

He was a taken aback by my comment and there was a short pause before he smiled. "Good point. See you tomorrow." And he was out the door. I leaned back on the sofa. If I read him right, his facial expression told me he enjoyed my company as much as I enjoyed his.

I slid the letter tiles into the box and closed the lid. I left it on the table and stared at the fire, just listening to its crackle and to Felix's purring. The only other sound was wind from the north rattling the windows. It was only eight o'clock, but I was ready for bed. The faint smell of Chinese food mingled with Nick's woodsy aftershave. I moved to the sofa and stretched out with an afghan over me and waited for the fire to die down.

My thoughts were a whirlwind akin to snowflakes in a blizzard. What was all this Jesus thing about? And the Good Samaritan? Are these people in my life all because I embarrassed myself at the grocery store? I didn't believe in chance or fate. I thought that was just nonsense. But is there a reason for all this? Why now all of a sudden? The thoughts kept buzzing around in my brain, like angry bees.

I fell asleep on the sofa, dreaming of an unseen force taking charge of my life like a puppet with the strings getting pulled in several directions at once. How did I know what was going to happen next? What if I made the wrong choice? Would one string pull harder than another, or break if I tried to go in a different direction? I saw images of things and places from my childhood.

My dream was in murky colors of red, yellow and blue. It was almost like watching a kaleidoscope of my life flashing off in my brain. I woke with a start about nine-thirty and felt like I'd had a nightmare. But I couldn't remember what was so scary. It was like someone was forcing me to do things I didn't want to, but I couldn't tell exactly what they were. It was a strange sensation and I didn't like it.

The fire was almost out, so I took the poker and stabbed the last log down to red coals, shut the glass doors and went up to bed. I brushed my teeth in a daze and hoped I could fall back asleep and dream pleasant things. I thought of Nick, wondering if he'd read my inscription yet. Did he stay up reading his students' essays? Was he still up now?

I fell into bed, my ankle not hurting as much and dozed off in no time.

The next morning my ankle felt a lot better, but I still couldn't put my full weight on it. I showered and put on a sweat suit, in Mascoutah colors, which were dark purple and white. These were my favorite kind of clothes, soft and comfortable, making it easier to work in. In the office I turned on the computer before limping downstairs.

I fed Felix and gave him fresh water and put away the clean dishes sitting in the drainer. I hobbled around the first floor, opening curtains and blinds. Fresh snow blinded me in the sunshine. I swept up ashes from around the fireplace and put the board game back on the shelf. It felt good to move around even though I wasn't doing a whole lot. In the sunshine, I could see the living room was pretty dusty, so I took care of that.

I just managed to put the feather duster away when there was a knock at the door and I went to answer it. "Good morning, Mrs. John, come on in."

"Well, good morning, Natalie. You're looking much better."

"I feel much better. I actually did some dusting this morning and I hate dusting."

She laughed, and I followed her to the kitchen. "I baked yesterday since it was chilly and brought you some muffins and oatmeal."

"Something smells wonderful. I'll get the juice unless you want hot tea?"

"Hot tea would be perfect. But I'll get it, you sit down." She waved me to a stool at the island.

"Oh, I think I'm fine," I protested.

"You may be dear, but I'm here and I'll make the tea. Just sit down there and tell me about your evening with our little Nicky."

The gag in my throat nearly choked me and I plopped on the stool, my head shaking. Nicky? Ick. She put on her oatmeal to reheat and the kettle of water for our tea. I watched her in amazement. It was almost as if it were her kitchen. "You could have warned me. I probably scared him half to death." I groaned.

"I'm sure you did no such thing. Besides, Nick enjoyed your company I'm sure. You two are perfect for each other."

We are? Why would she think that?

"Anyway," I went on, "he brought Chinese food from Twin Dragons, which was delicious. He brought in more wood for the fireplace and we played Scrabble. I think he had a good time."

"I'm sure he did. Who won the game?"

I laughed. "He did, naturally. I wasn't exactly mentally prepared and told him so. I also warned him that next time he better watch out, because I might whop him."

"So you two did have a good time, that's good." She sat down on the stool next to me. We stirred our tea and she said grace. I still wasn't used to that. But she prayed for me and my ankle.

"Thank you," I said.

"You're welcome." We ate in silence.

"These muffins are wonderful. What kind are they?"

"Apple cinnamon. I also made an apple pie. My kitchen smelled divine."

"I bet it did. Which reminds me, I also told Nick I would bake him a chocolate zucchini cake if he bought me the chocolate chips for one. He's supposed to bring them tonight."

"He's coming back tonight?" She sounded pleased.

"Yes. I might challenge him to a Scrabble tournament, now that I'm thinking about it. That might be fun. Since we're both word people."

Mrs. John didn't know what to say. "It does sound like fun. So when will you make this cake?"

"Probably tomorrow if I'm able to get around easier. The way I feel today, I'm sure I'll be fine by tomorrow."

"That's good. I think Mrs. White is bringing some soup for your lunch. She said she would let me know if she needed me tomorrow. But I think you're doing well."

"I think so too. It's probably due to all the spoiling I've gotten the last few days."

"It never hurts to spoil others once in a while."

We finished our breakfast and tea. She got up and washed our dishes. "Well, if you need anything, give me a holler. I'm glad you and Nick are becoming friends. You make a good match."

I didn't know what to say so stayed silent. It wouldn't last once Nick found out about one night in my past. I followed her to the door.

"Thanks again, Mrs. John. Tell Mr. John I said hi."

"You're welcome, dear. I'll tell him." Through the glass door I watched her walk down the sidewalk then shut the front door. I wondered if she knew something I didn't. It seemed like she was pleased Nick and I were spending time together.

I shook my head, puzzled at Mrs. John's behavior and hobbled upstairs, but a little faster than yesterday. I got situated at the desk and checked email first.

I had a message from Luke that he hoped my ankle was feeling better. I had thanked him for the gift card he gave me and made a small mention of my accident. Felix came in and sat in front of the desk, in his usual place. My story flowed along pretty well and then I came to a sticky spot. I looked at the clock. It was eleven-thirty already. I got up and stretched. I never checked the mail from yesterday, so decided to go get it. Today's was probably there as well.

I slipped into shoes I kept by the door and stepped down to the porch, holding onto the railing. It felt good to be outside in crisp, clean air even though it was freezing. There was always something about smelling clean air with no scent of pollution or gas fumes. I flipped through the small stack of envelopes. A couple had stamps on them. Wow, I actually got some personal mail for a change. I limped back into the house. I slipped the wet shoes off on the rug and sat down in the living room.

The junk mail I tossed into the kindling pile on the fireplace hearth. Two envelopes were sent locally but didn't have return addresses on them. I opened the pink one first. It was a get-well card from Mrs. White. How touching. The other one was in a blue envelope. It was also a get-well card, from Mrs. John. Boy, they sure were going over the top. The cards looked pretty and homey on my dusted off mantel. My plants around the room needed watering though, so I gave them their much-needed drink.

No sooner had I finished my task when the doorbell rang. "Hi, Mrs. White! Come on in," I said, holding the glass door.

"Well, aren't you a ray of sunshine this morning, Natalie. You must be doing better."

"Yes, I am. Thank you for the card. It's sitting on the mantle, along with Mrs. John's. They look so pretty up there."

"Well, I'm glad you enjoyed them. I've always loved mail myself."

"Me, too. I don't know how to thank you all."

"Don't worry about it dear, your appreciation is enough. Now, how about some hot soup on a cold day?"

"How perfect, thank you. I'll get some bowls."

I followed Mrs. White into the kitchen. She carried her pot of soup in her hands with pot holders, set it down on the stove and turned it on low. She pulled a tote bag off her arm and pulled out a bread basket.

"I have some fresh wheat bread to go with our soup. We just need some butter and silverware and we're set."

I took down two bowls from the cupboard and handed them to her. She filled them up. The soup was steaming hot and smelled delicious.

"What kind is it? It smells wonderful."

"It's chicken and noodle. It's an old family recipe from my mother's side of the family. Mom always made it when one of us was sick. We had it often in the winter time."

We sat down together and she prayed for our food. She prayed again for my ankle to heal. I tore into my soup. It was as delicious as it smelled. The bread was soft and tasty too. "This sure hits the spot, Mrs. White. Thank you."

"You're very welcome. It's one of my favorite meals. How did your evening go last night?" Where had I heard that before? What was it with these two ladies?

"It went well." I filled her in on our evening.

Mrs. White smiled. "Sounds like you had a good evening, then. I'm glad. Nick is one of our favorite young people at church. If he isn't busy, he's willing to help out with home projects for us older folks. He's good with a hammer and can get around nooks and crannies easier than we can." She put her spoon down and shook her head. "I can't understand though why he hasn't married before now. As far as I can tell, there's nothing wrong with him. I haven't ever seen him bring a date to church before. But the girls there all seem genuinely interested in him, it seems. I guess the right one hasn't come along yet."

I continued eating without comment. It was interesting to learn he hasn't been married and divorced like I thought. Did that mean she thought I was the right one, or was she just wondering aloud? I didn't know, so I just ignored her comments. I finished my soup and took another slice of bread. I got out the strawberry jam for a simple dessert. "Nick and I finished your cookies last night. I told him I would make a chocolate zucchini cake if I had some chocolate chips. He volunteered to get me some today."

"Well, now isn't that nice of him. It doesn't seem to me to be quite a fair trade, though. Him buying the chocolate chips and you doing the work and clean up." She tapped her spoon in her bowl, as if miffed.

I hid a smile. "I don't mind. I guess I shouldn't have been surprised he volunteered so quickly though."

"Definitely not. They say the quickest way to a man's heart is through his stomach. Must be some truth to it after all."

"The way he ate your cookies, I don't doubt it." We laughed. "I suppose as a bachelor, he doesn't get that many home baked goods."

"Oh, hold on a minute. Don't let him fool you, Natalie. He's had more than his fair share of our goodies over the years. Our Sunday school class takes care of him very well. Of course, he's usually taking care of a small fix-it job for us, but he's well taken care of in that department. He's had many a dinner at my house or at the John's, I know."

"Hmm. I remember him saying that whoever his wife turned out to be, she better know how to bake. Maybe that's why."

"Could be. He's so used to being spoiled; he wouldn't want it to stop."

I grinned. "I love baking, but haven't done as much lately. It seems like only yesterday I took cookies to Nick's uncle and met Nick."

"Love is like that. You feel like you've been together forever, but it's a good kind of forever, not a bad kind."

I didn't say anything about love, did I? What was she talking about? I took my empty soup bowl to the sink and filled it with water, chalking it up to her age.

"I'll leave this bread and soup with you and you can finish it tomorrow if you like. I'll get my dishes later. I know where you live," she joked.

I smiled. "Thank you very much. I think I'll sprain my ankle again next week."

Mrs. White laughed. "I'd think twice about that. But maybe you should skip a week." She filled the sink with hot soapy water and washed the few dishes.

"Yeah, maybe every other week. Then I'd have it made."

She put her coat on and I followed her to the door. "You and Nick have a good time this evening. Don't keep him up too late. Call me if you need anything."

"I will. Thanks again for the delicious lunch." I shut the door and went into the kitchen. I turned the stove off and moved the soup pot to the back. I wrapped her bread up in the cloth, left it by the stove and went back to work. Those ladies were something else.

I was looking forward to Italian tonight with Nick. I was feeling a whole lot better. I hoped he could stay late enough to play another game. Or a different game if he wanted. Tomorrow I would miss everyone not coming by. I might have to run errands to get out and be around people. As long as I didn't trip!

I sat down and worked for a couple of hours. After stretching, I picked up my mediocre novel. The problem with being a writer is that it's so easy to find flaws in almost every book. Either the plot is silly or contrived, the dialogue forced, or the book is just plain horrible and should never have gotten past the marketing department. Everybody and their brother wants to be a writer these days. Don't they know it's hard work? After finishing the next chapter, there was a knock at the door. I looked at my watch. It was five o'clock already. I hopped up and walked to the door, almost normally now.

"Hi, Nick, come on in," I held the door for him. He had several sacks in his hands, so I couldn't see any of him except his eyes.

"Hi, Natalie. I have a few things for you."

"Looks like more than that. Let me take a bag," I offered.

"Nope, can't let you. I've got it." I quickly shut the door against the winter wind and followed him to the kitchen where he plopped his bags on the counter. "These are for you," he said, handing me a bouquet of carnations with greenery.

I sucked in my breath. "How pretty! I'll get a vase." I found one in a kitchen cupboard. "Thank you. I haven't had carnations in ages." I leaned over the vase, taking in their sweet scent.

"You're very welcome. And here are the requested chocolate chips."

I laughed when I saw them in his hands. "Three bags? Is there a hint here?" I stacked them on the counter.

"Just a little one." He pulled out some trays from another bag. "And here is dinner which has made me very hungry on the drive over."

"Smells heavenly. I'm certainly ready. Do we need plates or just silverware?"

"Neither if you don't mind plastic." He held up wrapped silverware and napkins.

"That's fine. What do you want to drink? Tea, milk, juice, or water?"

"Tea would be great." I poured our drinks.

"Let's eat in the dining room. I'll bring the flowers, napkins, and drinks; you bring the food, please."

"Yes, ma'am. I'm great at following orders from bossy patients."

"Very funny. Actually, I don't think I qualify as a patient anymore." I walked in front of him to the other room. "See?" I turned around.

"No, I don't; would you mind doing that again?" He asked with a straight face.

I whipped back toward the table, trying to hide my flushed face. "Nick!" I almost dropped the vase onto the table. I set it in the middle and the drinks in front of our seats. I glanced at him before sitting.

"What?" His face was complete innocence.

I decided to never play poker with him if the opportunity ever came up. "Let's eat," I answered, downplaying my embarrassment.

"If we must." He set down a tray in front of each of us along with a package of wrapped silverware. We sat in the same chairs Mrs. White and I used when we played our game. "I'll bless the food."

I bowed my head. There was silence for several seconds, so I stole a peek to find him looking at me. "What?"

"Nothing." He quickly dropped his head down. What's up with that? Why did he keep looking at me as if he couldn't quite figure me out? Or as if he wanted to say something but thought better of it?

"Dear Lord, thank you for Natalie and her friendship and that her ankle is healing well. We thank you for this food and ask you to nourish our bodies. Be with us this evening and keep us safe. In your name, Amen."

"Amen," I whispered.

Nick looked at me again, but didn't say anything. I opened my tray and pretended not to notice. "This smells delicious and very Italiany."

"Italiany?"

I knew that would get his attention.

I grinned. "Writers make up words all the time. And start clichés."

He nodded, opening his package of utensils. "Well, let's see if it also tastes Italiany, then," and he dove into his chicken parmesan. I waited for a response. "Delicious."

I opened my tray and unwrapped my silverware. "How did you know chicken parmesan was one of my favorite Italian dishes?"

"I guessed. It's one of mine, too."

I stared at the flowers he brought. "I love the scent of fresh flowers and they're beautiful. Thank you." I was trying not to cry. I put down my fork. All the attention and visits, cards and flowers were almost too much. I gulped down some water to avoid tearing up.

Nick reached across the table and put his hand on my arm. I looked at him. I felt a funny tingling run up my arm. "You're welcome. I'm glad I met you, Natalie."

"Me, too." It had been a long time since I had a close friend. Even longer since having a male friend, one I could trust. Besides Luke, who was more of an acquaintance.

He let go and took another bite. "And I'm really looking forward to your cake," he tried to lighten the mood.

"Well, I have plenty of chocolate chips to make more than one. And cookies, too."

"Oh, yeah, those cookies you brought to Uncle Nick's were great too. Just let me know what else you need. I'm your man."

"I will. Trust me." I remembered what Mrs. White told me earlier. Maybe I could come up with some odd jobs of my own for him to do. Living in an old house certainly lent itself to projects. I thought of that annoying buzzing I heard upstairs periodically but haven't had time to investigate.

He arched his eyebrows but didn't say anything. I tried not to smile. After we finished eating, we took tea to the living room and decided to exchange the projects we edited for each other. My ankle wasn't bothering me as much and I finished his paper that afternoon. I read his suggestions with interest. I peeked over my paper to see his face.

He was intently reading my comments I left for him. Most of his mistakes were minor, as he was an English teacher after all. "Do you have any questions?" I asked.

"No. Do you?"

I shook my head. "I agreed with everything you said, thanks."

"You're welcome."

He pointed to the Scrabble game back on the shelf. "Feel up to a game?"

"Sure." I moved my papers and brought the game box to the table. We made small talk while playing our game, which he won. I was still getting used to being around him, and felt a little reserved. I couldn't figure out why he wanted to hang around me, but for now I enjoyed the company.

Chapter 6

The next morning after breakfast, I edited for several hours then walked to the library to return my western books. I had read enough to write the parts for my book. After a quick lunch of Mrs. White's soup, I baked a chocolate zucchini cake for our dessert tomorrow. Then took a small roast from the freezer to thaw.

When I checked the mail, I found another card in the small pile of envelopes. I didn't recognize the writing on the front and there was no return address. The front of the card read, I'm thinking of you...and the inside said, all the time. The sender wrote in a neat script, *I'm glad you're getting better. But I'll miss the dinner company. Remember you owe me cake! Yours, Nick.*

He's so sweet. Definitely too good for me. I added his card to the growing collection on the mantle. I really felt at home now, with personal mail and some new friends. Even if they were all religious folks.

Weak sunshine peaked through large clouds the next morning. It looked as cold as it probably was. Since I hadn't been to the gym all week, I thought I would go and do my usual routine taking it slow until I made sure my ankle could handle it. I fed Felix and left the house.

After a few errands and my uneventful workout, I was ready to shower and work at home the rest of the day. I put the roast and vegetables in the slow cooker, added herbs and seasoning, covered them with water, and turned the cooker on low. I worked in my office for several hours, the aroma tantalizing me.

Though Nick was coming back tonight because I offered to cook for him back before my ankle accident; it still felt like going on a first date. I tried reading, but had to read the same sentence five times and still didn't understand what I read. I tossed the book down in frustration.

I stirred the dinner contents and set the table in the dining room. The flowers still looked good sitting in the center, but I refreshed the water in the vase. The rooms had all been straightened and dusted.

Finally the doorbell rang. I gave my hair a quick finger comb and opened the door.

"Hi, Nick. Come in out of the cold."

"Hi, Natalie. How are you doing?" He shrugged out of his coat and I hung it on the wooden tree. I tried to ignore the musky scent coming from the collar.

"I'm fine. I don't think I qualify as a patient anymore."

"Well, I guess that's good and bad, huh?" He slipped out of his wet shoes. I peeked at his socks. Navy with a red diamond pattern.

"All the cards and the company and the meals have been wonderful. I should have Mrs. White and Mrs. John over sometime."

"I'm sure they would enjoy it." He followed me into the living room. "Thanks for the card, by the way. It made my day." I gestured toward the mantle.

Nick smiled at me. "You're welcome. I figured it was a small price to pay for some chocolate cake."

"Very funny."

"I meant what it said, though." He stared at the fire, with his hands in his pockets and not looking at me. I thought about what he wrote. He must have meant the part about thinking about me all the time. I felt my face flush. I didn't know what to say, so kept silent.

He broke the awkward silence. "Looks like your fire could use some fuel. May I?"

"Knock yourself out. What would you like to drink?"

"Water please, I haven't had enough today."

The awkward moment was over. Standing in the entryway, I quietly watched him stir the fire and add another log to it before I headed to the kitchen. How would it be if we ever did become a couple? As I poured our water, I dreamed of both of us living in this house as husband and wife. Lost in my thoughts, I hadn't realized I was spilling water onto the floor. Snapping back to reality, I grabbed a towel and wiped it up, thankful Nick was in the living room and had no idea I was acting like a silly school girl in the kitchen.

I handed him his glass after he replaced the poker. I sat on the sofa.

He sat in the chair opposite me. "Is your ankle back to normal?"

"Pretty much. I managed to get to the Y this morning without too much trouble. Then I ran some errands and worked in the office this afternoon." I wiped my wet hand on my leg, and put my water down. "Dinner will be ready in about half an hour."

"The aroma from the roast is making my mouth water. Certainly smells better than the cafeteria ever does."

I smiled. "Well, I hope it tastes as good as it smells."

"I'm sure it will." He turned as Felix entered the room. "Hi buddy," he said, rubbing his back. Felix had stopped at Nick's feet. Apparently Felix wanted more attention, because he jumped in Nick's lap. His contented purring could be heard across the room.

"You may regret that," I said.

He grinned at me, saying, "I'm washable." Nick's brick red oxford, navy tie and tan slacks now had an accessory of white fur.

We chatted about the weather and books we've read lately and then got ready to eat. Nick washed his hands at the kitchen sink while I carried the roast to the table. I pulled some bread warming in the oven and took out the salad from the fridge, already made.

We sat down and Nick prayed over our food. He thanked God for me, a new friend. I was touched. I still didn't see how we got connected so quickly, so comfortably as if we'd known each other for years. Yet, we've barely known each other for a couple weeks.

But I liked it. A lot. I just had to take this praying stuff with it.

"How is your uncle?" I reached for a slice of bread and buttered it.

"Getting better. He's slowly adjusting to a new rhythm."

"That's good. I can't imagine being married that long and then suddenly being alone again."

"Yeah, it's not fun to think about." We were quiet in our own thoughts before he spoke again. "This roast is delicious. And so are the bread and salad."

"Thanks."

We chatted about our last few days, Nick telling me about some of the funny excuses his students come up with for not having assignments done.

"Natalie," Nick hesitated before continuing, "would you consider going to church with me sometime?"

I gulped and digested his question before answering. "Sometime, perhaps. But probably not any time soon."

Nick seemed to consider my answer and nodded, satisfied. He asked another question. One I felt safer and easier to answer. "Would you mind going to a Christian book store with me? After supper—unless you have plans?"

"That might be doable," I answered. How bad could a book store be? "What's one like?"

"Similar to any book store except with more Bibles, greeting cards, and t-shirts, with a Christian theme. And of course lots of books, both fiction and non."

"That might be ok. Any store with books can't be all bad."

Nick grinned. "Great. I think they're still having some sort of after Christmas clearance sale. You might find a truck load of bargains."

"Sounds right up my alley. My ankle is the only concern, then. I don't think I can stand around too long." I stood up to start clearing the table. "Don't worry. I guess this means you won't get clobbered in our tournament tonight. But your day will come," I pointed at Nick. "You just wait."

"We'll see about that," he answered, pointing back.

After we cleared the table, Nick offered to wash, so I let him. I watched from my perch at the counter. He did a good job. Then we put our coats on and I grabbed my purse. From the porch, Nick took my arm since the ground was slippery from snow. "I'll shovel for you when we get back, if you have one."

"Oh, you don't have to do that," I protested. My breath came out in foggy puffs. The sky was clear with a spattering of stars. With no clouds, it was sure to be a cold night. I slid in Nick's car after he opened the door.

"I know. But I want to." He started the car.

I couldn't argue with that, could I?

"I do have a shovel and it's in the garage. Somewhere." The garage was an area I seldom went into except for parking my temperamental car.

"I'll find it. Don't worry."

I wasn't the least worried. I just didn't feel right about it. What was it about this guy that made me say yes to everything? Except church. No, not that, if ever.

When we arrived at the store, Nick offered me his arm as we walked across the parking lot. How nice it would be to stay there, but I couldn't let my mind wander in that direction.

Once in the store I looked around. The store was pleasing, with a quiet atmosphere and lots of things to look at. I wandered over to the Bible section, completely overwhelmed. If I'd ever seen Bibles in a regular store, I hadn't paid any attention. "I can't believe all the different kinds. Why are there so many?" I mumbled to myself. Nick was in another area of books. Bibles came in leather, hard cover, paper, Jesus' words in red, this version, that version. What on earth?

Nick came up beside me. "Do you want a Bible?" he asked softly. His look was sympathetic.

"I don't really know. But I seem to be standing here, so maybe I should." I gestured my arm across the whole aisle. "What do you recommend?" I certainly had no idea.

He pulled a Bible off the shelf and handed it to me. It was a New King James version, with Jesus' words in red. "The King James or New King James versions are the closest to the originals which were in Greek and Hebrew. Later they were translated into the King's English. But sometimes the archaic language is harder to understand. Some other good choices are the New International Version, the New American Standard or the Message versions which are in everyday language." He found me those as well, adding them to my pile.

"Good grief. Now I have to decide what color and between leather or imitation or hardcover? Are you serious?!"

"Someday you might understand," Nick said, looking hopeful.

I finally picked out a New King James version in blue imitation leather. And a cover to keep it in. Then I spotted the fiction section and got engrossed in the selection of historical fiction and mystery books. I was surprised at the selection of thrillers and mysteries, not knowing there were so many Christian authors. I picked a couple mysteries that sounded intriguing. It wouldn't hurt to read them, I supposed. But I doubted they were any better than 'regular' books.

Nick picked out a couple books on something he called theology or something or other. We went to the checkout counter where a guy with one pierced ear and a black t-shirt waited.

"Hey, that's a good pick, your Bible there. Have one myself. I try reading it every day, but sometimes I don't get to it." He rang my items up.

"That will be eighty-two thirty-eight. And here's a free bookmark listing upcoming local events."

I handed him my debit card. He rang it up and I moved aside for Nick. I looked at all the magnets, bookmarks, highlighters, stickers and mugs near the register. The store looked rather inviting, with a gray and maroon carpet, beautiful framed prints on the walls and glass and brass shelving. In the children's corner a video played some goofy vegetables with big eyes. Bright yellow, green and red games and books were also in that section.

We strolled to the parking lot and neared Nick's car. I jumped as a man came near us, getting into his car parked next to Nick's.

"Sorry, ma'am, didn't mean to startle ya," he nodded and got in his car.

I stood immovable for a minute, my heart pounding. I hugged myself tight, trying to get my heartbeat back to a regular, non-threatened beat.

"Natalie, are you ok?" Nick touched my arm.

I flinched, and tried not to stiffen further, grateful the street lamp was weak. I didn't want Nick to see my face. I broke in a cold sweat under my coat and started shaking uncontrollably.

"I'm fine." I quickly got in the car, taking a deep breath. My teeth chattered as scenes from a dark cold night six years ago flashed through my mind. I pushed them back as Nick slid in.

"What happened out there, you look like you saw a ghost." His voice was soft and compassionate. He started the car and turned down the radio and the heat up.

"It's nothing," I lied. I couldn't possibly explain it. I didn't know if I'd ever be able to. I clicked my seatbelt and stared straight ahead and then made crinkly noises with my bag, readjusting it on my lap, trying to forget the startling incident.

He slowly put the car in gear and pulled out of the lot. He was silent until he asked, "Do you know where to start reading your Bible?"

I shook my head.

"May I make a suggestion?" His voice was still soft, nearly bringing tears to my eyes. A part of me longed to tell him about my past and move beyond that night of terror, but I didn't know how. And what would his reaction be? I couldn't risk the betrayal.

"Of course." I relaxed, now in the dark comfort and security of Nick's car. I willed myself to stop shaking.

"Start with the book of John, in the New Testament. You'll get a quick overview of what Jesus' life was about." His voice was low and gentle.

"Thanks." I decided to read some before going to bed that night.

Nick pulled the car up to the curb in front of my house. He got out, came around the car and opened the door for me. I clutched my bag and he held out his arm. I hesitated, and then took it before walking to the door, arm in arm. It probably would be better for Nick to shovel off the path, even though several footprints tracked through it from my many visitors. I unlocked the door and Nick said, "I'll find the shovel and then leave it here by the door, if that's alright."

I stepped inside and turned the foyer light on. "Nick, you don't have to—"

"I already said I would. Besides a little exercise won't hurt me."

I nodded, since he insisted. "Will you have time to come in for cocoa when you're done?"

He looked at his watch under the porch light. "It's not quite nine, so sure."

"Good, I'll leave the front door open then."

"I'll be inside in no time." He was on his way to the garage, determined to shovel for some reason. I shook my head, going into the kitchen to heat the kettle. I took two mugs from the rack on the counter and found the canister of cocoa I wanted from the pantry.

Thinking about Nick shoveling, I thought I could really get used to this treatment. It wouldn't take him long to clear the snow; the path from the house to the sidewalk wasn't that long. Just then I heard Nick come in and shut the door. "I'm in here," I called. I poured the water and stirred.

"Told you it wouldn't take long." Nick had taken his coat and shoes off in the doorway. Now he rubbed his hands together and leaned on the counter a few steps from me.

I stopped stirring. "That wasn't the point."

"Oh? What was?" He tilted his head with a puzzled look on his face.

"All the trouble you and your friends are going to. I don't deserve it." I started stirring again faster, almost spilling the cocoa.

"Who says? That's the second time you've said that." Nick walked around to my side of the counter and leaned against it facing me. He was so near, his musky aftershave mingled with the steaming cocoa. I didn't answer.

Nick gently and slowly reached across the counter and placed his hand on mine to keep me from stirring. I held my breath. My hand felt as warm as the cocoa. My heart raced. I couldn't look at him, but stared into the depth of my mug.

"Natalie, who says?" he repeated his question, softer this time. He also squeezed my hand gently.

Heat spread across my face. I continued to look at our hands, not daring to look at those warm brown eyes resembling melted chocolate. I didn't want to continue this conversation. I couldn't.

The telephone rang, making me jump at the interruption. "Excuse me," I turned away from Nick's nearness walking around the counter the opposite way and rushed out of the kitchen in search of the phone. I never remembered where I had it last. I had to get a grip. I couldn't let myself fall for this guy. I wiped tears off my face and took a deep breath. I found the phone on the couch behind a toss pillow. I picked it up and hurriedly pushed the talk button before the answering machine upstairs kicked on.

I sunk into the sofa, listening to a recorded spiel about house siding. I didn't care if I didn't need it. This was an excuse to get myself back together. My heart slowly returned to normal. I looked up as Nick walked in carrying both mugs. "My house already has siding, thanks." I disconnected, my quiet reprieve up.

Nick handed me a mug, and sat in the chair across from me, our roles suddenly reversed. "Thanks," I whispered. I set the phone on the coffee table.

"You're welcome."

I avoided looking in Nick's direction. I knew he thought something was wrong with me, but I wasn't ready to deal with it.

He interrupted my thoughts. "Natalie, I—"

"I don't want to talk about it." I cleared my throat, glancing at him.

Nick arched his eyebrows. "Natalie, I was just wondering if you fed Felix. He was rubbing against my legs and meowing."

"Oh." I was relieved. "Sorry. I think I forgot to feed him before we left."

Nick nodded.

We sipped in silence. What was I doing with this man? How could I ever tell him? And if I did, what would he say?

He broke into my thoughts. "So explain your Scrabble tournament idea you mentioned at dinner. It sounds interesting."

His request threw me off guard and it took me a minute to switch gears. I explained it to him, relieved he didn't repeat his earlier question. We decided to play a game while we enjoyed our drinks and each other's company. The tension from earlier dissipated like the steam from the cocoa, and we were both able to relax. We agreed that this game wouldn't count in the tournament, but be a practice run.

I won, but only by ten points. Then it was time for him to go. We walked to the front door together. He slipped into his loafers and his long coat. "Goodnight, Natalie. I hope you enjoy reading your new Bible and if you have any questions, just ask." He gently gave my arm a squeeze.

"Thanks. Have a good day tomorrow. Good night." I leaned on the door, relief flooding my insides. I wondered how long I'd be nervous after dark in parking lots. Tears welled up in my eyes as I remembered Nick's compassionate looks at me throughout the evening. I couldn't remember a time when someone so concerned wanted to know how they could help me. I just couldn't bring myself to tell him. I moved away from the door, turning the porch and foyer lights off.

I finished picking up the game and left it on the table. I fed Felix who was practically wailing for his dinner and thought about the last few days. Nick was wonderful. He was funny, a true gentleman, trustworthy and kind. He seemed to think of others and did what he could to help them. From what I've gathered from Mrs. John and Mrs. White, he was a true catch. Except for the God thing, which I didn't understand.

Though he was a great guy, I still didn't think I could share my secret with him. He would probably run the opposite direction when he learned the truth. I wanted to enjoy his company for as long as I could, though. Why not?

I still didn't understand why people went to church each and every week and why they read this big book called the Bible or why they helped each other, sent cards and cooked for me, and all the other stuff they did. What does God do? Who does he love? Why is there a hell? Nick shared some things, but it still didn't make sense to me. I guess I wanted to buy my own Bible to try and figure this God out. If it were even possible.

The trip to the book store was a pleasant surprise. It wasn't much different from any other book or gift shop, really. If Nick hadn't helped me with my Bible purchase, I doubt I could've picked one out. The choices were ridiculous. I sat on the sofa and took out all my purchases. I put my Bible in the cover and looked at the table of contents to find John. I turned to the first page and read the first three chapters. I didn't understand it. In chapter three, I read that God sent us his Son so whosoever believes in him should not perish. I read that verse five times. I might have to give this stuff more thought. On another day.

As I got ready for bed, I thought about what I just read. Did I believe or not? What did I believe about anything? Where does a person go when they die? Is there some sort of afterlife? A holding place? How good does a person have to be to go to heaven or how bad to go to hell? Was there an alternative to either place?

Thinking about Nick and Mrs. John and Mrs. White doing all they had for me, I realized how selfish I was. These strangers were helping me, going out of their way. Why? What had I ever done for anyone? I decided to give this some serious thought and think about what I could do for others.

I would have to talk to Nick more about this stuff. But for now it was time to go to bed. Only time would tell if I could find answers to my questions.

****

We were now into February and still bitter cold with snow blanketing the ground. The temperature had only been in the low 20s all of January and February so far. But inside, Nick and I were nice and cozy with the fire blazing. We were playing our first game of the Scrabble tournament. We stretched out on the floor, near the fireplace with the game board between us. Felix wasn't far from Nick's feet.

We had gone to Luke's for a writing meeting on the first Saturday of February, and it had been a disaster for me. Luke had seemed to think he and I were closer than we were and Nick had suffered in frustration. A part of me had enjoyed it, only because it was fun watching Luke and Nick act like two school boys fighting over a pretty girl; but more of me found the whole situation stressful.

Tonight though was different and this time, I won like I predicted. "Game number one, Natalie. How many are we going to play?" I found a tablet on the end table and wrote 'Tournament' across the top.

Nick was thinking, staring at the fire. "I don't know, ten? Best of ten?"

"So what's the prize?" I tapped my chin with the pen.

"Hmm. How about a chocolate zucchini cake for me if I win, and a dinner and movie for you if you win." Nick held out his hand.

"Sounds like a deal to me." We shook hands. "Deal." Our hands stayed together a little longer than necessary.

Then Nick got up. "I better get going. I have some papers to grade before tomorrow and it's going to be a busy day." I took our plates and headed to the kitchen. "Let me cut some cake to take with you."

"Really? Since you twisted my arm, I'll take some." He followed me into the kitchen.

I took out a paper plate and added three large pieces to it. "This good?"

"Let's see, that's enough for tomorrow, Sunday and Monday. What about Tuesday through Friday?" He leaned against the counter with a lopsided grin.

"Hmm. I see a dilemma here. If I put some of this in the freezer, we can have some Wednesday at writers group. Will that suffice?"

"I guess that'll have to do." He sighed and watched me wrap it up.

"Here you go," I handed him the package.

"Thanks, this is great." Our fingers touched, sending an electric pulse up my arm. I barely registered what had happened and followed Nick to the door.

"Keep those kids in line and teach them a thing or two." I smiled at him.

"I'll try." He smiled back and added, "See you Wednesday."

"Good night." I made sure he made it to his car and then shut the door. I went back to the kitchen and put the remaining cake in the freezer as promised and cleaned up the kitchen. As I worked, I wondered what I was doing with a guy out of my league. Who did I think I was? Back in the living room, I slid the game pieces back in the box, poked the remnants of the fire to orange embers and sat on the sofa, rethinking the week.

On Valentine's Day, I received several surprises. The first was a flower delivery, compliments of Luke. His note said, *Thanks for your friendship, keep up the writing. Luke.*

In the mail I received two cards, one from my parents and one from Nick. I opened his first. It wasn't romantic, but welcome all the same. He included a gift card to a book store, which was right up my alley. My parent's card had a short note in it that said they missed me and hoped I was doing well. I put the cards on the mantle. The day for celebrating love was on a Tuesday, and Nick had prior plans, so I knew we wouldn't be seeing each other.

Instead, I stayed home and treated myself to watching a couple of my favorite movies, an oldie called Charade starring Cary Grant and Audrey Hepburn, and the Blind Side starring Sandra Bullock. I enjoyed caramel popcorn and Felix's company.

On a Friday evening in early March, Nick was over and we played another game in our tournament. The fire blazed, Felix purred, and something buzzed upstairs.

"Do you hear that?" I asked, sitting up from the floor.

"I do and thought I'd heard it before. What is it?" Nick leaned his ear towards the stairs.

"I don't know, but every once in a while I hear it and I think it's in the attic, though I have no idea what it is."

"Do you have a flashlight?"

"In my bedroom, on the nightstand."

He got up. "Lead the way."

Felix ran up the stairs ahead of me, as usual. "Silly cat," I said. "He does this every night."

I went to my room and, grabbed the flashlight and handed it to Nick. I gestured to the door which led to the attic stairs. I followed him, feeling like a chicken.

When we got up there, the buzzing was loud. I switched on the light and we didn't see anything out of the ordinary except a couple of bees. "That's weird. How can a few bees be so loud?"

I stood close to the door, Felix huddled at my feet. We both watched Nick check out the rafters, the corners and the ceiling. "I think it's more than a few bees, Natalie. More like a whole swarm." He looked at me with a worried look.

"Yikes. Really?"

"There's actually honey over here on the floor." He was kneeling down, looking at the drops on the floor. He stood back up and pointed the light toward the ceiling. "Natalie, I think you have a huge hive here with hundreds of bees in your roof. You need to call in some professionals." He looked at me with surprise.

"Oh my gosh."

"Let's leave them alone for now," he turned back toward me and scaredy cat number two, who still crouched at my feet.

"No problem, I'm out of here," I led the way back downstairs after shutting the door tight.

"I'll ask around to find a contractor that can take care of your pests. Depending on the possible damage to rafters and the like, you might need a few repairs. I'd avoid the attic for a while, if I were you."

"I agree; no problem. I'm glad to know what's been making that buzzing sound I've heard. Thanks for checking. Wow."

"You're very welcome. Here's your flashlight."

"Thanks," I put it back on the nightstand while Nick politely waited in the hallway. We headed back downstairs to our game. Well, at least that mystery was solved. We sat back down and resumed our game, which Nick won.

"Nick, three, Natalie two," I said disappointedly. "I'm going to have to work on my vocabulary if this keeps up."

"Me, too, actually. The scores have been a little too close." He gave me a serious poker face.

"You just want another cake."

"What's wrong with that?" He tilted his head, looking at me intently.

I shook my head. We wrapped up our evening and said our good-byes. I went upstairs, Felix racing ahead as usual, and went to bed a little fearful of being carried away by a massive bee swarm.

Nick called the next day to give me two names of guys who could take care of my infestation. I called the first one and he could come Monday morning, so I made the appointment.

When he arrived, I showed the Pest Controller where Nick had found the drips of honey. "Ma'am, I'd say you've got a big problem, if there's this much honey on the floor. That means there's a whole lot more up there," he pointed to the area above where the drips were coming from.

"Just do what you have to do," I led the way back downstairs. "And be careful."

He nodded, and I left him to it. He came back and forth, and up and down the stairs with an assortment of tools. After his assessment, he said he'd have to coordinate with someone who could repair the rafters and the corner of the roof and did I have anyone in mind? I said I'd get back to him.

Nick was pretty sure this job was out of his league and gave me the name of a guy from church who owns his own construction business and could either do it or recommend someone.

A few days later, my house was a beehive of activity, literally. I had a pest crew cutting out blocks of honeycomb and smoking out the bees and another small crew cutting two by fours and nailing them into the rafters. Luckily the bees didn't quite go through the roof, so I didn't have to have any roofing done.

I locked Felix in my room and kept the attic door shut as much as possible while all this was going on. The controller had to carefully remove each honeycomb through the house since it wasn't wise to toss them out from the roof. He carried large sections at a time, and I stayed away as much as possible though he reassured me the bees were calm in their smoky environment.

After the two crews left, and I was several hundred dollars poorer, I crashed on the sofa with a much irritated cat that wasn't happy with me. It was a great relief to have the problem taken care of. I at least got a few jars of fresh honey out of the deal.

****

I finally treated Mrs. White and Mrs. John to lunch and thanked them for all their help with my ankle. We ate at the local café which offered hearty soups and sandwiches.

They both asked me, almost at the same time how it was going with Nick. "We're just friends," I answered.

I knew why I was holding back, but I didn't understand Nick's reservations. And I wasn't ready to ask. He asked again if I'd go to church, but I declined. He didn't seem too surprised, though he tried to hide his disappointment.

****

Hints of spring arrived in early April. Each day was a little warmer, with fewer chilly days. Robins were seen flying around the yard and tulips had been poking up for several weeks now. Apparently I had some around two of my trees. Mostly red and yellow ones, but a few pink ones, too. I planned to plant more pink ones in the future.

I kept up my usual routine, going to the YMCA on Mondays and Wednesdays, working at home most days. And of course our writing meetings on Wednesdays. Nobody ever responded to our notice at the library, so it was just the two of us. At least this way, I had Nick to myself.

Then events beyond our control threw us together.

Chapter 7

The Friday after Easter I stepped outside to get the mail and was just turning around to go back in the house when I heard someone yelling my name. "Natalie! Natalie! Wait!"

I turned around to see Mrs. John running over in her slippers. "What's the matter?" I couldn't imagine what had her so upset and why she was outside in her slippers with no jacket. I had heard some sirens a few minutes earlier, but that wasn't anything unusual. A nursing home wasn't far from me and they transported patients to the hospital so often that I tuned out sirens most of the time.

"Natalie," she began with her hand on my arm. She caught her breath before she could continue. "Something's happened at the school. We heard it on the scanner. They've called in the bomb squad from O'Fallon. Some sort of explosion went off inside the school. We don't know how many might be injured."

She took a deep breath and regained her composure and walked into the house with me. "They've shut the school down and have called parents to pick up their students. I heard helicopters a few minutes ago; it's probably total chaos. Nobody has heard anything about the teachers yet."

I looked at her wondering what she was getting at. "You mean Nick? You think something might have happened—"

In an instant, we both knew we had to find out. "I'll go with you, Natalie. I know some of the school personnel. Get ready, and come get me. I'll go get my shoes and coat."

"Ok, I'll be ready in—" but she had already left. I bolted upstairs to brush my teeth and hair as fast as I could. I slipped on my shoes from last night and grabbed a heavy sweater. I ran to the car but it didn't start right away. It hadn't been driven in a few days. "Come on, Nellie, we don't have time for this!" The engine finally turned over. I backed out the driveway and drove the two blocks to Mrs. John's. She was waiting for me on her porch. We took off for the school. The streets were jammed.

Police were diverting traffic off of Main Street, so we snaked around emergency vehicles, traffic and pedestrians. Fire trucks from several cities were in front of the building with their lights flashing; ambulances were on standby and students, teachers and school personnel were being ushered across the street to the local park. We couldn't get any closer than three blocks down the street. Now there were ribbons of yellow tape around the schoolyard and orange barriers blocking the driveways. Only emergency vehicles were allowed in and out of the parking lot, and the buses were being diverted to an area around the park, two blocks away.

"What do we do now?" I wailed.

"Let's pray. I should have thought of that first before alarming you." She took my hand and we bowed our heads. "Dear Lord, we come before you now and ask that you protect those inside the school and get help to those who need it. Help those that are injured get treated quickly. Be with the doctors who help them and for the families of the victims. And we pray for those responsible that they may repent and ask for forgiveness if needed." I heard more sirens in the distance. I looked up and saw two more ambulances racing toward the school driveway. Mrs. John was still praying, and I put my head back down. I tried not to think about what may have happened to Nick. Was he fine, or was he hurt? "Please help us to get information on our friend Nick and we pray that he is ok. We pray all these things in your name, Amen."

    My amen was barely a whisper. We sat in the car staring out the windshield at the crazy scene from a distance. We could see students huddling together and police officers directing traffic and students away from the school.

    Some of the teachers and other school personnel as far as we could tell, were bewildered but were trying to help. They didn't know what to expect next, if anything. Buses were trying to get through, but had to wait for an officer to show them where to go. If school had started, it hadn't gone on for very long. It was only nine-thirty now. Who would think something like this would happen in our small town? Was it an accident or on purpose? With the increase of guns and school shootings, who knew.

    Police cars and ambulances and buses blocked most of our view, but we could see groups of people coming and going. A minute later sirens blared as at least one ambulance sped away. Who were the injured? How could we find out?

    "If they only took a few to the hospital, that's a good sign," Mrs. John said as she took my hand and squeezed. "Now, let's try not to worry. I'll be back in a few minutes."

    "I'll go with you," I started opening my door.

    "No, you stay here. I know some of the officers. I don't want you to get hurt." She got out of the car and walked down the street toward the chaos. She walked with a purpose and looked straight ahead of her. After a minute, I lost sight of her, wondering if she could get any information.

The constant noise and flashing lights made me feel like I was watching a rock video but it was completely out of hand and a bizarre scene. My shoulders felt tense, and I let go of the steering wheel to loosen up a bit.

I adjusted the heater and turned the radio to a classical station to help calm my nerves. I fiddled with the zipper on my sweater while I waited. A few minutes later, I saw Mrs. John heading back to the car. She had her head down, and it looked like she had a tissue to her face. Oh, no, what could that mean?

I sat up and turned the radio back off. She got back into the car. She put her hand on my arm and in a wobbly voice said, "Nick was taken to the hospital on one of those stretchers."

"But why? What happened..." I couldn't imagine what was going on. I'd never stepped a foot in the school. How could sweet, dear Nick be hurt? How bad?

"They think he was in the room where the blast went off. There was a lot of blood on the floor. Some of the students were hurt. It wasn't from a bomb or gun, that's the good thing. So far, they think it was an accident from mixing the wrong chemicals together, but the students in that chemistry class are being questioned at the back of the school before they can be released. The injured have been taken to St. Elizabeth's. I'll tell you how to get there." She wiped her nose.

Officers were directing traffic, but drivers were trying to ask them what happened, and it was slow going getting out of town to the highway.

I could only imagine what the parents were thinking or trying not to think.

It hurt to breathe, but because I wanted to know what happened and how bad he was, I followed Mrs. John's directions and we were at the hospital in twenty minutes. This was the first time I had been at one of the local hospitals. We parked in the visitor's lot and walked through the double doors, looking for the information desk.

We found a large counter behind a half wall with a blue sign suspended from the ceiling that read 'Information'. A kind looking elderly gentleman asked, "May I help you?"

"We need information on a patient brought in a few minutes ago by ambulance."

"The only thing I can do is direct you to the emergency department. Are either of you family?"

We both shook our heads.

"The emergency department is down that hall and then you take the first left. I don't know if anyone down there will help you unless you're family."

Mrs. John thanked him and we headed for the emergency room. The E.R. wasn't very busy. We couldn't find anyone to ask what we needed to know. We took seats against the wall to wait. I stared at the shiny blue and white tiled floor or at the walls of pale blue.

We sat in silence for a few minutes, not sure what to do. I wiped the tears from my eyes, not sure why I was crying. Of course I didn't want anything bad to happen to Nick, as we were still becoming friends. Already it seemed as if we knew each other for years. Mrs. John blew her nose. I patted her on the shoulder, for lack of something better to do.

For an E.R. it was pretty quiet. We could hear noises down the hall, but we also could hear the heater humming. At least there weren't noisy children around.

After sitting nearly an hour-and-a-half, a doctor in green scrubs came out. "Mrs. Norton?" he looked straight at me. I looked at Mrs. John. She nodded.

I stood up bewildered; torn between the deception of being called Mrs. Norton and wanting to know what was wrong. The fear won out and I turned toward the doctor.

"I'm Dr. Swenson. I'm afraid Nick is in critical condition. He may lose his hearing in one ear, and his face may be badly scarred. He has second and third degree burns covering most of his upper body. He's also in a coma from a concussion. If you believe in prayer, ma'am, this is the time for it. We'll be wheeling him into surgery shortly to try saving his ear and taking care of the burns. Someone will let you know when he goes up to recovery. Coffee machines are down the hall, help yourself." Dr. Swenson was quiet a moment, letting Mrs. John and I absorb his comments. "Do you have any questions?"

I was in shock and couldn't speak. First from the doctor assuming I was Nick's wife, and then from his prognosis. I shook my head, and said weakly, "Thank you." I plopped down in the plastic seat. Mrs. John spoke for the first time, "Is he going to make it?"

"Most likely yes, but it will be a long road to recovery with the chance of the hearing loss I mentioned. He'll have to get burn treatment and after this initial surgery he'll need further testing to see how things heal."

"Thank you, doctor. We'll be here, praying. Take good care of our Nick."

"Will do." Dr. Swenson paused a moment before turning back to the inner sanctum of life-giving treatment.

After he left, Mrs. John called the pastor and discussed something called the prayer chain. While she was on the phone, pacing and gesturing with her hands my thoughts ran wild. How could this happen? Why to Nick, one of the kindest people I've ever known? Who would take care of him, and help with any rehab he might need? Confusion and hurt overwhelmed me and the tears raced down my face, dripping on my lap, but I didn't care. I hoped and prayed Nick would be as good as new again. And soon.

Mrs. John came back a few minutes later with a cup of coffee. "Would you like some coffee?" I shook my head no. She sat down and patted my arm. "Pastor is on his way. I've left a message with the prayer chain coordinator and Mrs. White is going to check on Nick's place later.

"He'll be alright, dear. He's in good hands." She handed me a tissue and I wiped my face and nose.

I didn't know what she meant, whether the doctor's hands or God's and I was too shocked and angry to ask. I was almost too numb to speak. It took too much effort. Last night seemed days ago. Mrs. John and I had only been sitting here a few minutes and already it seemed like an eternity. I looked at my watch. It wasn't even noon.

Mrs. John sipped her coffee. Every once in a while her eyes would close and her lips would move. I didn't know if I wanted to pray to God. He didn't deserve it. How could he do something like this when he had the power to stop it? He probably wouldn't answer any of my prayers anyway.

We heard voices down the hall and a small crowd entered the waiting room and headed toward us. I recognized Mr. Norton, Nick's uncle. He looked tired and haggard. I didn't recognize anyone else, but guessed they were from the church. They started talking to Mrs. John. I stayed in my chair, half listening to the swirls of conversation around my head. I was almost too tired to listen and keep up. Another gathering met in a far corner, most likely for one of the students. They must have gone to different hospitals, because this one wasn't as busy as I'd think it would be after something like this.

I leaned my head against the wall and shut my eyes. Maybe if I kept my eyes shut long enough, this nightmare would go away. Incredibly, I almost dozed off before someone spoke to me. "It's Natalie, right?" a soft voice asked on my left.

I opened my eyes slowly to focus on a man standing over me. He looked faintly familiar but I couldn't place him from his polo and slacks.

"I'm Pastor Collins from First Baptist. It is *Natalie*, right?"

I nodded.

"May I have a seat?"

I gestured to the empty seat. He sat down. "I'm sure this is a shock to you, as it is to all of us. We're praying for a quick recovery both for Nick and the other patient as well."

I didn't respond.

"Unfortunately, we live in an evil world and these things happen."

No kidding. If anyone knew evil, I sure did. But I tuned back in to the pastor.

"...we still must do our best, never losing hope."

Hope? Hope of what? Hell on earth? How fair is that? I kept my sarcastic response to myself and simply brooded, worried about Nick. Where was his hope right now?

"We'll all have to pull together for Nick's sake, don't you agree?"

I nodded wholeheartedly. I at least agreed with that much, since he had done so much for me already. And he had barely known me before offering his help. The least I could do was be there for him. "Yes, he deserves that for sure. He's been so kind to me, I want to return the favor." I sat up straighter, looking at the pastor's gentle face.

"He doesn't even know yet, what he might have to face, does he?"

I shook my head, wishing I could keep the pain far from a man who only deserved kindness. And good things, not concussions and burns.

"All right, then. Let's make a pact, shall we? You and I can make this our pet project. We'll keep everyone posted on his condition. We'll need someone to visit him almost daily and let the others know how he's doing. We'll all pray for him of course. You can make a daily journal of sorts for Nick to read later when he's out of the hospital. This will help him not to forget these days, if you know what I mean."

I leaned forward. "I can do that. Should it be on paper or computer?" This was definitely something I could do.

The pastor paused a minute, thinking about an answer. "Whichever you prefer. You can update it as you like, and no one else needs to read it. This is between you and me, ok?"

Somehow, I felt important and honored to take on this responsibility. But why me? Why did Pastor Collins trust me with this? And why between just him and me? I was already thinking of getting a wire bound journal, one not too flowery that Nick would enjoy when he went home after his recovery.

"Why me, though? Why not someone else who knows him better?" I finally voiced some of my questions.

"Ah, well, you see," he looked away, seeming to stall for some reason, beyond my comprehension. He turned back to me. "Well, it's like you said, you'd like to return the favor. And I've heard you're one of those writer types," he kind of smirked and rushed on, "so this might be a good project for you." He seemed relieved and pleased with his reason, whatever the true reason was. I'm not sure how he knew I was a writer, somebody must have told him. "Plus, your schedule is a little more flexible, right?"

I nodded agreement, "True." I thought about it for a minute and agreed it would certainly be something I could do for Nick. "I'll do it. I'll get a journal this afternoon and return this evening if he's out of critical care." At least I could find out how Nick was each day first hand. Somehow I felt better, feeling like a part of something. Before the pastor got up, I touched him on the arm. He turned back to me. "Yes?"

"Pastor, will you do something for me?" The question popped out before I could retract it.

"Of course, Natalie. What is it?"

I couldn't believe I was asking this. "Could you please pray for me, too?"

He was quiet only a second before replying, "Of course, of course. I'll check back with you in a day or two."

I nodded.

He got up and talked with a few of those who had gathered. Not until after he walked away, did I realize I didn't specify what to pray for. But he didn't seem surprised I asked. So how was he going to pray for me? That was certainly something to ponder later.

I don't know why, but my inner turmoil calmed a bit after talking with Pastor Collins. He seemed like a nice enough guy. I watched his retreating figure go down the hallway, most likely going on to the next crisis. I forgot to tell him that Dr. Swenson was the doctor, and he thought I was Mrs. Norton. Somehow though, in the long run, I figured it really didn't matter.

Mrs. John came back over and sat in her original chair. "How are you holding up, dear?"

"I'm better now. I'm not sure why, but I really am."

She looked like she understood. She patted my arm again. "I'm glad. It helps to have friends who are highly connected." She had long since finished her coffee and thrown her cup away. She looked like she felt better, too. There seemed to be some sort of peace that came over the room while everyone had gathered.

I smiled, despite myself. I didn't even consider Pastor Collins a friend yet, for I barely knew him. But I've heard a little about him from Nick, Mrs. John and Mrs. White. With this new project, there was certainly a strong possibility of him becoming a friend. And maybe that wasn't so bad.

Chapter 8

    While Mrs. John and I waited or prayed, and before there was a journal to record things in, I already worded today's entry in my head. The first day of a long journey, I was afraid. But I would do this one thing for Nick. If anyone deserved kindness, a favor done for, or a chance to show gratefulness to, it was Nick Norton. He deserved it and so much more. The members of Mrs. John's church left one by one, not knowing any more information than we did. After a while it was just the two of us again. "Shall I go search for some sustenance?" Mrs. John asked.

    "Yes, please. I'm getting hungry just sitting here. After we eat, I'll find the gift shop and look for a journal. At least while I sit here, I can doodle or do some writing, too."

    "Right. I'll see what I can find. I have no idea of the nutritional or flavor value, but we'll make do."

    "I hope at least one of those is good," I said.

    "Let's hope for at least the flavor, shall we?"

    I smiled and she left with her purse. How is it possible to become starving, merely sitting down and waiting for bad news? It was nearly noon, and breakfast seemed days ago, not just a few hours. On a table in the corner, I looked for a decent magazine to look through. I knew I couldn't focus enough to read anything, but I could at least flip through and read photo captions of whatever caught my eye. I found a magazine filled with model homes, perfectly spotless and probably where no child or pet ever stepped foot. Some of them intrigued me, the

Victorian ones with charm but updated for today's lifestyle. I was halfway through the magazine, when Mrs. John came back.

"I found a little kiosk on the third floor. They had some salads and sandwiches. I hope turkey and American suit you. I grabbed some condiment packets too, if you like."

"This looks fine. Thank you." I took one of the sandwiches and packets of mayo and mustard. She also found bags of barbeque chips. We devoured our lunch as if we'd never see food again. I took our trash to the can by the magazine table. "Want anything from the gift shop?" I picked up my purse.

"Would you pick out a nice card from both of us?"

"Sure. I won't be long."

I left her reading my magazine. I went back to the information desk where an elderly lady now sat in a pink lab coat. She gave me the directions I needed and I took the elevator to the second floor. The shop was well stocked with all kinds of snacks, cards, flowers, t-shirts, small games, coloring books, and stationery and pen sets. I looked through the stationery and notebooks finding one that wasn't too feminine for my purpose. I found one that was wire bound, with a geometrical design in metallic colors on the cover. Then I looked through the cards for one appropriate from Mrs. John and me. I added gum, mints, and a deck of cards to my basket and then paid for them at the counter. Another elderly lady also in a pink coat rang up my purchases.

I sat out in the hallway outside the gift shop and quickly signed the card. I also opened the mints and popped two in my mouth. Then I quickly put everything back in the bag and headed back to the E.R. waiting room. I wondered how long it would be before we got any news.

When I rounded the last corner, I saw Mrs. John standing with a doctor. I hurried over. "I was just telling your mother-in-law—," at this, I raised my eyebrows and Mrs. John silently patted my arm—"that Nick pulled through and we're monitoring his vitals. If they stay normal for the next twelve hours or so, he should rally. We aren't sure about his hearing yet, until he regains consciousness and can be tested. But the worst is over. He'll remain in critical but stable condition until those twelve hours are over and if they're good, we'll move him to satisfactory condition. He won't be able to have any visitors until that point.

"Do you have any questions?" The doctor's mask was still around his neck and blood splattered his green surgical scrubs.

I shook my head. My body felt numb. What had happened to our Nick?

"Thank you, doctor. We'll come back in the morning."

He nodded and left. We went the opposite direction. "I feel like we're abandoning him," I whined.

"I know. But it won't do Nick or either of us any good to just sit here all day and all night. He would understand. Besides, we have things we need to do. When we get back to my house, we'll notify the prayer chain with Dr. Swenson's update so everyone can pray more specifically. And I'll have Mrs. White check in on Nick's place and stop the paper, water his plants, feed his fish and all that kind of stuff. Then I'll call the school and talk to Mr. Keller, the principal. He'll need to know Nick will be out for some time and to get a substitute. At least this is Friday and he'll have more time to find one."

We were out to the car by this point, and we got in. "Mother-in-law, huh?" I cracked a grin at her. She didn't look at me, but just patted my arm again, looking out her window and muttering something about all of us being God's children. I just let it go; what did it hurt?

The bright sunlight made me realize that the world keeps spinning regardless of our circumstances. Soon the sun would set and my world would be dark. The fresh air brought relief after the stuffy and medicinal smell inside the hospital. I cracked open both front windows letting the breeze blow through my hair until we wound our way out of the parking lot. "Do you mind if we stop by the flower shop in town first?" Mrs. John turned to me.

"No, not at all, *Mother*." I grinned despite my anxiety. "What do you have in mind?"

She chuckled, relieving some of our tension before answering. "Something simple, perhaps a bouquet of balloons and a plant. We don't know how long he'll be unconscious and we certainly don't want to get flowers that might die before he even knows he got them."

"Good point." I drove to the flower shop on Main Street, the one next to the café Nick and I met at for breakfast weeks ago. It seemed only a few days ago.

I walked in behind Mrs. John. The store was very busy for this time of day, I thought. "Hi, Velma. We need something encouraging for Nick. Perhaps some balloons and a hearty plant?"

Velma, who stood tall with red hair and a flowery apron nodded. "Of course. What a tragedy. How is Nick, do you know?" She walked over to her aisle of plants. "I saw and heard the commotion down the street and feared it was a school shooting."

"We just came from the hospital. He'll pull through, with the possibility of losing his hearing in one ear. He's still in critical and has a long road of recovery ahead of him." We walked closer to Velma.

"Such a shame. I'll be praying for him. I guess the other one taken to the hospital was a student, Jim Peterson. I don't know him, but people have been ordering flowers and plants left and right for him. And the other two were treated and released I'd heard."

"I don't know Jim either, poor young man. I still don't know exactly what happened, but time will tell."

Velma turned to her plant display. "Well, I have some peace lilies, pyramid bamboo and mixed greenery. Let me know which balloons you'd like, I'm running a special today, three for the price of two. Please excuse me," Velma left us to help incoming customers. We looked over the plants and chose a healthy green mixed plant with three varieties in an eight-inch pot. We went over the balloon section and looked at the display on the wall. We discussed the ones we liked and agreed on three. One was bright yellow and said, "God loves you,", the middle one read, "Get well" and had squiggles on it, and the third read, "We love you," in red letters on a silver background. They weren't anything flowery of course.

Velma was back at the counter, ringing up a customer in front of us. We told her which balloons we wanted filled and paid for the plant as well. I gave Mrs. John money from my purse. I carried the balloons and she carried the plant, which we put it in the back seat. We would take them with us to the hospital in the morning. We planned to go together right after breakfast.

When we arrived back at Mrs. John's, there were a few cars in her driveway. I didn't know whom they belonged to, but she didn't seem surprised. I pulled up and parked in the street.

"Pastor Collins is here, and Mrs. White with Mrs. Nixon, I reckon. They'll want our news."

We quickly gathered our purchases since they couldn't stay in the car in the frigid temperatures and I followed her into the house. "Good afternoon, everyone." We hung our coats on her hall tree while she updated them from what the doctor said. We bought a Milky Way to hold the balloons down and left them by our jackets. Mrs. John told me in the flower shop it was Nick's favorite candy bar.

Everyone had come to the hallway when they heard us pull up. Now, Pastor Collins said he'd get back to work at the church and would update the prayer chain. Mrs. White said she'd taken care of Nick's paper and set his thermostat for the moment. She'll go over periodically and air it out and run the faucets, things like that.

"We'll be praying for you, too," Pastor Collins whispered in my ear. He put on his coat and was gone.

Mr. John joined us the kitchen where Mrs. John and I collapsed into kitchen chairs. "Hi, Natalie, how are you holding up?" He squeezed my shoulder in a grandfatherly way before sitting down.

"Ok, I guess. Tired. I feel like I've been up for days. I don't know how families do this every day with loved ones in the hospital for cancer or something serious."

He nodded with understanding. "It's tough, but you just have to take one day at a time. We'll all be praying for Nick. He's dear to us. I think Mrs. White has tried calling his parents in Pennsylvania. She's left a message for them to call Pastor. No doubt they'll be on the first plane out here."

I was learning all kinds of things about Nick. Who knows what else I'll learn while he's in the hospital? Mrs. John started some chili and invited me to stay. I accepted. I hadn't been home all day, and was in no mood to cook. Let alone work. I set the bowls and spoons on the table as Mrs. John informed me where she kept them. Before I sat down, I retrieved the card from my purse I purchased for Nick and laid it on the counter.

Mrs. John took out crackers, butter, cheese and corn chips. Mr. John offered grace and said a special prayer for Nick. I added a silent one of my own, before adding my Amen.

"It feels good to eat something hot, especially since it's delicious," I commented to the cook.

"Thank you, Natalie. It's nothing special, but it's quick on a day like this."

"Will Nick's parents stay at his place?" I asked, taking a handful of corn chips.

"I don't know. I think he has a studio apartment, so it may or may not suit his parents. They may prefer a hotel; the nearest one is off I-64 at the edge of town. They'll probably stay with his uncle, which is really his great-uncle."

"Of course, I'd forgotten about him."

"Nick's father is an insurance salesman I know and owns his own business. His mother does some sort of consulting. I bet they can both find help to take care of their business while they're here."

She picked up my card and said, "This is a nice card, Natalie. I'll sign it in the morning before we return to the hospital." She set it on the counter and said, "I'll clear the table."

"Let me help you with the dishes."

"That isn't necessary, dear. It won't take long at all."

"I don't mind. I'll dry," I insisted.

"All right. It won't take two shakes, then. While we work we can plan our day tomorrow. Maybe we should pack a lunch, huh?"

I grinned. "The sandwiches were a little dry, weren't they?"

"You could say that again." She ran the hot water, adding soap.

As we worked, Mrs. John told me about Nick and his family. Nick had gone to school back east and they waited to see where he would find work. They came for visits occasionally. Mrs. John told me his parents wanted him to join his dad's business, but Nick didn't think that was right for him.

I listened to the information, taking in what she shared. I didn't want to ask any questions though. It didn't seem right. We made quick work of the dishes and decided what to bring tomorrow. Then I made the short walk home, oblivious to the sharp wind.

I didn't know why, but the house felt extra quiet and lonely. I ached for Nick, not knowing what happened and if he would be ok. If there was a God, I hoped he was listening to everybody's prayers on Nick's behalf.

I turned on the television to await the evening news and then went to fill Felix's empty food and water dishes. I walked back to the living room just in time to hear an anchor say, "...earlier today in Mascoutah. We have since learned it was not malicious, but a chemical experiment gone wrong. Judy, what can you tell us?" The screen went to a remote location near the school. Judy was standing outside the yellow tape, the wind blowing her hair behind her. "Earlier today an explosion sounding like an M-80 was heard shortly after the school day had started. With the increase in violent acts in schools and universities nationwide, there was instant pandemonium.

"As you can imagine, students and teachers were panicky and didn't know if they in were in danger of a militant or further explosions. When it became known it was an accident in the chemistry lab, it was too late to calm everyone down and reassemble the students and teachers. To be on the safe side, the school was evacuated and those injured were rushed to St. Elizabeth hospital in Belleville."

I'd heard enough and switched off the set. It still didn't explain why or how Nick got hurt unless his classroom was next to the chemistry lab, which was possible. I had no idea where his classroom was.

I went to bed with a slight ache in my stomach and in my heart.

The next morning, was cloudy and breezy. We still had some chilly days, but spring was on its way. Tulips and crocuses were blooming; the early variety already bloomed out in some places. It was always a joy to see the yellow and red tulips peeking up through the ground.

I quickly got ready for the day, packing my laptop in its carrier, and packing up my lunch. I also took the bag with the journal and other gift store items and put it by my purse. I fed Felix and ate cold cereal for breakfast. I washed up the few dirty dishes and headed to Mrs. John's. If I kept hanging out with Mrs. White and Mrs. John, my dishwasher would soon become a relic.

I had to warm up the car for a minute first and turned up the heat for Mrs. John who was waiting by the door. She put on her coat and picked up the balloons and plant purchased yesterday.

"Good morning, Natalie, how are you?" Mrs. John put Nick's gifts in the back seat and put a quilted bag and her purse at her feet.

"I'm good. Got everything settled?"

She nodded, buckling her seat belt. "Oh, it's a cold one this morning."

I nodded. It was supposed to get up to sixty today, but right now it was pretty chilly. "I hope we get some information from the doctor this morning. I hate not knowing. Has Mrs. White said anything about his parents?"

"She got a hold of them last night, and they said they would fly in this morning after getting cover for their jobs and the house. They said they would stay with Nick's uncle here in town. That way they could help him as well."

"That's good. I hope they have a good flight."

"And somebody took care of letting Mr. Keller, the principal, know to get a substitute. I can't remember who it was, though. So much has been going on." We got to the hospital a few minutes later and hauled our gifts and bags through the doors. We stopped at the information desk to see if Nick was in a room yet. This morning, there was a middle-aged woman with tight curls and big glasses sitting behind the desk.

We found out Nick was in a room on the fifth floor. We re-gathered our belongings and headed for the elevator. There was a nurse just coming out of room 537. "Excuse me, is Nick Norton in that room," Mrs. John, asked pointing.

"Yes, ma'am. He's still unconscious, but he can receive visitors. He's one lucky man."

After she left, we both shrugged, not knowing what the nurse meant, whether it was that Nick was still alive or that we were visiting. Anyway, I followed Mrs. John into the room.

"Oh, my." Mrs. John stopped and I almost bumped into her.

She and I stared at Nick, not recognizing him at all.

Mrs. John took a tissue from the bedside table and wiped her eyes. I busied myself with the balloons and computer bag until she regained her composure. It took me a minute to collect myself as well. I had to swallow the growing lump in my throat. I couldn't believe all the equipment hooked up to him, and all the bandages covering his left side, from his head to his chest. He looked like half a mummy. Mrs. John put the plant on the shelf and dropped her bag beside the chair on the right side of the bed. She patted his good hand before we each took a chair and sat down. Neither of us broke the silence.

Nick had the bed on the far side of the room, away from the door. The other bed was empty for now. The top blanket on his bed was light blue. Apparently the hospital got in on a big sale, all things blue. The walls in this room were also light blue, and the white tiled floor had specks of gray and navy in it. A volunteer brought in a bouquet of flowers and set them on the shelf next to our plant. She also had a couple of cards she put up there.

"He looks so peaceful," I whispered.

"Yes, he does, poor fellow. I hope he isn't in much pain."

I took out the journal and a new pen. I opened it to the second blank page, skipping the first for a title page. I wrote today's date at the top. I wrote 'You are asleep in your room on the fifth floor. Mrs. John and Natalie Alexander visit. They bring balloons and a plant. A volunteer brings in flowers and several cards. The nurse tells Mrs. John and Natalie that you are a lucky man.' I put the journal down for now and we just sat, silent.

I wouldn't have recognized this person in the bed as Nick without his name on the sign on the wall outside the door and the nurse's confirmation. Here was a man who was partly burned, bandaged and broken, who looked nothing like the handsome and healthy man that was our Nick. Would he be ok? How would he handle his condition once he woke up? Would he be angry? Accepting?

Mrs. John had brought some knitting with her and took it out, starting her needles to a rhythmic clacking. Following her lead, I took my laptop and turned it on, but didn't know if I could write in this strange place, under the circumstances. I read what I had written a few days ago, hoping to get into the flow of the story. I kept glancing from the computer screen to Nick's face. I wanted to hold his hand and take all the pain away. It almost scared me how deeply I cared for this man who I hadn't known long, yet it seemed like forever. I think I was starting to fall in love with him, and I wasn't sure that was a good thing.

I had to be careful. My heart was still fragile in the love department. He didn't know my past and the trauma that happened to me back in college. And hardly anybody knew about my daughter, the daughter I didn't know the name of, the daughter I scarcely had seen before she went to her adoptive parents.

I worked on my book, in starts and stops. I would write a few sentences, stop, think, look up at Nick and look back at the screen. There were noises in the hallway, constantly. Nurses and doctors going back and forth, carts of food, medical carts, volunteers filling water pitchers, phones ringing, buttons buzzing, machines beeping. How did patients ever truly get rest unless they were unconscious? Maybe it was a blessing for Nick in that regard.

A tall man wearing tan slacks and a white lab coat came in. "Good morning, ladies. How is our patient this morning?" Dr. Swenson, I gathered. His face looked familiar, though his clothes made him look like someone else. He looked from us to Nick.

"He's just resting; peacefully we hope." I finally answered.

"Good, good. He needs lots of rest. He may sleep for days or he may wake up any time. He's on some pretty good drugs, through the IV. He may feel disoriented and confused when he does wake up. He may not recognize you, Mrs. Norton," he turned to me.

"But, I'm not—"

Just then, two more visitors I didn't recognize entered the room. The female one said, "Oh good, doctor, you're here. I'm Mrs. Norton,

Nick's mother." She turned to look at her son. "Oh, my..." and started to cry. Her husband, Nick's father, I assumed, hugged her and squeezed her shoulder.

"Hi, I'm Dr. Swenson. Your son is quite the fighter. He'll pull through, provided the burns don't get infected. And we still don't know about possible hearing loss. But he's through the worst already and just needs lots of attention from his loved ones."

"Hearing loss?" Mrs. Norton's question came out like a squeak and she leaned on her husband. She was nearly six feet tall, with short hair, and his dad's was graying at the temples. Nick's dad wore glasses making him look like a kind professor.

"Whatever blew up at the school exploded very close to Nick and splattered. I'm not sure how loud it was or what it was made of. Depending on those things and testing when he wakes up, we can determine how much or if any hearing loss he will suffer. He's very lucky it didn't get him in the eyes. He would for sure be blind, looking at the kind of burn on his skin."

"Otherwise, doctor, will Nick be... normal?" Mrs. Norton hesitated before she finished her question.

"I think so. We'll do our best to keep the burn clean and from infection. He may have scarring, but it should be minimal. I don't think the fracture will affect the use of his left arm, but we'll keep an eye on the burns."

"Any more questions I can answer?" Dr. Swenson looked around the room.

We all shook our heads.

"I'll check on him in the morning, unless someone calls me. Have a good day." Dr. Swenson strode out with purpose, on to another patient.

Mrs. Norton went to the bed and took hold of Nick's good hand. She sat on the edge of the bed and rubbed his hand with her thumb. Mr. Norton stood behind his wife, his hand on her shoulder.

Mrs. John and I got up to leave. Mr. Norton turned to us and said, "Please don't go on our account."

"Mr. Norton, I don't know if you remember me, but I'm Mrs. John from First Baptist and this here is a new friend of ours, Natalie."

"How do you do," he asked us both. "Thank you for being here with Nick. What exactly happened? Mrs. White mentioned some sort of explosion and we had visions of half the school being gone."

"We still aren't sure. He must have been standing in for a teacher in the science lab for some reason and something went wrong." Mrs. John shook her head, looking down at Nick.

"The doctor seems to think I'm Mrs. Norton, his wife," I tried explaining. "We met a while ago and Nick helped me when I twisted my ankle. If there's anything I can do, please let me know."

"Did you say you were Natalie?" Mr. Norton asked me. He turned away from Nick to talk to me.

"Yes. Somehow the doctor assumed I was his wife when he gave us an update after his surgery yesterday." My cheeks grew warm at the memory.

Mr. Norton smiled. "Well, I can certainly see why the doctor assumed so. And why Nick likes you. I probably would have done the same thing. So you're a writer, is that right?"

I nodded, not quite being able to get my voice working.

"Very good. Nick has told us a bit about your writing group. Hope it goes well for you."

"Thank you," I squeaked out.

Mrs. Norton turned to us. She smiled at Mrs. John and me. "Thank you for being here for our Nick. I couldn't bear thinking he might be all alone. I should have known better."

"Well, we did what we could, which wasn't much," Mrs. John said.

"You did more than we could have, not being here. We appreciate it. Thank you so much." She took a tissue and wiped her eyes, smudging her eye liner.

"Pastor Collins might stop by later. We've started the prayer chain and I'm sure Mrs. White has told you about his place."

"Yes, thank you so much. It's comforting to have church family, isn't it?"

Mrs. John nodded and I didn't answer. I didn't have a church family and didn't know what it was like. But I guess it was like having others help and comfort you when you needed it.

Mrs. John and I left then, leaving Nick with his parents. "They seem nice."

"They are. They adore their Nick. They didn't like it when he accepted a job here and didn't stay in Pennsylvania. But he needed to and they had to let him go. It's all part of the parenting process."

I took Mrs. John home and then went to the library to work for a while. I didn't feel like sitting in an empty house. I watched patrons come and go and listened to their conversations with the librarian more than I worked. But I didn't want to be alone, even though I wasn't really with anyone either.

I wrote drivel, but at least it was something. I could edit later. I worked for a few hours, and then went home. I fed Felix and ate my lunch, still packed. I took out Nick's journal and added that his parents arrived safely and thanked us for coming.

After a quick supper, I watched an old Pink Panther movie and read a couple chapters of the Bible. I still didn't understand it. I went to bed, hurt and lonelier than ever.

Chapter 9

On Sunday morning a cool breeze blew though the sun was shining. The overnight clouds kept the night air a bit warmer than it would have been. But below 40 degrees is still freezing in my book, no matter what the exact temperature. Dressed in jeans and a sweater, I went downstairs to feed Felix and fix myself breakfast.

While eating my oatmeal and banana, I figured most of Nick's friends and possibly his parents would be at church. This might give me a chance to visit Nick alone. I took the bag with the journal.

When I arrived, nobody else was in his room. I noticed additional cards and plants on the shelves. Nick was asleep, so I sat down quietly. I took out my Bible and turned to my place in John. I read the next two chapters when a noise startled me.

I looked at Nick but his eyes were still closed. Maybe he groaned. I moved to the bed and took his hand, rubbing it gently. "Nick, Nick; are you there?" I whispered. No response. I kissed his hand before sitting back down. Our first kiss, and he was unconscious. Go figure.

I closed the Bible and opened the laptop. I found my place and continued the story. The characters were almost a third of the way through their stories. A few were getting tired of the project already. Some writers were energized by it and kept going.

After writing for a while, I took out the journal and added a few notes that he was still asleep today and had many more cards and gifts. Around 11:30, I left and drove to a small café nearby. After eating, I went back to the hospital. This time I only took a paperback mystery with me. It was one of the new ones from the Christian book store.

    Nobody was in his room, so I sat down in the chair by the bed. A short nurse with dark curls came in and checked his vitals. Her white nametag read 'Nancy'. "How is he doing? Everything good?"

    She nodded. "He seems stable. Nothing out of the ordinary."

    "Thank you, Nancy."

    "You're welcome. I hope he wakes up for you soon. He looks like a nice guy." She blushed as if she shouldn't have voiced her statement.

    "Thanks, and he is." After she left, I turned to the first page of my book. It was pretty good, actually. I read twenty pages before I noticed a presence in the room. Nick's parents were walking in, holding hands.

    "How's he doing?" his dad asked.

    "The nurse just checked his vitals and said he's holding steady."

    I got up from my chair. I needed to stretch, anyway.

    "You don't need to leave, Natalie," his mother said.

    "I don't mind. I need to stretch for a while. I'll come back later." I went down to the gift shop and looked around. I picked out another card for Nick and after paying for it sat down on a bench outside the shop. For a while, I mindlessly watched people coming and going. I wondered how long Nick would be unconscious. What if he was deaf in one ear after he woke up? Would it bother him? We still didn't know what exactly happened at the school, but somebody probably knew by now. Maybe even his parents knew already.

A little after two o'clock, I wandered back to his room. The Johns were there, and Nick's parents and Mrs. White. Extra chairs had been brought in from somewhere and the other bed was still empty, so Nick's visitors were able to spread out.

"Hi, Natalie. How are you holding up?" Mrs. John asked.

"Fine, thanks."

"Pastor Collins just left after praying with us. You can have his chair, if you like," Mr. John offered.

I sat in the chair he indicated.

"We understand that Nick was standing in for his friend, Mark Zuckerman in the science room," his dad explained. "His friend had an important phone call to take in the office and since Nick didn't have a class that hour and was down the hall a couple doors, he sat in for him. The science students were doing an experiment with magnesium, which is highly flammable. A student was fiddling with a cigarette lighter and started the flames and thus the explosion. Lucky for him, they didn't blow the whole wing up. But unfortunately, Nick and a couple students were standing nearby and got injured during the accident. Apparently, according to Mark, it could have been much worse. He feels terrible. That's what we know from the principal. He stopped by earlier."

"That's too bad. How are the students, then?" I asked.

"Two of them have been treated and sent home, but there's one here who's conscious, but has worse burns than Nick. We don't know which room he's in."

"The big plant there," Mrs. White pointed to a large peace lily on the floor in front of the nightstand, "is from the school. And that balloon bouquet is from students in one of his classes."

"His room sure is getting crowded, isn't it?" With our plant and balloons, and the ones from the school so far, there were an additional four plants and three groups of balloons. If we hadn't been in a hospital room, you would think it was decorated for a birthday party or graduation.

"Earlier, this morning, I thought I heard Nick groan, but then I didn't hear anything else," I offered.

"We heard him do that a while ago," his mother said. "I thought he might wake up, but he didn't." Her face was pale and her eyes dull. She wiped her nose with a crumpled tissue.

"The doctor said he might wake up briefly, but because of pain could go right back to sleep," his dad added.

After the update about Nick, we chatted about mundane things for a while. I was tired of sitting, so decided to go home and work out. I said goodbye and walked into a biting cold wind. The sunshine had been replaced by gray clouds. I think it was supposed to rain tonight.

I drove home thinking about the last few days. How crazy! I was so glad to meet Nick, but was worried about the outcome from his accident. How would he handle possible deafness? How would he look? Would he have scars? Would it bother me? Did it matter if it did? I wondered if I was falling in love with a man I was still getting to know.

Three weeks later Nick hadn't woken up, but occasionally someone would hear him groan and thought he might. His parents had gone back home for a few days to tend to their lives, but Pastor Collins gave them a report every couple of days. I kept Nick's journal up, with help from the pastor.

Most of his visitors were Pastor Collins, the Johns, Mrs. White, his uncle and I. I met Nick's teacher friend, Mark Zuckerman, who felt awful. Mark was about six foot three, with sandy brown hair and didn't look the type to use the school gym. I tried to assure him that it was an accident and could have happened to anyone. Anyway, he hadn't stayed long and didn't seem to feel any better when he left. Other friends and coworkers came from work in the beginning, but had tapered off. Life gets in the way. Each day I would take my laptop, Bible, and a book.

I got used to working around the constant hospital noise. I longed to see Nick's eyes open and hear his voice. Three-and-a-half weeks was too long. I wondered how his substitute was handling his classes. I know Nick was planning to have most of his students work on essays or reports toward the end of the school year. Who knows what they were working on now.

Some days I would wonder what I was doing, hanging around a guy who deserved better. Other days I wondered why Nick wasn't married already. Was there some flaw in him I hadn't uncovered yet? After all, he's generous, kind, funny, compassionate, and a great companion as far as I was concerned. He had many qualities I'd look for— if I was looking.

Did I even have a chance?

Chapter 10

By the first week of May the days were getting brighter and warmer. Spring was in full bloom with its welcome sight of magnolias and begonias blooming all over town. Pink azaleas swayed in the breeze and late tulips still dotted many flower beds around yards and local businesses. Some days the wind was a bit strong, but spring was definitely here. Robins and monarchs flitted about, bringing spring to reality.

Neighbors were working in yards, washing their cars or watching their children play and I waved when I saw them. Since I had moved in during late summer and had been busy settling in, I hadn't seen them much in the fall.

I had been reading through the book of John, though I still didn't understand it. I could have asked someone, I guess, but since Nick was the one who suggested I start there, I wanted to talk to him about it. Since Easter Sunday, I had been going to church and sitting with the Johns or Mrs. White. I still didn't understand half of what was said, but felt drawn to attend, knowing I at least had friends to sit with.

When Mrs. John asked me the first Sunday after Nick's accident, I hesitantly accepted. If I was going to hang out with these people, might as well join them. And maybe God would answer my prayers if I prayed them there.

After the service, either Mrs. White or the Johns would invite me over for lunch, or sometimes all of us together, then we would visit Nick in the afternoon. I was getting to know these people and felt more at home than ever.

My novel was now half finished, and I had been doing some extra editing for a client. Today, I brought some editing along and one of the books from the Christian book store. I sat in the shaft of sunshine coming in the window of Nick's room. The book I brought was a historical romance and was pretty good. It was clean, of course, which actually made it better somehow. After reading twenty pages, I stopped reading because something felt different in the room. But when I looked up, nobody was there or in the hallway. I went back to reading. Something wasn't quite right and the feeling wouldn't go away. I visually checked Nick's machines and they seemed to be humming along fine. As I moved my eyes from one side of his bed to the other, I glanced across Nick's face. His big brown eyes were staring at me. Goosebumps raced up and down my back. I shivered.

"Nick! You're awake! How are you?" I stood up, the book dropping to the floor.

He groaned and answered, "Not sure. Where am I?" His voice was hoarse, but it was as sweet as hearing the first robins in spring.

"How do you feel?" Out of habit, I sat down on the bed and took his good hand.

He grinned at that. "I've been better, apparently. What is all this stuff?" He looked at the wires and tubes hooked up between him and the machines. He gingerly touched his bandages on his face and shoulder.

Relief swept through me like a warm blanket. I pushed the call button so a nurse could notify the doctor. "We have to make sure you're alright. You've been unconscious for several weeks."

"Weeks? Why, what happened?" Nick gave me his full attention. He wouldn't let me let go of his hand, though I tried and gave up.

"Some sort of accident in the science lab. Do you remember anything?"

"Not really. How long have I been here?"

"About four and a half weeks. Give or take."

"Wow." He tried sitting up, but frowned. "Guess I won't do that." He slid back down.

"Here, try this." I raised the head of his bed just enough to not make him dizzy.

Nancy his nurse strolled in. "Well, hello there! Nice to see you awake. I've called the doctor and he should be here shortly. At least he's in the building, so it shouldn't take long. Just hang tight and don't try to move too much, too fast. I imagine you're a little stiff?"

"Yeah, I think so. Have I really been out that long?"

"Yes, ever since you came up to this floor from Critical. You got burned, and there's a possibility you may have lost some hearing, but it doesn't seem like you have. And you might have some scarring from the explosion," I whispered.

Nick was quiet. "What explosion?"

"There was an accident in the science lab that sent you and a student to the hospital. You were standing in for another teacher."

A visitor interrupted us. Dr. Swenson strode into the room. "Well, well. So you're Nick; glad to see you awake. Pain anywhere?" He pulled out his stethoscope, ready to assess Nick. Today his scrubs were blue.

"Everywhere, but not too bad."

"I'm Dr. Swenson, by the way. Nice to meet you. You're wife here has been keeping a vigilant front, not giving up. She's a keeper."

"My wife..." Dr. Swenson missed Nick's look of astonishment and at the same time made me smile. Still, the doctor's assumption was embarrassing.

"Dr. Swenson, I'm not—"

"Could you give me a few minutes with your husband?" Dr. Swenson turned back to me.

I looked from him to Nick, who was now grinning ear to ear, or trying to. I'm not sure if his grin was from my embarrassment, or the doctor's assumption. "Of course," I said, rushing out of the room. Hot with embarrassment, I walked up and down the hall, hoping Nick was as good as he sounded. I tried fanning my hot face with my hand. Mrs. Norton, indeed.

I actually heard Nick laughing from down the hall. I was so relieved, butterflies danced in my stomach. Now there was something positive to write in his journal for today. Sunshine shone through large windows where I was waiting for the doctor to finish his assessment. Thank goodness he woke up. What if he hadn't? I didn't want to think that way. I wondered what the doctor was doing, and if he would have a good report. I gazed down at the parking lot, watching people driving in and out.

After several minutes, I glimpsed the doctor walking in the opposite direction. I hurried back toward Nick's room.

"Mrs. Norton, huh? I definitely like the sound of that." His amusement embarrassed me. I tried to ignore it. He now had a much smaller layer of bandages on his face and I could tell he was trying to smile, despite them. He was sitting all the way up. He slowly moved his good arm around and above his head. His voice was a little stronger, too. It looked like they had sponge-bathed him again and given him a clean gown and sheets.

"Well, you still have a sense of humor, that's good." My face blushed again. I didn't answer his question, but instead said, "Well, Mrs. John is claiming me as her daughter, so I guess we're just one big happy family, aren't we?" I dropped into the chair at the foot of the bed. "Are you feeling ok?"

"I feel pretty good, considering what the doctor said happened. He said I'll have a scar along my ear, but it won't be that noticeable. And possibly some scarring along the side of my face, but it shouldn't look too bad. Not that I care that much anyway."

It was such a gift to hear his voice. I had to concentrate on what he was saying.

"Natalie, have you really been here every day like Dr. Swenson said? For over four weeks?" His voice was soft, and so wonderful to hear after all this time.

I nodded, swallowing hard, suddenly emotional.

"Nat, that's incredible. I can't believe you'd sit here every day just for me. Why?"

I looked up at the surprise in his voice.

Why did he have to ask? "What do you mean why? Because...you helped me with my ankle... I wanted to return the favor. I..." I knew the real reason, but I couldn't tell him. Not yet.

"How is your ankle by the way?"

"Oh, gosh, it's fine. I haven't thought about it in weeks."

"Can you move your chair closer? I can see you better over here."

I got up and slid the chair over to the side of his bed.

"That's better. Can you help me slide up a bit?"

"I can try." I wasn't sure if I could with all those bandages, but I gave it my all. I put one arm under his good one, and my other around his chest and together, on three we half shoved, half pushed. Nick smelled like antiseptic, cotton, and soap, all mingled together. I could imagine myself in those arms in a better circumstance. I tried not to think about it.

"How's that?"

"Much better. Thank you." He took a sip of water before asking, "What day is it?"

"Today is Tuesday May 25th. Do you remember anything that happened?"

"Hmm. Not really." He drank more water.

"Are you hungry?"

"Starved. I don't remember when I ate last."

"Is this the first time you woke up since the accident?" I didn't know, since I obviously wasn't there round the clock.

"I don't know. All I know is I'm stiff and starved. How is that for alliteration?" He gave me a small smile.

I returned his smile. "Maybe we should buzz the nurse."

"Do we have to?"

I didn't know if he was kidding or not. "Well, I guess it could wait a minute…"

"Good, because I'm enjoying your company. And I don't want to be bothered. Except for being hungry. I guess we'll have to buzz her after all." He reached for the call button and pressed it. A voice came over the intercom, "Yes, may I help you?"

"This is Nick, in room…" he looked at me.

"Five-thirty-seven," I answered.

"-in room five-thirty-seven. I guess I've been asleep for a while. I'm kind of hungry. Can you order the Hungry Man special?"

I heard a chuckle through the phone.

Nick replaced the receiver by the bed. "I have no diet restrictions, which is a good thing since I'm not dieting, that I remember."

I laughed. It was so good to talk with him, not *about* him.

"Now, where were we?"

"You're not in any pain?" I asked.

He considered my question, looking over his bandaged body. "Not much. They probably have stuff dripping through me. Except for a slight headache and being stiff, I don't feel too bad."

"Well, that's a relief. Your parents will be relieved. I met them when they were here right after your accident. I'm sure they'll be thrilled to hear from you."

"I better call them later. I'm sure they've been worried. I understand they've been going back and forth not knowing I'd be here that long."

"They're very kind and concerned about you."

"You'll have to talk with them again. I'll call them later." Nick changed the subject. "Natalie, what have you been doing here every day? I can't believe you've been here all this time."

I focused back on Nick, not sure why he was so surprised. "I worked on the novel, read the Bible some, read the books from the store we bought...do you remember that?"

"Yes! We went to the book store after we had dinner at your place, right?"

"Yes. That was a week or so before the accident. The explosion happened on a Friday morning around nine.

"They brought you here by ambulance. Mrs. John came running to my house right away to tell me. Not knowing what or how it happened, Mrs. John and I went to the school and saw you taken by ambulance, though we didn't know it was you at first. When we did find out, she called the prayer chain and half the church and Pastor Collins came to the E.R. Then Dr. Swenson came out when it was just her and I left in the waiting room and he assumed I was your wife—"

Nick smiled when he heard that.

"Anyway, he told us you might lose your hearing and that you could have some scarring from the burns."

"Well, I'm thankful I have my hearing. If I could get these bandages off everywhere, I'd feel even better."

A volunteer knocked on the door, with a food tray on a cart. "Hungry man special?" he asked, coming in.

"Most definitely. I'm starved! I feel like I haven't eaten in weeks," he joked.

I laughed.

The volunteer didn't get it. "He's been unconscious for several weeks," I explained.

He broke into a grin, "Oh! Enjoy," he said, leaving.

"This looks great. I hope it tastes as good as your cooking. Would you like something?"

"Goodness, no. Dig in!"

He looked at the tray, at his arm, and at me. "Here, let me help." I removed the cover off his plate, and unwrapped his silverware. Since one of his arms was still in bandages, it wasn't going to be of much use. I slid the plate closer and took the lids off of his juice, and salad dressing, and opened his carton of milk.

"There you go." I felt his eyes following my every move.

"Thank you, Natalie. You're a godsend."

"Just doing what any kind and considerate person would do."

"Well, I appreciate it." He put his head down and closed his eyes for maybe three seconds for the shortest record-breaking silent prayer.

"You are hungry, aren't you?" I'm not sure he even formed words during his prayer.

He nodded, a bite of salad already in his mouth. He ate in silence, while I contemplated what he said earlier about me being here almost every day. I didn't mind really, at least I could get some work done, too.

He's a nice guy and a perfect gentleman and all.

"I think I'll live now." He wiped his mouth with the paper napkin using his good arm and then pushed the tray back. "Now, about our Scrabble tournament—"

"What?"

"You remember, don't you? As I recall, I'm only ahead by one game."

"Yes, but you mentioned it, as if we were talking about it a few minutes ago."

"To me, it was a few minutes ago," he answered.

I thought about what he said. I guess to him, it seemed like yesterday when we discussed it, though it had actually been several weeks. "I'm sorry. I'll have to get used to your different frame of reference. So, the tournament, yes?"

"How would you feel about continuing it here? I know you've been here all this time already and I understand if you don't want to. It seems I'll be here a while, getting burn treatments and therapy. Doctor Swenson says I'll be here for at least three weeks if not longer, depending on any skin grafts or whatever."

"Sure. I can bring the board next time I come. Are you prepared to lose?"

"I don't need to be, but thanks for asking."

"Very funny. We'll see about that."

Nick looked around his room. "Would you mind handing me that pile of cards?"

I got up and took them from the shelf on the wall and handed them over.

"Thanks. Let's see who cares." He gave me a wink.

He's so goofy. I slit them open for him and silently watched him read one after another, speed reading them. When he got to the second one from me, he read it three times. He looked at me, and said, "Thank you." He stood it on the nightstand.

"You're welcome. The least I could do."

A volunteer came and took Nick's empty tray.

Nick handed me the cards back and I tossed the envelopes for him and stood some of the cards up on his shelf. "How is your novel coming? Are you still working on it?" He changed subjects after the volunteer left.

I nodded. "It's not spectacular, but it's only the rough draft."

"I'd be glad to take a look if you want. I have plenty of time on my hands for a while, you know."

"You really want to?"

"Sure. I can't turn pages of a book very well." He held up his bandaged arm. "Of course, I could hire you as a personal assistant and you could read to me." His smile could light up Paris.

"You've got to be kidding."

"Who, me? I'm not joking."

I looked at him, not believing what I heard. His face, though half covered with bandages, was very serious. "But, you'll be in and out with treatments and you have visitors besides me, all day long."

"No, I won't. Everyone will go back to their own lives. Not that you don't have one," he added quickly. "But, you can do your work here. And we can continue our tournament after your work is done each day."

"Nick, people have been visiting you for almost a month. And I don't know how you'll handle your treatments. You might be really tired. Besides, I don't want to wear you out or hinder your healing."

"Natalie, please. I need your company." His brown eyes were dark, almost pleading.

I didn't understand his urgency.

"Do you remember when we talked about being in a room full of people, but still feeling all alone?" he asked, trying again. He took my hand and held it in his own.

"Yes." I still didn't know where he was gong with this.

"I tend to get depressed, if I'm alone too much," he whispered. He gently squeezed my hand as if to say, please understand.

"Nick..." I couldn't believe this. Nick, gorgeous Nick, with tons of friends from his church, a good job with coworkers, and everything? Well, he had me there. I tended to too, but tried to forget about being alone most of the time.

"Natalie, I mean it." He sat up as straight as he could, limited by his attachments. He continued, "I know I met you for a reason. And I need you." He brought my hand to his lips and kissed it. Then he leaned back against his pillow, looking out the window.

For a few minutes, the only sounds were his machines running and noises from the hall. I considered what he was asking. I looked at our interlocked hands and felt torn. Being there while he was unconscious was one thing, but now?

When he spoke again in a softer tone, he explained his loneliness. "I used to have a brother."

My eyebrows rose in surprise.

He nodded before continuing. "We were close. Did everything together." He blinked hard, controlling his emotions. "Skiing accident in high school. Broke his neck." He turned to me with wet eyes. "I never got to say goodbye." He looked away again, out the window, lost in his memories.

It finally sunk in how serious he was. Though flattered by his request, I wasn't sure if I wanted to do it. It would be hard to keep my heart from falling in love completely if we were together nearly every day. The last few weeks didn't count since he wasn't conscious. I didn't think I could handle that kind of pressure. And if I did fall in love with him, which was only a kiss away, I would have to tell him about my past. I wasn't ready for that.

"Can I think about it? For a day or two? And see how you do after your first couple of treatments?"

He turned back to me, relief sweeping across his face. I really didn't want to commit to anything right now, with his emotions raw, and my own in a quandary.

I decided to leave since he had many phone calls to make. Somehow his cell phone had been found and was left on the nightstand. I handed it to him. "I'll see you sometime tomorrow, ok?" I squeezed his hand, reassuring him as much as myself.

"Thanks, Natalie. I appreciate your understanding."

"You're welcome. Get some sleep and follow doctor's orders. Ok?"

"I'll try. Good night."

I strolled down the hallway, lost in thought. I was so relieved he was awake, but didn't know about visiting daily. Could either of us handle it?

Chapter 11

I didn't make it to see Nick the next day but called him instead, explaining I had to get some work finished. The warm weather was tempting me to putt around the yard instead of working, so I set a writing goal with the reward of working outside once I reached it.

Satisfied once I met my goal, I rewarded myself by cleaning out the flower bed bordering the wrap-around porch. I started down at the west end, moving across the flower bed slowly. First I raked out dead leaves from the oak trees in the yard, bagging them for the trash. Then I got a workout pulling weeds and grass sprouting up through the river rock, adding them to the leaves. Feeling like I accomplished a great deal made me feel good and it was a fun way to get in some exercise and fresh air. I was more for fresh air than exercise, but this job met both criteria, a win-win for me. I worked outside for a few hours while Felix roamed nearby, jumping at grasshoppers and other doomed prey.

The fresh air and spending time in nature rejuvenated me and I finished my current project that afternoon. I would Fed Ex it in the morning.

While working in the garden the day before, I thought about Nick's idea of me working at the hospital. I wasn't completely sold on the idea, but we could try it for a few days.

When I arrived at his room, Nick was finishing his breakfast.

"Good morning, Nat. How are you?" Despite the ruffled hair, growing beard, bandages everywhere, Nick sported a more rugged, but still handsome look. Even his arm muscles bulged through his gown. His dark eyes were always kind and bright and he rarely frowned.

"I'm well. And you?"

"Slightly improved after eating." He gestured to the chair closest to the bed.

"You look darling in your pink gown."

Nick's face flushed. "I have been informed that the laundry staff is having trouble with the washing machines leaking down in the basement and the only gowns clean and dry are these lovely things—," he pulled it off his chest—"from the maternity ward. Go figure."

I laughed out loud. "I'm sorry. I just think it's funny."

"Glad I can be of service," he said dryly. While he finished his pancakes, I updated his journal with notes from yesterday and today.

"Have you thought about my proposal?" he asked. At least he waited until I finished writing.

I nodded. "I'll try it for two days, and take it from there. I don't want to conflict with your healing. Deal?"

"Deal. Did you bring your laptop?"

"Not today. I'll bring it after the trial period, depending how it goes."

"That's all I can ask. But I hope you say yes," he added before pushing aside his tray.

Just then a short nurse with dark skin wearing aqua scrubs came in to check on Nick. "How we doin' this fine morning?" she asked. She was from the south.

"I'm doing great now that I've eaten. I just wished I could get up and around."

"In time, in time. Let me check them bandages." She lifted some of them up and clicked her tongue. "I think we better change them. Can you give us a few minutes, honey?" she turned to me.

"Sure. Nick, I'll be back in a few minutes."

"I hope so."

I shook my head on the way out. What have I gotten myself into? The outdoor air felt good and smelled a whole lot better than the medicinal air in the hospital. I took a short stroll around the inner courtyard and then searched for a kiosk inside where I bought a hot chocolate and a bagel.

I took my small breakfast back outside and found a bench. I chewed on my bagel and thought about Nick reading my novel and working in his room. If I did let him read it, and I read books aloud to him, it would sure keep us from being lonely.

As it turned out, I didn't have to worry about it right then. When I walked back up to Nick's room, he had visitors. Mrs. White, Mrs. John and Nick's parents were surrounding his bed. Mrs. White spoke first, "Hello, dear! How are you?"

"Fine, thank you. I can come back later." I turned to go.

"Oh, no, no, no. Mrs. John and I were just leaving. We have to take a delivery to a classmate from Sunday school."

"Oh, yes. We're glad to see you doing so well, Nick. I'll bring you some goodies as promised," Mrs. White said.

"Thanks for coming by. I appreciate all your gifts." They each leaned over for a brief hug.

"You're welcome. See you later." The two of them walked out.

I noted clean bandages and a fresh gown—that wasn't pink.

"It's good to see you, Natalie," his mother said.

"Thanks. Has Nick been behaving himself?" I tried to get a reaction.

Nick looked at me, in disbelief. "You doubt? Of course."

Nick's dad snorted. "He's been begging for more food. I understand he had quite a breakfast already."

"Let's see; pancakes, bacon, fruit, yogurt, juice, and milk, I think. Was that all?" I asked, looking at him.

"Yes, that was *all*. I ate every bite."

"You're not pretty in pink anymore, I see."

"Thank goodness," he said to me, before explaining to his parents. They got a chuckle out of that. "Sorry to have missed it," his mother teased.

"At least nobody took photos." He turned to me. "Back to our deal," he started to say.

His dad interrupted, "What plan? You're not trying to blackmail dear Natalie into staying here with you every day, are you?"

"Of course not, Dad! I just asked her to read to me and offered to help her with her book, that's all."

"Not if Natalie is uncomfortable being in a hospital so much, son. It's not exactly the most aromatic or exciting place to be, you know."

Nick was quiet for a minute, realizing what he had asked of me. "Natalie, I'm sorry if I asked too much," Nick apologized.

"Well, let's ask Natalie, about that," his dad said. He turned to me and they both waited for me to say something.

"Well, I have thought about it. But, I..."

"We could at least try it for a few days, right," Nick piped up.

"Nick! Let the poor girl finish," his dad scolded. "Go ahead, dear," his dad looked back at me.

"That's what I offered..."

"For three or four days and see how it goes?"

"Is Nick strong-willed," I burst out, looking at his parents.

"Yes!" They answered simultaneously.

I nodded. "Thought so." We all laughed. "As I recall it was for *two* days. On one condition."

I noticed a smirk on Nick's dad's face and saw him wink at his wife.

"What's that?" Nick asked quickly. He missed the gestures from his father.

"No nursing duties. I can't stand blood, goo or anything else that's supposed to stay inside the human body. The only blood I can stand is the kind from an editor's pen."

They laughed again, his parents looking at Nick. "Sounds fair to me," his dad said.

"I have several nurses available for that, I promise. Do we have a deal?"

"Deal." I shook his good hand but he wouldn't let go. I looked down at him. He worded silently, 'Thank you' before letting go. I nodded and sat back down.

"Well, now that that's settled, your mother and I need to do some shopping. Do you need anything, Nick?"

Nick looked around the room at his plants, flowers, balloons, cards, gifts and then at me. His eyes rested on me and he answered, "No, Dad, I'm fine. Thanks."

"Natalie?"

"Oh, no, thank you."

"We'll see you this evening then. Natalie, make him respect you."

"Dad!" Now it was his turn to squirm.

I grinned before answering, "I will, sir. I'll hold my next chocolate zucchini cake over his head."

"Sounds good. You kids have a good time, we'll see you later," Mr. Norton squeezed Nick's shoulder and his mother kissed him on the cheek. We were silent for a minute, waiting for them to leave. I heard his dad say, "She can handle him," before their voices faded. I smiled. I hoped he was right.

"About that cake..."

"What about it?" I countered.

"When can you make one? Would you? Please?"

"Maybe after our trial period is over, depending how it goes."

"That's fair enough. What kind of books do you like? I don't like sci-fi too much."

"Me either," I agreed. "Contemporary, thriller, mystery, and a few others. So what do you want me to read, and how are you going to get these books?"

Nick pointed to his nightstand. "Open the top drawer."

I did and found the books he bought at the Christian book store. I looked back at him for an explanation. "Mrs. White brought them from my place. They were still in the bag by the door."

I picked them up. "Which one do you want me to read?"

"Which one interests you?"

"Let's see." I took the stack and sat back down, looking at each one. The one on theology or whatever, I quickly put aside. He had three fiction ones that looked intriguing. I've never heard of Frank Peretti, or Robert Whitlow. "Either one of these might be good," I held them up.

"How about the Whitlow--he's into courtroom drama. That should keep us both interested. Will you please sit in dad's chair, closer?" Nick gestured to the chair on the side of his bed that his dad vacated.

I sighed. "If I must." I picked up the bag and replaced the other books back in the drawer.

"That way you don't have to read as loud."

I rolled my eyes. "Right."

"Actually, I just wanted to see you roll your eyes."

I didn't respond. I moved the chair to a better angle. "Are you ready to listen or not?"

"Almost." He reached down and with one yank of his good arm, pulled me and the chair closer to the bed.

"Hey!" I was definitely seeing a different side to Nick since he's been in the hospital. He was still ever the gentleman, but with a little bit of sarcasm and strong-will tendencies thrown in for good measure. Apparently he was strong *and* strong-willed. Oh, joy.

"Now I'm ready." He closed his eyes and leaned back on his pillows and sighed.

Shaking my head, I opened the book and turned to page one. I read the first three paragraphs before Nick stopped me, "You have a nice, easy voice to listen to. I like that." I looked up but his eyes were still closed. He gestured with his hand to keep going.

I read the first chapter and stopped. I needed water. "I'll be back in a minute. I need some water." I wasn't used to reading long passages out loud.

Nick opened his eyes. "Here, let me. I have extras." He poured water in a Styrofoam cup and handed it to me with a straw.

I took the cup, his warm hand lingering over my fingers, sending tingles up my arm. I put in the straw and took a long drink. "How long do you want me to read?"

"As long as you can. It's very peaceful." He leaned back again, closing his eyes.

I read chapters two and three and closed the book with the included bookmark. My own eyes were getting tired and I closed them for a minute. A warm hand on my knee jerked me awake. I sat up. "Ow!" I rubbed my stiff neck.

"Are you ok, Nat?"

I loved it when he called me that. I felt special. "I'm fine. I'm sorry I fell asleep." I was embarrassed and put the book on his bedside table. My neck was quite stiff.

"Natalie, come sit." Nick patted the bed.

"Why?"

"Just come sit. I won't bite." He held his arm out.

Reluctantly, I moved from the chair to the bed. I felt his hand move my hair out of the way which sent goose bumps down my spine. He gently massaged my neck and shoulder. My heart beat ten times faster. But I dropped my head anyway, because his touch felt so good. After a few minutes, I stretched back out. It felt better. He dropped his hand, and I turned around to thank him. At the same time, he leaned forward, and his lips brushed my cheek. "How's that?" he whispered. He brushed my hair out of my face. I felt warm, tingly and cold all at the same time. I looked at him, and knew in that moment that it was too late. I was in love. It was all I could do to get out, "Much better," in a normal voice. I couldn't and didn't want to get up. He still had his hand on my shoulder, gently squeezing it. He finally dropped his hand and asked, "Are you hungry?" I got up and moved back to the chair.

Just to change the subject, I nodded.

"I can get meals for guests for a nominal charge. What would you like-tonight they have roast beef, meatloaf or beef and noodles." He read from a card on his tray.

"Is the food any good?"

"Actually, it's not bad. Of course, you have to realize that except for mom's, yours, and Mrs. John's or Mrs. White's cooking, I have little to compare to."

"Do you want me to stay?"

Nick looked at me as if he was puzzled. "Why wouldn't I?"

"I thought you might be tired."

"I'm fine. We both took a little cat nap. I enjoyed your reading very much and I'm grateful you're willing to give up your time."

"All right then. The roast beef please. But I'm paying." I reached for my purse.

"Sorry, Nat. I'm paying and no use arguing."

"But—"

He already picked up the phone and ordered. "Besides, it will be a working dinner."

"It will?" I was suddenly alarmed, having no idea what he meant.

"We have to work out some sort of schedule."

"Oh." That kind of work.

"I've been told I'll have burn treatments on Mondays, Wednesdays, and Fridays starting Monday. I'm really looking forward to it."

I looked at him, realizing he was being sarcastic.

"After my burn heals enough, they'll put a cast on my arm. Right now it's wrapped in gauze and a sling. Will you try to come often?"

"Only if it doesn't wear you out."

"Good, it's the only thing that's going to get me through. Except for God's strength, of course." He rubbed his eyes and picked at the blanket.

"Will it be bad?" I asked softly.

"Bad enough. But that's not until next week." He was putting on a brave front, and we both knew it. He changed the subject. "I'll ask Mrs. White to bring my laptop and my folders I need for my book. At least we can make good use of this incarceration by being productive. And the food is fairly decent."

I laughed. "It's not that bad," I swatted his arm.

While we ate, we worked out a tentative schedule for next week. When his parents returned, we talked for a few minutes and I left so they could visit. I told Nick I wouldn't see him over the weekend. I knew he needed time with his parents and I needed a respite myself.

Today had been another step closer to the inevitable doomsday.

Chapter 12

The following Monday morning I found Nick's bed empty. He must be getting his first treatment. I settled down in a chair with the novel I was reading. A few minutes later, orderlies wheeled Nick in on a gurney. He looked pale. They swapped him back to his bed and left. "Nick?"

He peeked an eye open. He lifted his hand up a little, and I moved to the bed. "Do you need anything?"

"Pain meds." He tried to reach for the button, but I pushed it for him. A few minutes later after a nurse gave him what he needed, I asked, "Did you have breakfast?"

He nodded. He rested with his eyes closed.

"Are you ok?"

He nodded again. I rubbed his hand. "I don't want to do that again. Today."

"You don't have to. Can I do anything?" I felt so helpless.

He shook his head. I sat on the bed holding his hand until he fell asleep. I kissed his forehead before moving back to the chair and continued reading. He woke up about an hour later.

"You're beautiful, did you know that?" Nick asked as he adjusted the bed back to a sitting position.

It had been so silent; he startled me when he spoke. He looked a lot better. He drank some water keeping his eyes on me.

"No, I didn't." And considering my casual attire of jeans and long-sleeve t-shirt, I didn't agree.

"You are. Don't let anybody say otherwise. Did you bring your laptop?" He set his cup down on the bedside table.

I nodded, still embarrassed about his comments. I took the laptop from its bag and turned it on.

"I'm anxious to read your story. Anything to take my mind away from these surroundings."

I'm not sure if it was drugs, his strong-willed nature or the hospital fumes, but Nick was starting to push too hard. I didn't think he was being bossy just to be bossy, but I didn't want to wear him out. After all, it wasn't like he was in the hospital for a broken leg. This was a little more serious. I didn't want to be the one to hinder his recovery, just because I didn't want go home to an empty house. Or because I was in love with the patient.

"Ok, but only for an hour. You need your rest."

"Patients can't get any rest."

"You might not get much, but if you're not careful it will wear you down faster. Then, it might slow your healing. And you'd have to stay longer…"

"Natalie, do I sense some concern on my behalf?"

"What's wrong with that," I huffed. The laptop was still booting, and I didn't look at him.

"Natalie?"

I didn't respond.

"Natalie, if you don't look at me, I'll have to get out of this bed, tubes and all."

I jerked my head up.

"I'm sorry. I wasn't trying to make fun of you. I just want you to stay because I enjoy your company and I truly won't get much rest here. But you're right. I could slow the healing process down. I didn't consider that. I'm sorry. Will you forgive me?" His chocolate eyes pleaded for mercy. There was no contest.

I nodded.

"One hour?"

"Sure."

"Come sit." He patted the bed again. And wheeled the tray down to the end of the bed.

We maneuvered the laptop so it wasn't resting on any bandages or his bad arm. I sat next to him on the bed, trying to leave space between us, which was difficult on the narrow mattress. We could both see the screen, and I kept the mouse on my side. "How's this?" I asked.

Nick nodded. He was already reading the first chapter. "It's about a group of writers who try to write novels in a month?"

I nodded, too embarrassed to look at his face. After a few minutes, I peeked at him while he read. He looked at me after reading several pages and said, "Natalie, this isn't bad."

"Ha! Yes, it—"

He put his hand on my arm. "Natalie, it isn't. I'm an English teacher, and believe me I see drivel every day. This isn't bad at all," he argued.

"It's only a rough dra—"

He squeezed my arm. I looked back at him, waiting. "It needs polishing, yes, but it's good. Very good." He gently took the mouse from my hand and scrolled down a couple more pages.

"I think you could teach my class a few things," he commented.

I laughed.

"I'm serious. Would you like to be a guest speaker after I get back to class?"

"And speak," my voice squeaked.

"You'd be great. Would you?" Nick stopped reading the screen to look at me.

I looked away. "No thanks." My answer came out gruffer than I intended.

Nick looked at me. "Why not?"

"I don't like crowds or speaking in front of others."

"Even if I was there?"

"Especially if you were there." I shuddered at the mere thought.

"Why?" He gently covered my hand with his.

My cheeks grew warm and my hands grew sweaty. "I can't talk about it," I whispered, turning away.

"I'm sorry, Natalie. I'll drop it." We moved our hands and he went back to reading.

I looked away. I tried forgetting my memories and fear. I looked around the room, at all the cards, plants, and balloons. So many had shown their love to Nick. Would I ever be a part of that? Would I ever feel clean and whole again? Would I ever be able to go out at night and not be jumpy in parking lots? I didn't think I could ever tell him why I couldn't speak to his class or any other.

It seemed like yesterday, the day I was raped, resulting in an unwanted pregnancy. I gave the baby up for adoption. My family still blamed me, and that is why I moved so far away. I still felt shame and wondered if I did the right thing, giving my baby away to strangers. But I was too young to be responsible for another human being and didn't have a way to support us, anyway.

Would I ever feel like I belonged to anyone, like Nick? He was so obviously loved, and by so many. Tears dripped off my cheeks and I hadn't known I was crying, until a tissue wiped them away, bringing me back to the present. Nick had noticed them when I hadn't answered his questions. "Nat?" He asked gently, while rubbing away my tears.

"I'm sorry," I cried and ran out of the room.

I ran into the restroom down the hall and locked myself into a stall. I tore off a long piece of toilet paper and blew my nose. I cried harder, having not thought about the incident in a long time. Where was my baby now, and how old was she? I tried to figure out the months, but was too upset to think straight. Now I felt like an idiot, running out on him like that. I cried until I couldn't anymore. Then I washed my face at the sink and ran my fingers through my hair.

Except for my purse and keys, I thought about leaving everything at the hospital and going home. I was forced to go back to Nick's room.

I took a deep breath and re-entered his room. Nick had the laptop closed and was reading his Bible. I slowly walked back in and sat down on the chair. Nick looked at me with such compassion, his eyes like melted chocolate. It almost made me cry again, but I refused. I stared at the floor.

"Natalie, I'm here if you need me. I'm sorry if I-" He spoke softly.

"It wasn't you. I just can't talk about it right now." I picked up the laptop and put it in my bag. "What are you reading?"

"The book of Ruth. It's in the Old Testament."

"What's it about?" I sat back in the chair.

"Ruth loses her husband, and her mother-in-law loses her husband and a sister-in-law, loses hers. They start traveling to another country away from the famine, and Ruth insists on following her mother-in-law, saying her mother-in-law's God and people will now be her God and people. Ruth eventually marries again. It's a very touching story."

I didn't need touching stories at the moment; I just wanted to forget. I pushed the pain and shame back down into dark secret spaces where I could keep them hidden. "Is it time to order dinner?"

"Sure. Can you hand me the phone?" He put down his Bible.

I picked up the receiver and handed it to him. He had the order card on his table. After he ordered, I took the phone and hung it up.

"What's your favorite kind of chocolate?"

"What?" That question came out of nowhere.

He repeated the question.

"Why?"

"Just answer the question." His tone said, work with me here.

"Pecan Delights, Hershey's dark chocolate and homemade fudge are some."

"Thank you."

"What are yours?" Two could play this game.

"Chocolate-mint ice cream, rocky road ice cream and double fudge brownies."

"Well, those are good, too."

"And a new favorite, too."

"What's that?"

"Chocolate zucchini cake."

I grinned. "Me, too."

A volunteer came in, wheeling two trays on a food cart. "Turkey and potatoes?" she asked.

"That's mine," I took the tray and set it on my lap. "Thank you."

"The meatloaf must be yours, then. Let me help you get settled, honey." Why was everyone calling him honey or dear?

"Anything else I can get for you?" The volunteer stood at the foot of Nick's bed.

We shook our heads. She left the room and I took a sip of my ice tea. I waited for Nick to say grace. I looked up from my tray. "What?"

Nick's eyes were soft chocolate again, full of compassion, but I didn't know what he was thinking. Finally, he said, "Thank you."

"For?"

"Staying with me for the better part of your day when you could be doing something else. Somewhere else. I know being in a hospital is not the top place to be on most people's list. I appreciate it, Natalie. I really do."

"I owe you one, you know."

"You do?" It was his turn to be surprised.

"For coming over to my house and bringing me dinner."

"That wasn't anything at all."

"It was to me. The visits, meals, and cards were greatly appreciated. I felt like somebody. After everybody stopped coming, I was a little lonely. Felix isn't a great conversationalist, you know."

He laughed. "I'm sure he's not. I'll pray now." We bowed our heads. "Dear Lord, thank you for this food, please bless it to our bodies. Thank you for Natalie, and her friendship. Please let her know you love her and there's nothing in her life you can't forgive. Be with us this evening. Amen."

I stared down at my tray, unable to look up. I was afraid if I looked at Nick, I would start crying again. The tears were already gathering in the corners of my eyes. How does he always know how to pray for me? He doesn't have a clue what happened to me in the past, but yet his prayer was almost like he did. I finally looked up since I was really hungry, and the food smelled good. I took a deep breath, and unwrapped my silverware.

I removed the top cover of my plate and sniffed. It smelled delicious. Beside the turkey was broccoli with cheese sauce and small red potatoes. A separate dish had a green salad with cherry tomatoes, cucumber and shredded carrots. I opened the ranch dressing and drizzled it over the top. On the last plate was a piece of cherry pie. It all looked good, considering it was hospital food. I took a bite of the meat and it melted in my mouth. "Mmm," I said.

"Good?"

"Mhm. Yours?"

"Pretty good, considering where we are. And the lack of ambience doesn't help, but it will do."

I smiled. I took a bite of salad.

"I couldn't ask for better company though."

"Thanks. I'm glad I met you." I stopped before I said anything else. I didn't feel like getting emotional again.

"Me too. Remember the cookies you brought to my uncle's?"

I nodded. That day seemed like ages ago.

"They were delicious. I ate most of them, since he wasn't eating much at the time."

I smiled, not surprised by his confession. "By the way, I got your card in the mail weeks ago. That was very sweet. I put it on the mantle."

"You're welcome. I hope it wasn't too corny."

"Not at all. It was nice."

For the next few minutes the only sound in the room was the clatter of our forks on our plates as we ate. We were both lost in our own thoughts. I wondered how I was going to resolve my issues so either we could move forward in our relationship, or most likely Nick would end it. I didn't know what else to talk about and kept eating. Nick had a faraway look on his face when I glanced at him between bites.

I wondered what he was thinking about. Then I caught a slight grimace cross his face.

Alarmed, I put my fork down. "Nick?"

He closed his eyes and dropped his hand to the tray. He still held the fork.

"Nick, are you ok?" I got up and put my tray down. I walked over and touched his hand. He slowly turned his head toward me. "I'm fine," he whispered. I took the fork out of his hand and put it on his plate.

"Should I call the nurse?" I brushed his hair off his forehead and felt his skin. It was warm.

"No."

"You look a little pale. Are you in pain?"

"Just give me a minute." He looked at me, but I wasn't sure he saw me.

I cautiously sat back down, ready to hit the call button if necessary. I watched his face for any more signs of distress. Another brief grimace crossed his face. I was starting to worry. Where was the pain? Under the bandages? Somewhere else?

After a minute, he picked his fork back up. I continued to watch him the rest of the evening. I resumed eating, but with a nagging sense of doubt about something not quite right.

We left our trays at the foot of the bed and sat quietly, letting our dinners digest. Nick still looked pale and he wasn't talking as much. I got up and sat on the bed and picked up his hand. It was warm. Too warm. I felt his forehead again and it was wet from perspiration. "Nick, you're burning up."

"I'm just tired."

"Nick, if you're burning up, you might have an infection or something. The nurse needs to look at you." I spoke urgently, a little nervous at how warm he felt to the touch.

"I don't want to be messed with. I'll be fine in a minute." He kept his eyes closed and though he argued, his voice and intent were weak.

I was getting desperate. "Nick, if you don't push that call button, I will." I got up, showing him I meant business.

Nick opened his eyes and looked at me. I still held his hand. "You wouldn't," he dared, his voice cracking.

"I would and I will right now, if you don't." I reached for the cord with my free hand. My heart picked up speed and I didn't like how pale he looked.

Nick simply dropped his hand and it fell to the bed. He whispered, "Push it."

I did and a minute later a nurse came in. "He's burning up and says he doesn't feel well."

She pulled out a thermometer and pushed it under his tongue. She checked his pulse and read his machines beeping nearby. She entered notes into Nick's computer chart. "I need to call the doctor. He may need further treatment." She left the room. I sat back down on the bed and rubbed his hand with my thumb.

"Don't talk. I'll stay here until the doctor comes, ok?"

He barely nodded his head. "Thirsty," he whispered.

I picked up his water and held the straw for him. He took several swallows and plopped his head back down again. I resumed holding his hand, afraid to let it go. Now that I knew I was in love with him, I didn't want anything to happen to him. I would be devastated.

For the first time in my life, I prayed. Really prayed. I asked God to please do this one thing for me, to please help Nick.

A minute later the doctor came in. It wasn't Dr. Swenson, but a Dr. Givens. "Ma'am, we're going to have to wheel him downstairs. He might have to go back into surgery. Somebody will let you know." He left the room and came back a minute later with a gurney and a few nurses who wheeled him out. I watched him go, my heart beating faster and my own hands starting to sweat. I slumped into the chair and sat there for a long time. I didn't feel like crying anymore, but tears threatened anyway. The phone in Nick's room rang, startling me. I didn't know if I should answer it or not. After the third ring, I picked it up. "Hello, Nick Norton's room. This is Natalie."

"Natalie, this is Pastor Collins. How is Nick doing?"

"I don't know. They just wheeled him back downstairs for possible surgery. He started to sweat and said he wasn't feeling well."

"Oh, no. Is anybody else there?"

"No. But his parents should be by soon."

"I'll be there in just a few minutes."

"Thank you."

I hung up; relieved someone else was coming to share the burden with me. I didn't think I could carry it alone.

I took out the journal and added notes from what happened today. I didn't know who all the visitors were besides the ones I saw when I arrived. I'm sure there were others in between my visits, too. I was just writing down that he had to be wheeled out when Pastor Collins walked in.

"Still keeping the journal?"

"Yes, although I didn't think I would need it anymore. I hope he's ok."

"Me, too. Before leaving the church, I told the folks about Nick. The prayer chain will be started up again."

Mr. And Mrs. Norton walked in. "Where's Nick?" his mother asked.

"They wheeled him out for more tests a few minutes ago. He was starting to sweat and said he didn't feel well."

"Oh, no! What could be wrong?" she asked. She looked almost as pale as Nick had. She plopped on Nick's empty bed. Nick's dad stood next to her, rubbing her shoulder. The room felt empty, even with us in it.

"An infection somewhere, possibly," I said. "Or something in his arm not healing right." I closed the journal and dropped it back into my bag before standing to stretch out my legs and arms. I'd been in this room for several hours and was ready for a break. "Please excuse me for a few minutes," I said, walking out into the hall.

I walked up and down the long hallway, trying not to worry about Nick. I walked, my arms crossed hugging myself, fingering my sleeves while I waited. I took deep breaths, letting them out slowly. I couldn't believe how quickly I fell in love with this guy. A guy I didn't know existed six months ago. I considered his kindness, compassion, generosity, stubbornness, confidence, humor and his love for words and writing. What more could I want in a man?

I ignored the comings and goings of nurses and volunteers roaming the halls with all kinds of carts. The beeping and buzzing and telephones ringing barely registered on my brain. I thought only of Nick and how he was.

I just didn't know if I could tell him what happened to me on that awful day years ago. But if our relationship got serious, I would have to tell him the truth. Just the thought of how he might react made me cringe.

I shuddered as I walked back towards Nick's room. As I reached the doorway, I heard Pastor Collins praying. "...heal Nick of his wounds and let there not be any infection. And Lord, please show us how to love Natalie..." I slowly backed out of the room and into the hallway again. It felt strange hearing Pastor Collins praying for me, even though I asked him to several weeks ago. How many people did that make praying for me? For all I knew, Nick did too, besides at the meals we ate together. That was at least four or five people. What did they pray for about me? And how long had it been going on?

I lingered outside the door. Other visitors smiled when they saw me standing there. They too, have waited outside the room of a loved one for different reasons. Waiting there, I realized I was very tired. I decided to go home, even if it meant not knowing about Nick until tomorrow. I was too emotionally spent to sit and wait, possibly for hours.

A few seconds after hearing three Amen's, I walked in. "I'm sorry, but I'm going to go home. I hate not knowing about Nick, but I'm really worn out." I picked up my bag.

"We understand, Natalie. Thank you for all you've done. We know Nick enjoys your company," his dad said.

"You're welcome. If there's anything I can do for you while you're here, let me know." I turned to the pastor, "Good night. Thanks for coming."

"I'll walk out with you, Natalie," Pastor Collins offered.

"Thanks."

We all said good night. His parents were staying until they got news of Nick's condition of course. I couldn't blame them. I would have too, but I couldn't physically or emotionally handle it.

Pastor Collins and I walked out to the parking lot. As we walked, I asked him if there was anything God couldn't forgive.

"Not a thing. Not stealing, lying, murder, or anything. Jesus covered it all when he died on the cross. Every sin for you, me and even those not born yet."

I didn't know if I believed that or not. I simply nodded. I didn't want to tell him why I asked. And who I needed to forgive.

"Can you be forgiven if you don't forgive someone else?"

"Unfortunately, no."

I let out a short gasp, stopped in my tracks and turned toward him. My heart plunked to my toes. Did I hear him right? He went on, "The Bible says if you do not forgive your brother, God cannot forgive you. Forgiveness is a two way street, between us and God and between us and others."

Well, there that goes, then. I could never face the guy that raped me. Never. "My car is this way, good night," I said, moving on.

"Natalie, wait a minute. You seem upset."

That was an understatement. I took a few more steps. What was the point? But I stopped on the sidewalk at the end of my row anyway. I turned back around but didn't dare look at his face. He had to catch up to me.

"Do you mind if I pray for you right now?" He stood at a distance, in case I bolted or hit him. Either one was tempting.

I tried not to cry again. I nodded, not trusting my voice or emotions. Not that it mattered. Apparently I was doomed.

He slowly closed the gap between us and put his hand on my shoulder and we bowed our heads. "Dear Lord, I come before you now on Natalie's behalf. Please put your arms around her and show her your love. Help her to heal from whatever is hurting her. Let her know your true peace and love that only comes from you. And we pray for Nick's healing as well. In your name, Amen."

At this point I couldn't stop the sobs. I ran to my car to get away from all these people who kept praying for me. I wished they would stop! I can't forgive the creep, so what good would it do, if I believed in Jesus now? It was so unfair!

I drove home, wiping tears away with my hand. I couldn't wait to go to bed after a long hot shower. I ran into the house, dropped my purse and bag on the sofa and ran upstairs. Felix could eat whatever crumbs were left in his dish. I started the shower and took out clean pajamas. Afterwards, I brushed my teeth and fell into bed.

After another crying spell, I fell asleep from sheer exhaustion.

Chapter 13

I didn't wake up until almost ten the next morning. Felix purred and pawed at my chin something fierce. "Ok, ok. I'll feed your royal majesty." Since I completely ignored the fellow last night, he had a right to be heard this morning.

Sunshine glittered through the slits in the blinds welcoming me to a new day. A spring breeze blew against the north side of the house. After I fed Felix, I wasn't sure I wanted to eat anything myself. I didn't know if I wanted to visit Nick anymore, either. How could I love him if I couldn't face or forgive a creep from my past? It was hopeless. And how could I love Jesus or he love me if I couldn't forgive this guy? That was not what I wanted to hear last night. I had tossed and turned all night, trying to figure this mess out. It was beyond me and I didn't like it.

I was torn. I wanted to know how Nick was, but I didn't want to get close to him anymore. I couldn't drag him into my problems.

I was stuck with nowhere to go.

I stayed home, listlessly roaming from room to room. I ran my finger along dusty tables, pinched off dead plant leaves, stared through the windows at tree limbs blowing in the wind. Boredom, fear, anxiousness, and hopelessness weighed me down.

Maybe some soft music and a good book would help. I opened the living room windows to let the fresh air clear out the musty house. Felix came in, thinking it might be safe to be around me. He settled on the hearth. I sat on the sofa, hugging a pillow. What was I supposed to do?

I dug out my Bible from the bag sitting on the sofa. I turned to the concordance in the back and looked up verses on forgiveness. There were many. I started writing them down so I could look them up. I didn't know all the book abbreviations, so I had to keep flipping to table of contents in the front to figure them out. There were verses on forgiveness all through the Bible, but I didn't know which ones applied to me.

Some were listed in the book of Psalms, Jeremiah, and a bunch in books after boy's names like Matthew, Mark, Luke and John. I read several verses that didn't help.

The last one on the list was from the book of First John (how many Johns are there?) chapter one, verse nine and it said, "If we confess our sins, he is faithful and just and will forgive us our sins and purify us from all unrighteousness." I could ask to be forgiven, but that won't help me, according to Pastor Collins. What in the world am I supposed to do? I groaned, frustrated and tossed my pen onto the coffee table where it bounced to the floor. I rolled my eyes.

The doorbell rang. Who could that be? I peeked through the sidelight beside the door. It was Mrs. John.

"Hi, Mrs. John. Come in."

"Hi, Natalie. I saw your car out front and stopped by to see if you wanted to visit Nick with me."

I walked into the living room and sat down. "How is he?"

She followed me, but didn't sit. She eyed my Bible without comment. "He's out of surgery. They had to do a skin graft and cut away some infected skin. He's in pain and it's a setback, but he's out of danger."

"Oh, that's good." I really was glad.

"How about it, then? Do you want to go with me?" She held her purse over her arm, tapping it with a finger.

I shook my head. "I have things to do here. Maybe tomorrow."

Mrs. John frowned. "Nick will be disappointed. Are you sure?"

I nodded. "I'm sure. Go ahead without me and tell him hi for me."

"All right, dear. Take care of yourself now."

I followed her to the door.

"See you later," I closed the door. I plopped back on the couch. I no sooner sat down than the phone rang. Now what? I didn't feel like talking to anybody. I let the answering machine pick it up. I stretched out on the couch and fell asleep.

After waking up, I went upstairs to work. I hadn't turned on the laptop since Nick closed it the other day. I didn't know how much of my work-in-progress he had read. I guess it didn't matter. I continued where I left off, writing out scenes and dialogue for my characters. Today they were meeting in a coffee shop to write and discuss their stories.

After a few hours, I saved my work and was about to turn the machine off when I noticed a document saved on the desktop. It was titled, 'For Natalie'. I opened it to find a letter from Nick.

"*Dearest Natalie,*

I hope you find this note soon and read it. I don't know what trauma you've experienced, but I want you to know that whatever it is, God cares. He loves you and wants to help you. I see the pain in your face when you think I'm not looking. I feel your resistance and longing to share your story. There isn't anything you can't

tell me. After being a high school teacher this long, there isn't much I haven't seen or heard. And if you think I'll be horrified by whatever it is, I'm here for you. Let me know if there's anything I can do. I'll help any way I can, I promise. Please don't carry your burden alone. I'm here for you day or night. I'm praying for you.
    Yours,
    Nick"

    I stared at the screen, getting blurry through my tears. I read it several times, with tears dripping off my nose and chin. I wiped them away with a tissue from the desk. I sat back in the chair and closed his letter before turning the computer off.
    I sobbed, leaning on the desk. I felt torn between the fear and shame and the urge to reveal my secret once and for all. I wanted to, but was afraid of the outcome. How would Nick handle it? How would I feel afterward? And what about this Jesus stuff? How was that supposed to work?
    I sat up and wiped my face with a fresh tissue and tossed it in the trash and noticed the blinking light on the answering machine. I'd forgotten somebody called before my nap. My finger pushed the 'play' button. "Natalie, Pastor Collins here. I was hoping to catch you and see if you were ok. I'm headed over to see Nick; maybe I'll see you there. I hear he'll be all right. We're praying for you. Take care."
    I reasoned with myself, if I didn't go at all, Nick's journal would have a blank page for today. That didn't seem fair, in spite of my reservations on seeing him. But I did want to see him. I needed to see him, to see for myself he was alright. Forget

about everything else. I'll just have to take things one at a time, and hope for the best.

I changed quickly into jeans and a sweater and brushed my teeth and hair. I scrubbed my face and applied lip gloss. The worst thing that would happen, is either I wouldn't be able to tell him, or I if I did tell him, he would send me away. I was used to that, so it shouldn't have mattered that much. Except it did.

I fed Felix and told him to be good. I dashed to the car with my bag in tow. I didn't bother with the laptop. By the time I got to the hospital, it was just after the supper hour. I knocked on Nick's door before going in. He was alone. Good.

"Hey, there. How are you doing?" Nick gave me a welcoming smile.

"I should be asking you." I stopped by the other bed, not walking in any closer.

"Better now, thanks. I'm missing some skin and I'm sore but nothing horrible. They upped my antibiotic. Come sit." He held out his hand for me to come closer.

I slowly walked closer to his bed, sitting on the edge of the chair. I hoped he couldn't hear my heart beating a hundred miles an hour. I wiped my palms on my pants and tried to keep my knees from jiggling.

"I meant on the bed." He patted the narrow space on his mattress.

I looked at him and then the floor. I didn't know if I could do this. But I had to. After I took a deep breath, I said, "I saw your note. On the laptop. There's something—"

His soothing voice interrupted me. "Natalie, please come sit. I promise I won't bite. Besides I just ate," he smiled.

I reluctantly moved over to the bed, knowing he wouldn't be satisfied until I did. Another breath. My hands fidgeted with the zipper pull on my sweater. I looked down at the blanket, not daring to look Nick in the eyes. How would he take this? In a few minutes, I could be walking out of this room, never to see him again. Tears threatened again. This was so hard but I didn't want to lose him. I had to at least try.

"What's wrong, Natalie? You can tell me." His hand slid down my arm and into my clammy hand which he gently squeezed and held.

Breathe in. Breathe out. "I was raped," I whispered. I continued in a rush, "I had a baby. I don't know where she is," I started to cry. So much for subtlety. I started to get up, but Nick sat up and pulled my arm back. "Oh, Nat, I'm so sorry. Come here," he wrapped his arm around me, his hand pulling me to his shoulder. He hugged me tight which made me cry harder. He brushed my hair with his hand and whispered, "I'm so sorry; I'm sorry." He rubbed my back like I was a little child, repeating his words in a soothing voice.

I sobbed until I was dried up. I took a tissue off his bedside table. "I don't know if I can forgive him," I wailed, sitting up. I took a deep breath and blew my nose.

He continued to rub my back. "Hey, one step at a time." He turned my chin toward him, brushing tears away with his thumb. "I'm here. We'll deal with this together, all right?" He rubbed my hair, looking straight at me. His face held such compassion; a sense of relief filled me. He leaned his forehead on mine and in a low voice, said, "First of all, it wasn't your fault. Second, it doesn't diminish my feelings for you. If anything, you need me even more. Third, God loves you way more than you can possibly imagine."

I cried again, falling against his shoulder.

"Nat, Nat. You poor thing." Though his voice cracked with emotion, he nearly crushed me in his arm. I never wanted to leave his embrace. I felt safe and secure for the first time in years. And a great relief from the release of my secret.

"I thought you would hate me," I whispered.

"Never. Why would you think that? You're a wonderful girl, Natalie," he whispered in my ear.

I sobbed harder. He kept rubbing my back and hair. He smelled of antiseptic, burnt flesh, bandages and soap. Not the best aroma in the world, but it was sweet to me. I probably should have been consoling him, considering the circumstances, but instead, he was consoling me.

I had to blow my nose. I sat up reaching for a tissue. "I was afraid—"

"Natalie, honey, never mind. I'm glad you told me, but you don't have to say anything else. God will help us through this. Together."

I hadn't thought about Nick offering to help me. I had just thought he'd consider me as damaged goods. I should have known better.

"The truth takes guts," Nick said softly.

"Heart and lungs, too," I said. My smile was weak.

We sat in silence for several minutes, just the machines beeping and his hand rubbing my back the only sounds. His question broke through my thoughts. "Have you gotten any counseling?"

I shook my head. I'd never considered it. I had been so shamed and fearful of the guy, I never thought about it. And after moving here, it hadn't occurred to me. Not that I had known where to go anyway.

He took my hand again and said, "We can talk to Pastor Collins if you want. We can go together or you can go alone. But you need to deal with it in a healthy way. I'm sure he'll help you if you ask him. When you're ready. There's time enough for that."

His voice was husky with emotion and compassion. For me. I couldn't believe it. I let go of his hand and twisted around so I could see his face. "When I ran out yesterday, it was because—"

"Natalie, you don't have to explain." He scooted all the way over on his side of the bed and pulled me back to his shoulder, hugging me tight. "You can tell me the whole story or bits and pieces at a time later, when I get out of here. Right now, we both just need to heal." I pulled up my feet, letting my shoes slip to the floor, and curled up in his good arm. In a whisper he said, "We'll get through this. I'm so happy that I met you." He kissed my forehead.

The only sounds in my ear were Nick's breathing and the hum of his machines. All other distractions faded away. A heavy weight had been lifted from my shoulders. Not only in the sharing with someone else, but in the fact that Nick took it so well. And I thought he'd drop me faster than a slippery bar of soap. We sat there a long time, each in our own thoughts. My heart skipped a beat, knowing that Nick knew my secret and didn't blame me or turn me away. I reveled in his muscular arm, holding me tight, his hand rubbing my back and shoulder.

Nick's acceptance and comfort eased away my hurt, fear and shame. It was such a relief, I soon fell asleep. Sweet dreams of spending my life with Nick filled my head. There was something different to the quality of my sleep, it was noticeably more peaceful. Somehow during the night, my whole body got arranged next to his on the narrow bed.

The next thing I knew, the shining sun woke me up. I had a kink in my neck and couldn't figure out what the noise was. Where was I anyway? I opened one eye and saw blue walls. I sat straight up and gasped.

"Good morning, Sunshine," Nick said, turning his head to me.

"I didn't—"

I looked at him, and then saw a blanket over both of us that I didn't remember seeing before. "We didn't—"

"Yep. We slept together."

"Nick!"

"And it was so sweet," Nick smiled. "Did you know you have a soft snore?"

I hit him on the arm, softly. "How did this—"

"Here, lean back and I'll tell you." He readjusted the pillows.

I ran my fingers through my hair and wiggled my stiff legs. Nick rubbed my shoulders. Did he ever stop during the night?

"You fell asleep just as visiting hours ended and I pulled the curtain around the bed and let you sleep. I think when the night nurse came in she didn't know what to do, so she just left us alone.

"I think you needed some peace, and I let you sleep knowing what you told me had to be a heavy burden. I rubbed your shoulders and your back until I fell asleep. As they say, the rest is history."

Nick hugged me to him. He whispered in my ear, "You're just as beautiful to me as you ever have been, Nat."

I saw the compassion in his eyes and melted there in his arm. My heart swelled higher than ever. I leaned back and closed my eyes, thanking God for the peace in my heart.

It was a new day, in more ways than one.

A knock startled us, and I quickly moved to the chair. I stifled a yawn.

"How are the lovebirds this morning?" Doctor Swenson asked.

"Just fine, Doc, just fine." Nick answered. He gave me a quick wink while the doctor looked at Nick's chart. I smiled back.

"Good, looks like your vitals are all good." He flipped the computer open, reading the info. "Any complaints?"

"Just one."

"Oh?"

"When can I get out of here?"

The doctor and I chuckled.

"Let's not rush things. I know hospitals aren't the best place to be, but we have to make sure everything is healing properly." The doctor turned to me and before he could ask, I got up.

I took my purse into the bathroom down the hall and brushed my teeth and my hair. Luckily I kept a toothbrush in my purse, for emergencies while traveling. Never knew when I would need one. Though I never dreamed it would come in handy because I slept with Nick in a narrow hospital bed!

Chapter 14

After freshening up, I found a kiosk on another floor and bought a dry muffin and juice. I walked back to Nick's room and found him digging into his pancakes drenched in syrup.

I moved back to the chair and we talked out a tentative schedule around his burn treatment schedule. Our trial plan fell through due to his infection.

"Yes, commander, I think that'll do." I looked at my notes.

"Sounds like a deal then. I may need you to occasionally get things from the library for research."

I nodded. "I'm on a first name basis there."

Nick arched his eyebrows. "Really?"

I nodded. "I go there once or twice a week."

"Doesn't take you long to get settled."

"I'm a writer, Nick. I go to the library all the time."

"I guess so. Well, now you might go more than twice a week. I also need some new highlighters and markers and a red pen. Could you get those for me?"

"Sure. Anything else?" I added his shopping list to my notes.

"Yes, a pint of rocky road and two spoons."

I laughed. "I don't think so."

"Why not?"

"I doubt it's allowed."

Nick wrinkled his eyebrows. "Who cares?"

"I do. I'm a rule follower, you know."

"I am too, but there isn't any rule against bringing me my favorite ice cream."

"I'll have to check with the proper authorities."

"You don't believe me?"

"That would be a no."

"I'm crushed."

"Sorry." I was enjoying this little game. After my confession, it was so much easier to feel relaxed around Nick. And of course, I didn't think ice cream was against any rules. He wasn't on any restricted diet.

"You should be." Nick stuck his chin out and I chuckled. He was as goofy as ever. I think it was the hospital stay and the meds. He certainly wasn't this silly when we first met. But he was just as gentle and compassionate.

Just then his parents walked in. "Hello, you two. How is everyone?" his dad asked.

I turned to his mom and said, "Nick's giving me a shopping list."

"Oh? Cross off rocky road ice cream," his mother said knowingly.

I stared at her. "Ok..."

She gave me a knowing smile before saying, "Here you go, Nicholas." She held a small bag out to Nick and kissed him on the cheek. Nick looked at me and we laughed. It was the first time I'd heard anyone call him by his full name.

"Now Natalie doesn't have to break any rules." He took out a plastic spoon and opened his frozen pint. "I can ask for more spoons," he offered, setting the lid down.

"No thanks," his parents said.

"You go ahead."

He leaned back on his pillow, a bite of ice cream in his mouth. "Mmm. This is wonderful. Thanks, Mom."

"You're welcome dear. I thought I would treat you since we have to leave in the morning. I'm so glad you'll be all right. I thought it would be so much worse," she admitted. She dabbed at her eyes with a crushed tissue. Today she looked casual in her matching navy and green sweat outfit, though the gold and silver necklace with matching bracelet dressed it up.

"I love you, too, Mom. I'll be fine. Natalie has promised to visit each day to get me through."

His mom looked at me. "Thank you, dear."

"You're welcome. I'm happy to be Nick's assistant."

"Don't let him push you, Natalie. He can be a bear sometimes."

"Mom!"

"Well if anyone ought to know, it's me. I'll give you a few tips later, Natalie."

I grinned at her and she winked at me out of Nick's line of sight.

Nick shook his head, taking another bite of his ice cream.

"Son, I'm glad you're ok, too. Now you treat Natalie right."

"That will be easy."

We chatted for a while longer and then it was time for his parents to leave. They were having lunch with some friends and Nick's uncle. After they left, Nick and I got to work.

We wrote on our individual laptops until a volunteer brought in his lunch. "Nat?"

"Yes?" I picked up my purse and waited.

"Will you share mine?"

"Oh, no. You need to eat it. I'll go get some tacos or something."

"Nat? After eating that ice cream, I'm not really hungry."

I laughed. "Are you sure?"

"Very. Here," he scooted the tray towards me.

"I feel awkward eating your lunch."

"Don't worry about it, nobody will know but us." He sat back against his pillows looking tired. He pulled the curtain back around, giving us privacy.

"I'll eat quickly then let you rest. I'll be back later, ok?"

He nodded. I watched him for a minute making sure he was just worn out from company. I didn't want him to get another infection. I ate rapidly so I wouldn't get caught in an embarrassing situation, leaving the tray on his bedside table. I took my purse and quietly left.

I drove home with the windows down, enjoying the late spring breeze. The grass seemed greener and the sun shinier since my heart was lighter. I just couldn't quite figure out how to forgive a guy so I could be forgiven by God. How does that work?

On a whim, I decided to drive by the church and see if Pastor Collins was in. I waited for his secretary to get off the phone, so sat in a chair in front of her desk, trying to look like I wasn't interested in the conversation.

A few minutes later, she said I could go on in.

"Hi, Natalie. Come on in. What can I do for you?" He set some books and papers aside.

I sat down in the offered wing chair, suddenly nervous.

Pastor Collins saw my discomfort and ventured a guess as to why I was here. "That night that you asked me about forgiveness, is that why you're here?"

I nodded.

"You need to forgive someone who did something to you or a family member?"

"To me." I looked down at the floor. "I was raped," it came out in a whisper.

He got up and came around his desk. He leaned over to pat my shoulder. "I'm sorry, Natalie. I guessed it might be something like that." His touch was like a warm blanket and I started crying and couldn't stop. He sat back down and offered me a tissue from the box on his desk.

"I can't forgive him! I just can't!" I wiped away tears in anger.

He was silent for a few minutes until I could contain myself. "Unfortunately that is one of the hardest things to do. Especially in that kind of situation. The only thing I can do is share some scriptures with you and pray for you as you go through this. I can offer some counseling sessions if you want them, or from another counseling center." He sat in his chair, letting me digest this information.

"I don't know," I admitted. "I don't even know where he is. Or my daughter."

"You got pregnant and gave her up?"

I nodded.

"I'm sorry."

"I was still in school. I thought it best at the time."

"I understand. Was he someone you knew?"

"We were in debate together. We were on opposing sides and I won."

"Is that why?" His voice was incredulous.

"I guess. Maybe it was just a part of it. I made him look bad."

After a few minutes of silence he said, "There are ways to forgive others when you don't know where the offender is and even if they're dead."

I perked up at that. "Really? You mean I don't have to search for him or talk to him in person?"

Pastor Collins looked stunned. "Oh, Natalie. Goodness, no."

I wasn't sure I heard him right. Not having to get near the guy to forgive him was like winning the lottery without having to buy tickets. This had been the sticking point for me since he had first answered my question in the parking lot that night. Now the relief was so overwhelming, I lost it. I cried harder knowing I could forgive the perpetrator and never had to face him again. I realized Pastor Collins had more to say. "I'm sorry, I just feel so relieved...I was afraid I had to see him in person."

He smiled. "No, you just have to forgive him in your heart and move on. I know you'll never forget, and that's normal. But you don't have to let it hold you back or keep you from living a healthy and whole life."

"How do I do that?" This was great news to me. I took a deep breath, feeling like another boulder had been removed from my pile.

"Let me read some scriptures and we'll discuss how."

I went back to the car for my Bible and we read scriptures together. I prayed to forgive him, the best way I knew how. I would never forget the trauma or the fear and the resulting daughter I gave up. But it would no longer hold me hostage. I took a deep breath and a calming peace settled in my heart. I was finally free of the chains that once held me prisoner.

I started to cry again, but for a much different reason. Pastor Collins looked startled. "Are you ok?"

"I think so. I just feel so much better and cleaner somehow."

He nodded in understanding. "That's the power of forgiveness. When a person accepts the forgiveness of their sins, they feel that power and it changes their life forever."

"But how do I get that forgiveness?"

"All you have to do is ask for it. There's a prayer called the sinner's prayer and if you believe in your heart that God sent his only Son Jesus to die on the cross for your sins, you can accept his free gift of eternal life."

"How do I pray it?"

Pastor Collins smiled and folded his hands on the desk. "Repeat after me, Natalie."

I bowed my head and repeated his words of the sinner's prayer. If it was at all possible to feel even lighter and cleaner, I did. I couldn't believe how great I felt-like a brand new person.

Tears of joy ran down my face. How could I possibly have any tears left? I took another tissue from the box on his desk. "I'll have to get you a new box if this keeps up."

He smiled. "That's what we're here for."

"Thank you." I got up, a totally different person than when I first walked in.

"Welcome to the family, Natalie. If you need anything, just ask."

"I will, thanks." I turned to go when he stopped me.

"I think there's someone who will be very happy to hear your news."

"Oh? Who is that?" I couldn't fathom who he was talking about.

"He's currently being held in a prison, according to him, going stir crazy and demanding rocky road ice cream."

I laughed. "You mean Nick?"

He nodded. "He's been praying very hard."

I turned fully to face him, holding my Bible in my hands. "Why?"

"I think you'll find out in time, Natalie. I don't want to overstep my bounds."

I had no idea what he was talking about, but I wasn't worried about it. I was anxious to get to the hospital and talk to Nick in person.

"Tell him hi for me," he called as I turned to leave.

"Sure will. Thanks again," I said.

"You're welcome."

But first I had to get home and take a shower and fix my hair. It was probably the fastest shower I'd ever taken. I could barely contain myself while driving to the hospital and tried to go the speed limit. I pulled into the closest spot to the door I could find and ran across the parking lot.

I tapped my foot, waiting for the elevator. The ride up seemed longer than usual, but I knew it wasn't. I stepped off the elevator and headed down the hall toward Nick's room.

When I got there it was empty. I gasped. I didn't know what happened to him or where he might be. Plopping into a chair, my elation suddenly turned a one-eighty into anxiety. Where could he be? I prayed for him, not sure what else to do. He shouldn't be in burn treatment, so I hoped it wasn't an infection or worse.

The ringing phone in his room startled me out of my thoughts. "Hello? This is Nick Norton's room."

"Natalie? Pastor Collins here. While we were in my office, Mrs. John left a message with my secretary that Nick was taken to the burn center in Springfield where they could care for him there. You must have missed her on your way out earlier."

"Oh, no! Is something wrong?" I fell onto the empty mattress. "How long will he be there?" I noticed his room was pretty cleaned out, but not totally. I opened the nightstand drawer and took out his books, stacking them with one hand onto the nightstand. How far away was Springfield? Being a newcomer to the state, I've heard of it, but couldn't even tell you which direction it was in my flustered state. I gathered up the cards on his shelf, adding them to the books.

"I'm not sure. Mrs. John didn't know but went on home and called his folks. She took what she could carry and planned on coming back later."

"There's not much left, just a few books and cards. I can take them to her. I guess I'll have to wait and see him when he returns. I'll be out of town this weekend at a book signing."

"If I hear anything, I'll leave a message for you at home."

"Thanks for everything, Pastor Collins."

"You're welcome. Have a good afternoon. Nick will be alright."

I hung up, deflated. Oh, well. Nothing I could do but gather Nick's things and see what Mrs. John knew. I turned back the same way through the halls, going much slower this time.

A pop-up thunderstorm caught me unaware and I ran through the parking lot to the car, all the while trying to keep Nick's books dry. I was drenched by the time I got to the car.

I guess when Nick didn't feel like eating, it wasn't only from the ice cream. I hoped he was ok and it was nothing real serious. I turned the car back towards town and to Mrs. John's, the wipers on the car going full tilt.

Mrs. John and her husband weren't home either. I couldn't believe it. I had the best news to share in the world, and nobody to share it with. And the person I wanted to share it with most was unavailable and possibly seriously ill. I drove home and put Nick's books on the table in the foyer.

I fed Felix and plopped on the sofa, tears of frustration streaming down my cheeks. After a short nap, I packed for my morning flight. Tomorrow afternoon I would be signing books at a large independent store in Oklahoma with a small reception after with other authors. On Saturday morning I had a brunch planned with the same authors along with a book signing in a smaller store. I hoped to have time to sight see on Sunday before coming home that evening. Now I wasn't sure I felt like it.

Not only was I disappointed at not being able to talk to Nick, but I was worried for his health. And I didn't feel the greatest, either. Several sneezes had interrupted my packing. Probably a cold coming on.

I had to retrieve the laptop from my office and saw the answering machine was blinking twice. I played the messages. The first one was from Mrs. John letting me know what was going on. The second one was from Nick. "I'll miss you,

Natalie. Can't wait to see you again. I'll try to call when I can." His voice sounded echo-ey and weak. He called right after Mrs. John, so maybe he hit redial after she left his room.

I called Mrs. John and left a message that my key would be in the mailbox. I had asked her a while ago to take care of Felix and the house while I was gone. I planned to take a taxi to the airport.

I went to bed that night feeling as lonely as ever. I was so frustrated. My flight was at nine, so I had to be at the airport by seven. It would be an early morning, provided the night ever ended. Since I couldn't sleep, I turned on the lamp and took out my Bible and read through the first chapters of John again. Now more of the verses made sense, but not all of them.

It was an incredible feeling to have the love of God poured over me and to know what would happen to me when I died. Peace once again settled over me and I turned out the light, praying for Nick to get better and for a safe flight and a good signing.

The flight went well and I checked in at the hotel. The weather down here was windy and there was talk of a possible tornado. The whole state of Oklahoma was under a tornado watch according to the weather channel I had on in the room. Thunderstorms were forecasted for the entire day. Not my idea of fun, carrying books and papers in the rain. Oh, well.

I changed into my signing clothes and took a taxi to the store.

The red and yellow décor along with bright lighting made it a cheerful place. It was a perfect place to read or browse. I introduced myself to the lady at the checkout and she rushed me to the area where tables were set up. "We have stacks of each author's books and you can place any items you have on this table."

I took out my bookmarks and cards and a small basket into which I poured out a bag of wrapped chocolates. If there was anything that was a draw to a table, it was chocolate!

The clerk introduced me to the other guests and we prepared ourselves for a fun afternoon. I met a nice older lady, probably in her 70s, was my guess, who wrote cozy mysteries and a middle-aged author who wrote military suspense. He told me he was retired from the Navy. When they asked me what I wrote, I explained about the adoption stories. They both nodded with appreciation.

I unwrapped one of my chocolates and popped it in my mouth. We were soon busy, signing books and chatting with readers. Though the weather was lousy, we had a successful afternoon.

During the lags, Helen, the mystery writer, asked me where I was from. We chatted about our writing life and she offered to drive me around, since she had her car with her.

"Thank you, Helen, I appreciate that."

She drove a Cadillac convertible. Hmm, should be an interesting drive. She had the top up as it was still raining. "How long have you been writing?"

"About twelve years. Been published for the last five."

She nodded. "It's a rewarding career, though it won't make you rich."

"I know. I just can't stop. Most of my bread and butter comes from writing and editing booklets and white papers for corporations."

"Ah. Mine comes from my dead husband's estate."

I smiled. I'd never heard of her, so didn't know how popular her books were. She pulled up to the door. "Thank you so much, Helen. I hope this storm blows over soon. Here's one of my books." I slipped a card into it in case she wanted to contact me later.

"Oh, here's one of mine. Good idea." She pulled one from the back seat, slid a bookmark into it and handed it over. "Thanks, and take care," and she was off.

I ran into the hotel to find the desk clerk franticly checking out guests. I sprinted up the stairs to my room, grabbed a towel from the bathroom and dried off my clothes and hair. I tossed it into the floor, grabbed my toiletries and threw them into the cosmetic case and tossed it on the bed. I pulled my clothes from the closet and jammed them willy-nilly into the suitcase. I called a taxi and waited for it in the lobby after checking out of my room.

I didn't know how the airlines would handle this mess, but I wanted to go home. The rain was still coming down, huge puddles around the parking lots and sidewalks. I just missed one, stepping out of the taxi. I paid the driver and took my suitcase inside where I searched for the nearest restroom to again wipe off. People were scurrying everywhere, pulling suitcases and sporting backpacks. Travelers who just landed wanted to get back on a plane and fly out. Those from out of town like me wanted to leave as soon as possible. When I got up to the counter, the frazzled ticket agent looked at my ticket and frowned. "I don't know what I can do."

"Just get me out of here, and I'll take it from there." I figured I could sight see somewhere else.

"The best I can do for now is get you to Denver this afternoon with a connecting flight at 7:30 p.m. to St. Louis." Denver? That's the wrong direction. I didn't dare complain with the grumbling passengers all around me.

"Fine. I'll take it." I had an hour wait, so went to the nearest restaurant and sat down. I took out my paperback and waited for my chicken sandwich. I couldn't concentrate, so kept checking my bags and my purse. The hot chocolate I ordered with dinner didn't help the chill I felt. I hoped I could get home this evening before I felt any worse.

Nick wasn't at home, and neither was I. I wondered when we would see each other again. I couldn't wait.

Chapter 15

I had to spend the evening in Denver, and when I arrived, I found a quiet spot to sleep before I could get the connection to St. Louis. But first, I pulled my suitcase from the baggage claim rack and then searched for a gift shop to find a Get Well card for Nick. He had been on my mind all while I was traveling and signing the few books customers purchased.

I pulled out a stamp from my purse and dropped off his card in a mail slot near one of the restaurants in the airport. I dug through my suitcase and found a sweater to put on before lying down for a couple hours before leaving.

By the time I got back home from my trip, I was exhausted. The toll of my emotions, the trip, and Nick's illness wore me out. I sneezed on the plane and had more chills in the taxi from St. Louis. Coffee was the only hot drink the plane offered, so I sipped it, grimacing with every swallow. I must be coming down with something. After getting the mail and dropping my suitcase by the door, I drank some orange juice. I fed Felix and let him rub against my leg. I took my temperature and was dismayed at its reading.

I hauled my suitcase upstairs, unpacked, and got into pajamas. I flipped through the mail and set it all aside. I played the messages on the answering machine. There was a short one from Nick, "Knock 'em dead, honey. See you soon." My heart melted at his husky voice, even though it was hoarse and weak. I saved his message and deleted the others, all from telemarketers or the wrong number. I brushed my teeth and fell into bed, dreaming of a life with Nick in it, permanently.

****

I must have slept a long time, because Felix pawed at me something fierce. I pushed him away, barely able to lift my arm. I rolled over and was out again. Dreams of tornadoes, rain and book signings all swam together and sometimes I thought I heard voices, similar to Mrs. John's and Mrs. White's, though I wasn't sure. Dreams can be powerful sometimes. I could have sworn a hand felt my forehead a couple times, too. And thought somebody gave me sponge baths and covered me with blankets. But surely not, since I was the only one home. Sometimes I felt a presence, but it didn't seem like Felix. My fever must be affecting my brain. I was just too tired to care. I just wanted to sleep and nothing else seemed to matter.

I woke up to a light caressing on my cheek. I peeked one eye open and knew I was dreaming for sure. Nick stretched out on my bed, with a sling on his arm and his good hand brushing my cheek. Dared I open the other eye?

I slowly reached for the hand that I dreamed rested on my face. I felt something solid and a soft gasp left my lips. "Are you for real?" I whispered.

"As real as I can be." Nick kissed me on the hand, soft and slow.

"This must be a dream. Can you do that again?" I didn't seem to quite understand what was happening. Was I still sleeping? Or was I half-awake?

"With pleasure." His lips were tender and more than willing. He kissed each finger before taking my hand in his.

"Did I die and go to heaven?" I was afraid to keep both eyes open at once.

"Not quite."

"Are we married?"

Nick grinned before answering. "Not yet."

I inched myself up, looking around. I recognized my room. And realized Nick sat on my bed. Very close. And he was grinning at me. I took in the scene before me, not sure I was conscious. Then I heard purring. Sounded like Felix' purr. I eyed him taking a bath at Nick's stocking feet.

Traitor.

Nick wore a pair of gray sweats and a navy t-shirt.

"Why are you here? How come you're not in Springfield?" I noticed my pajamas, not recalling dressing in this set when I got home. "How come I'm in different pajamas?" I pulled up the covers in alarm, not sure what in the world was going on.

"One question at a time." He sat up and leaned against the headboard next to me. I drew up my knees under the quilt. "Because Mrs. John told me you most likely had mono, and I had to get out of there. So, I pleaded with the doc to be an outpatient and they moved me back here for a few days, and I started to heal faster so they let me go." He looked at me before adding, "My strong-willed personality is good for a few things."

"Wow. How long have I been sick?"

"A couple weeks."

I sucked in my breath. "Weeks? You're kidding!" I flung the covers off, forgetting how I was dressed. "My work—" Nick touched my arm.

"All taken care of. When your agent called, I filled him in and said I would send what you had so far. He liked it and said try to finish it by Christmas."

Stunned at this news, I recovered myself and leaned back against the headboard. Then I remembered Nick's situation. "How are you? Your arm?" I took his hand, not wanting him to ever leave. I brushed my fingers on his cheek, where a new scar appeared, next to his ear. It didn't diminish his looks at all; it was so far to the side. He was as handsome as ever. Good as new with a distinguished scar. I gulped.

He squeezed my hand in return and said, "My arm is fine, just in a sling now. I'm much better. But you scared us. Me." He let go of my hand and wrapped his arm around my shoulder, kissing my ear.

"Really?" I pulled his hand to my lips and kissed each finger, desire warming me almost as much as my fever.

"The only thing that kept you at home was all of us, taking turns to watch over you and bathe you. A couple times we thought we had to call the doctor, you were out of it so much. But then we could get you to drink some fluids before you fell back to sleep."

I looked at him in alarm when he mentioned the word 'bathe'.

He tried not to grin. "Don't worry; the old ladies wouldn't let me help."

I sighed in relief. "How long have you been here?"

"Not long enough," he sighed.

We were quiet for a minute, while I digested all that had happened over the last few months. I still needed to tell him my news about being a new Christian if he didn't know already. But right now didn't feel like the right time.

Suddenly I wrapped my arms around Nick, squeezing him tight, avoiding his bad arm. Nick hugged me back. No words were needed.

Later that morning, after I ate breakfast in bed, we caught up on what each other had missed while sick. I showed him his journal and explained how Pastor Collins asked me to keep it. Nick read it with interest, reading each page thoughtfully. "Thanks, Nat. I'll treasure this always." He hugged me and kissed my forehead.

I was still weak, but wanted to shower. Mrs. John and Mrs. White apparently had kept up the house and took care of Felix while Nick mowed and weeded the lawn and took care of the garden, and informed my agent I was sick. He also changed the oil in my car and washed it, though his arm was still in a sling. I had a feeling he removed it whenever it suited him according to the task.

I guess it was a good thing Mrs. John had my key and checked on me after I got back when I hadn't answered the door or the phone.

"I hate to kick you out even for a minute, but can I take a shower?"

Nick thought about it for a minute. "I guess so. Be careful. I'd gladly help if I could."

Too weak, I didn't respond. He helped me stand up. I was wobbly and fell back on the bed. Nick sat beside me. "Are you sure you can handle it?"

"Just weak." I leaned my head on his shoulder, not really wanting to get up. He wrapped his arm around me. "I love you, Nat," he whispered in my ear.

"I love you, too." After a minute, we tried again. I slowly walked around the room. "I think I got it, thanks."

Nick gave me a bear hug that made me quiver. It was just as I imagined. Then he kissed me on the top of my head before he and Felix went downstairs. I'm sure Felix was bewildered after the last few weeks. I gathered clean clothes and took a short shower, not wanting to stand too long. I dressed and dried my hair quickly, putting it up in a ponytail.

The partially closed guest room door drew my attention, so I pushed it open. Apparently someone had made themselves at home. Aftershave and toothpaste sat on the dresser as well as a pile of books and a Bible. It looked like a heap of dirty clothes sat in a pile under the window. Had Nick been sleeping here? And did the old ladies know? The plot thickens.

I held onto the banister as I plodded downstairs. Nick appeared, taking my hand and helping me down the last few steps. We went to the living room and sat together on the sofa. I think we both knew our relationship had taken on a new dimension. We held hands, neither of us speaking.

I must have fallen asleep again. Sometime later I found myself under a blanket, lying on the sofa. Nick sat at my feet, rubbing them gently.

Felix walked in, looking a little rebuffed. I chuckled at his behavior. "I have a feeling you're slowly being replaced, Felix," I said.

"I sure hope so. I'd love to be king of this castle."

"Only if I can be queen," I returned. I slowly sat up, covering myself with the blanket.

"Of course." I put my head back on the couch, and closed my eyes. I needed to rest for a minute. Nick still held my hand, rubbing it with his thumb. In his presence, in his arms, I was at complete rest. And so I fell asleep again.

When I woke up later, Nick sat reading in the chair by the fireplace, Felix on his lap. Well, at least if Nick and I ever married, Felix would already be used to Nick.

"What time is it?" I stretched my arms and slowly sat up.

"How are you feeling?" Nick put Felix down and came over to the sofa, sitting next to me.

"Starved and very tired." I yawned to prove my point.

"I can help take care of that. How about some of Mrs. White's soup?"

"Sounds wonderful."

I wondered what the work schedule had been like over the last couple weeks, and how Nick ended up sleeping in my house. Did they feed Nick here, or did they all eat elsewhere? I haven't been through the house yet, so I had little clue as to exactly what had been going on. I knew two things: one, I was too tired to care; and two, I was grateful for these neighbors I now called friends.

Since we were now into June, I'm sure Nick never went back to work. Which meant he had a lot of time on his hands.

"Here we are, and some fresh bread to go with it." He handed me a tray and I prayed silently. Nick sat down next to me with a cinnamon roll. Hmm, I hoped there were more of those somewhere.

"This hits the spot. Thanks."

"Thank Mrs. White. She and Mrs. John have tag-teamed the whole time, not knowing when you'd wake up. Sometimes we all ate dinner here and played games quietly, taking turns in your room to watch you. Even Mr. John took some turns. We laughed so much; we thought you'd wake up for sure. But it took a while." He was quiet for a minute before he said, "I'm not sure what I would have done if we'd lost you."

I nearly choked. Had I been that sick? I was completely unaware. "I couldn't have gone yet."

"Why not?"

"I haven't won our Scrabble tournament yet."

His hearty laugh warmed my heart. "I almost forgot about that with all the excitement around here." I put the tray on the table and leaned into Nick's shoulder. "I have something to tell you."

"Oh?"

I gathered my thoughts before continuing. "The day you went to Springfield, I went to visit Pastor Collins at the church office. We had a long conversation about my past and how I could get beyond the forgiveness part. He shared how I could do that without seeing the guy and then told me how I could accept Christ. I became a Christian that day."

"Oh, Nat. I'm so happy for you. I'll help you anyway I can. I promise." He kissed the top of my head and gave me a quick hug.

"Thanks." I knew he meant it, too.

Nick took my hand, and said, "I have a question for you."

I turned to him and waited. He slid off the couch and got down on one knee. "I know we're both still weak, but I have to ask you something. Natalie, will you marry me?"

A gasp escaped my lips. Did I hear what I thought I heard or was I still dreaming? With as much energy as I could muster, I answered. "Yes! Absolutely!"

He pulled me to him and gave me one of his hallmark kisses, slow and tender. He pulled away first and said, "I have a ring for you, but it's at my place. I'll get it later. Is that ok?"

I nodded, tears of joy running down my cheeks. He sat back down and held me in his arms until I fell asleep again.

Chapter 16

When I woke up again, it was twilight. I opened my eyes and noticed Nick was still there. He was typing away on his laptop. Without moving or making any sound, I watched him for a minute. His brown eyes were serious as he worked, his focus solely on the screen. His sling was off his arm and he wore a navy polo and tan shorts. His feet were bare. I smiled. He indeed had made himself at home.

He looked up and noticed me watching. "You're awake; how do you feel?" He shut the laptop and set it on the table.

"A little better." I sat up and stretched my arms above my head. "I think I'd like to sit on the porch. Can you get us some ice water?"

"Sure. Let me get it and I'll walk out with you."

I ran fingers through my hair, not sure how improved I looked over the last few days. But at least the shower earlier helped revive me a little bit. Had Nick really proposed or had I been dreaming? My heart was so full, I thought it would burst. Had I the energy, I'm sure I would have felt giddy from head to toe.

We walked out to the porch and sat on the swing. A light breeze swayed the oak and maple leaves and I could hear a cricket's chirp in the background. The metal thwak of a bat hitting a ball at the park and children laughing were the only other sounds. I hated to break the silence with words, but I needed to know some things. "What is today?"

Nick looked surprised. "I guess you're a little disoriented, aren't you?"

I nodded.

"Thursday June 14th."

"Oh. My birthday is next Saturday." How weird. I didn't like this feeling of not knowing what day it was. But it couldn't be helped.

"In that case, a celebration is in order. If you're feeling up to it, may I take you out?"

I grinned. "Of course. It will give me an incentive to get out of my fog faster."

"I know what you mean. Remember when you told me about my accident?"

I nodded in understanding. "I know; it's weird. I remember how you thought it had just been a day or two since our last conversation. In reality it was, but there was a big gap in time." I swallowed some ice water and then asked, "Um...how long have you...been staying here?"

He hesitated before answering. "A few days." He cleared his throat before adding, "I couldn't bear you being here alone after Mrs. John said she found you passed out and couldn't wake you."

He swallowed a sip of water and then said, "When Mrs. John and Mrs. White made the trip to see me, I could tell they were worried about something. I couldn't figure it out, because I knew it wasn't about me. It was like pulling tough weeds in dry ground to get them to tell me they were worried about you. They had left Mr. John with you while they came to visit." He took my hand and said, "After that, I fought for them to release me, I'd had a couple treatments and they were satisfied the burns were clearing up and I begged them to treat me outpatient. I had to come home, to see you and take care of you." He squeezed my hand before letting go.

I sipped my water while gazing out on the lawn, now a lush dark green. It was a good thing I had such caring neighbors and Nick to watch over me. I don't know what would have happened otherwise.

"But how did you know it was mono?" I couldn't figure out how they knew what to do if I hadn't gone to the doctor.

"The Johns have a friend in town who is a retired doctor and they explained to him your situation and he came over and checked your vitals and ruled out pneumonia because your lungs were completely clear. He said he couldn't be totally sure without doing blood work, but because of a normal temperature and clear lungs, he thought it was mono and you just needed lots of sleep."

"Good grief. All kinds of things happen while you're sleeping."

Nick chuckled. "Tell me about it."

A few minutes later, he asked, "Do you mind...me staying here? Does it make you uncomfortable?" Nick held his breath, staring at the porch floor.

Did I mind? Not in the least. Should I mind? Probably. "Not at all. Just wished I could've been a better hostess."

He let out his breath before laughing. "Oh good. Don't worry about the hostess part; the dear ladies have filled in superbly in that area."

"Do they know you're staying here?" Though I was fearful of his answer, I still had to know.

A look of guilt passed over his face. His answer didn't come right away. "To be perfectly honest, they probably suspect, but considering the circumstances, they haven't said anything. At least to me. And they're not gossips, so I think we're safe. If you know what I mean."

Ah. Now I knew. Of course Nick was a gentleman in every way and I had nothing to worry about. It didn't surprise me, his protective behavior, even if it made others suspect something other than his honorable intentions. He was wired that way and it was his nature.

"To put it another way, they haven't asked and I haven't confessed." I nodded. "Tonight will probably be my last night since you're getting around now."

I leaned back against the seat and closed my eyes. "After a bite to eat, shall we wrap up our tournament?"

"If you feel up to it, sure. There's plenty of food in the fridge to choose from."

"Somehow, that doesn't surprise me." We went into the house and warmed up leftovers and played our last game. Nick won, because I let him. He didn't need to know that, did he?

He circled his score on the tablet with a wide grin. "Victory! Now I can finally get some more of that awesome cake. When you're up to it that is. No hurry or anything." A short pause. "Do you think you could have it by Saturday?"

I tossed the nearest throw pillow at him.

****

The next morning Nick asked me, "So what do you think you'd like to do for your birthday?" We were sitting at the breakfast bar, polishing off some sweet bread and fruit we found in the fridge.

It was strange to see Nick in sweats and t-shirts or shorts and a polo like he was wearing this morning. But he looked as handsome as ever. It hadn't taken his skin long to tan while taking care of my yard. I'm sure he was tired of his sling and wore it less than he should.

I toyed with my fork. "Oh, I don't know. It doesn't matter."

"Doesn't matter? How come?" He put his hand on my arm.

"Birthdays are overrated."

Nick was silent for a minute and I had to turn to face him. His eyes looked sad. He picked up my hand and rubbed my thumb. "Oh, come on Nat. They can be lots of fun. If Mrs. John and Mrs. White hear you talking like that, you'll have a birthday you'll never forget." Nick swung his fork back and forth.

"How's that?"

"I'm not sure you want to know. I've heard some horror stories from people at church. If you don't make plans for your birthday, they'll be made for you. Ones involving hearses, black balloons, kidnappings, funny clothes, photos, all kinds of crazy things."

I gulped, just imagining myself in a hearse wearing funny clothes. I wouldn't put it past them to do something like that. "In that case, can we go out for a simple dinner? Seafood or Italian, for instance?"

"Certainly. I'll pick you up at six."

I nodded. I needed to get into the office, but didn't want Nick to leave either. "Can we work in the office?" We both stood up.

"Do you feel up to it?" He put his hand on my shoulder.

"For a little while at least. I can at least catch up on email and the snail mail." He gave me a bear hug. "Ok, I'll be up there in a few minutes. I'll clean up the kitchen."

"Thanks."

He nodded and shooed me away. The first thing I did was fire up the computer and blew the dust off the keyboard. I flipped through the small stack of mail sitting on the desk. A square pink envelope caught my eye. I recognized the strong masculine writing immediately. I tore it open. Inside was a card with flowers and an inscription that read 'Get Well Soon' and inside it said, 'Better yet?' Just like Nick. He signed it, *Lots of Love, Nick*. I set it on the shelf above my desk. Felix wandered in and sat in his usual spot. I cleared a space off the table against the wall so Nick could sit there. He'd have to bring up a chair from the kitchen.

I scanned my email contents and deleted everything that wasn't from my agent or a family member. That brought the list down from 183 to twenty. I read those and responded accordingly. I updated my agent that I was indeed alive but not completely well yet. I said I'd get back to work on Monday. That gave me a cushion to regain my bearings and clean out my office.

Nick came in, carrying a chair. "Thanks for the card," I pointed to it.

He kissed me on the cheek before sitting down. "You're welcome, Nat." We worked in our own worlds until the doorbell rang around noon. "That's probably one of our lady friends, checking on our purity."

"Nick!" I threw a pen at him, but he was already out the door, chuckling. I'd have to improve my aim if this stuff kept up. I closed out my computer window and followed, but much slower. Sure enough, it was Mrs. White. She was sporting a scarf over her hair, a knit top and slacks.

"Hello, dears. It's good to see you up and about," she said to me. "How are you feeling?" She gave me a quick hug.

"Much better, though I'm still weak. Not doing much."

"That's understandable. You gave us a scare. You take it easy and let Nick take care of you this time. We trust him," she said, winking. "I'll have lunch ready in a jiffy. You kids go along and I'll call you in a few minutes."

Nick and I looked at each other and shrugged. We went into the living room and I turned on the stereo to a light classical station. I didn't really know what food I had in the kitchen right now, and it was disconcerting a little. But I'll let them do their stuff as long as they want to. They've done it before and it seems to be their trademark.

She whipped up some sandwiches, relishes, and leftover potato salad. We chatted about things going on at the church, and in town. After lunch Mrs. White cleaned up and left.

Nick stayed just a few minutes longer and gave me a kiss on the cheek before he left. I hated to see him go, but knew he must. At least one day, we wouldn't have to leave each other at night anymore. I was looking forward to that.

I took advantage of the now empty house to do something important-I took a nap.
****

The night of my birthday, Nick picked me up at six. I didn't know where we were going, as I left that to Nick. I was just glad I wasn't driving. I hadn't done much all day, and didn't have a lot of energy yet. Each day, I got up earlier than the day before, but still had to take long afternoon naps.

Nick drove into St. Louis, to an Italian neighborhood called the Hill, famous for its fine restaurants. We pulled up front to find valet parking and Nick took a jacket from the back seat before opening the door for me. I was glad I dressed up in a new outfit. Nick moved comfortably in his sharp gray slacks and striped oxford with matching maroon tie that completed his ensemble. His scars were barely noticeable anymore and his sling was nowhere to be seen.

Nick put on his jacket and then we walked in to find antiques, soft lighting, and classical music in the background. We were ushered to a table in the back left corner and seated by a host in a tuxedo. All the tables were covered with crisp linen tablecloths, with small candles in the center and heavy silverware resting on cloth napkins. I slipped my sweater on since the air conditioner made me chilly.

"Thank you. This is a nice place." I took in the oil paintings and mirrors along the walls, chandeliers around the room and the cozy romantic atmosphere. The plush carpet was cushy under my sandaled feet.

"I heard about this restaurant from some teachers at work. They serve good seafood, steaks and pastas. I hope you like it."

"If they have shrimp scampi, I'll love it."

He smiled, but didn't look away. He reached for my hand. "You were pretty quiet on the drive over. Are you sure you feel like being out? We can pick something up instead." He tilted his head to the side, his concern melting my insides.

I squeezed his hand. "I'm still really tired. I hope I get my energy back soon."

"It takes a lot out of you. You'll be yourself soon." He patted my hand and then held it, his other hand opening his menu.

We ordered our beverages and studied the menu. I did order something on the menu called Scampi Alla Grigua, that sounded close to my scampi. A hefty scent of garlic and tomato sauce floated around from a nearby table. My stomach let me know it was dinner time.

"I'm afraid I'm not much of a conversationalist tonight." I pulled the small vase holding a red rose closer to me and breathed in the flower's scent.

"I'll just admire you and make up stories."

I smiled. "Sounds good to me. The story part."

"What about the admiring part?" Nick feigned a hurt look.

"Not necessary." I didn't really like being the center of attention, and never have. His admiring glances and smiles made me blush.

He shared tales from his younger days as a student and from the first years as a teacher while we nibbled on bread. I was glad he had something to say, because my mental state was still slow.

Our plates came and the food was delicious. I hadn't had shrimp scampi like that in years. The salad was also very good. It looked like Nick enjoyed his steak, too.

So far the evening had been a success. Before leaving for our dinner, Nick gave me a dozen pink carnations, my favorite flower in my favorite color. He also gave me a card and signed it, *'Love, Nick.'* A wrapped package, in flowery paper revealed chocolate and pecan candy, another small box held a dozen pens in bright colors. How did he know I loved small packages and pens, especially?

After the table was cleared, we sat talking while we let our delicious dinner settle a bit. When our server came back, he asked Nick if he was ready. Nick nodded. The server left our table and I gave Nick a puzzled look. Ready for what? The check? Nick's eyes had that twinkle in them, and I suspected he was up to something. But what?

The server came back with a large slice of chocolate cake with white frosting drizzled across it and set it before Nick. Nick turned the plate around to face me and I noticed the frosting wasn't in a random design, but in a pattern. In words. I read them slowly, out loud. "Will... you... marry... me?" I read aloud. "Will I marry you?" I said louder.

Nick smiled, came around the table and kneeled on one knee. "I know I asked you the other day, but now I have one more birthday present for you." From his jacket pocket, Nick took a ring box out and opened it. "Would you, beautiful Natalie, be my lovely wife?"

"Yes! Yes, yes, yes." I didn't care if others in the restaurant heard me. I gave him a hug and let go. He kissed me and my heart swelled.

I looked at the ring he held. "It's beautiful," I breathed. He took it out of the velvet box and I held out my left hand. It fit perfectly. The diamond danced in the candlelight. I leaned over and gave him another kiss.

The entire restaurant erupted into applause. We looked around, unaware we had been watched. We grinned, embarrassed.

I sat staring at my hand. I couldn't believe it. Nick kissed me again and sat back down. "How about some cake?" he asked, laughing.

"Oh, I don't think I can. Now it's my turn to admire." The diamond was a perfect marquis, and sparkled like sunshine on a lake. I looked at Nick and felt such longing, and total joy and peace all at once. He winked at me and took a bite of cake. He had cut it in half. I thought I'd just take my half to go.

"Now, if you can stop admiring your new jewelry long enough, when would you like to get married?" Nick grinned from ear to ear.

"Heavens, I don't know. That's something to think about, isn't it?" I looked back at my hand.

"It's up to you." He put his hand on mine and squeezed. "We can get married later this summer or next year if you want. Whatever you're comfortable with. I don't know what you want as far as a wedding goes."

"I don't know either actually. I never thought much about it...after..."

Nick nodded. "It's ok, Nat. I understand." He took my hand and gave me a reassuring squeeze.

Tears slid off my cheeks onto the table. What an emotional rush! Nick brushed the tears away. "We can talk later, in private. I understand if you're not up to it right now." He squeezed my hand again and let go.

"Excuse me. I'll be right back." I found the ladies room and wiped my tears away. What a night! I blew my nose and washed my hands. A lady in a navy suit walked out of a stall and looked at me, whispering, "Are you ok? I don't mean to pry."

I laughed. "Yes, I'm fine. I just got engaged at the table." I held out my left hand to show her my ring. How it sparkled under the lights!

"Congratulations! That's wonderful."

"Thanks." I left the bathroom with a smile on my face.

"I think I'm ready for cake, now." I smiled at Nick, warmth spreading down to my toes.

"Are you alright?" Nick looked concerned.

I nodded. "Just a little overwhelmed all of a sudden. But nothing a little chocolate won't cure." I smiled at him before taking a bite. I ate a few bites and left the rest to take home. I was too emotional and too full from dinner to eat much more. Even chocolate.

"I love you," I whispered.

"And I love you," he whispered back.

We left the restaurant arm in arm. I was so tired, but so excited, I didn't know if I'd sleep tonight or not. Excitement built up inside me so strong, I wanted to shout.

Nick didn't start the car right away. I waited for him to say whatever was on his mind. I didn't know if it had to do with our engagement or something else. Darkness was just descending and lights were coming on in the parking lot. Traffic was heavy on the main road nearby.

"I have to confess that I wanted to ask you sooner, but I couldn't." Nick put the keys in the ignition, but didn't turn the engine over. He turned toward me and took my hands.

"Why not?" I was so tired; my mind didn't have a clue as to where he was going.

"For one thing, I didn't even know your name yet."

"What?" Now I was really confused. I turned toward him, with my head leaning against the headrest. This mumbo jumbo was making my head hurt.

"I know it sounds unbelievable, but that day you came to Uncle Norton's, I opened the door to a beauty on the inside and the outside. I knew then you were the one for me, and I didn't even know your name."

"Are you serious?" I sat up straighter, unbelief stirring my brain. I thought about the past few months and the day I took the plate of cookies over that I thought he would never take.

He squeezed my hands, rubbing my new jewelry. "It was such an unexpected force and feeling in my soul, I can't really explain it. I felt it in my heart." He put our hands over his heart. "Then when I found out early on you didn't go to church, I started to have doubts. I thought, what is going on? Did I hear God right, or was it just my hopeful imagination? It seemed like the more we got to know each other, the more you pulled back. Then it finally dawned on me that there must have been something from your past you couldn't move beyond, so then I asked Pastor Collins and our dear lady friends to pray for you to somehow get beyond it. I couldn't stand not being able to help or comfort you."

Tears slid down his cheeks and he turned his eyes toward the windshield. "It hurt so much to watch you, not knowing what it was. Too afraid to ask, I just pleaded with God to help you. Mrs. John and Mrs. White somehow knew we were meant for each other early on, too. But we couldn't figure out why things weren't working out."

I was flabbergasted. Tears streamed down my cheeks. How did he know? What if I'd never taken those cookies over that day? Would we have ever met? "I don't know what to say." I took tissues from my purse, handed him one and blew my nose.

    He wiped away tears before he spoke. "That's ok." He chuckled softly. "I know it's a lot to absorb, but I wanted you to know. I love you, Nat. I really, really do. I'll do my best to honor and cherish you for the rest of my life." His voice was soft and full of emotion.

    I nodded. "I probably wouldn't have been ready anyway, until I told you about the other stuff."

    "I know and I'm so glad it finally worked out. I had no idea what it was, and braced myself in case it was something I couldn't deal with. Pastor Collins told me not to think the worst scenario, but I couldn't help it. I just had no idea what you were dealing with, and I so hoped it wouldn't end our relationship permanently." He wiped moisture away from his eyes. "I've never prayed so hard for anything in my life. You know I'm stubborn, right?"

    We smiled, deflating some of the tension. "I sure do. I guess it can be a good thing sometimes, huh?"

    He nodded. He reached over for a hug and we stayed that way for a long time. The stars came out one by one and we listened to the muffled traffic and crickets in the distance, rubbing each other's backs until we were uncomfortable leaning over the console. We reluctantly separated and Nick said, "I can't wait to tell mom and dad, and everyone. They've all been praying for you, you know."

    My cheeks grew warm. "Is that why your parents were so interested in me at the hospital?

How long had they known?" I tried remembering things that had puzzled me.

"I told them at the funeral. They didn't believe me at first, that I had met the girl I was going to marry. But knowing me, they decided to wait and see."

"I've got goose bumps." I shivered. Nick rubbed warmth back into my arms before he started the car. We drove back to my place, silent in the awesome wonder of true love and total peace.

Because I was still so weak, we decided to discuss wedding plans the next afternoon after church. He promised not to announce our engagement until I was ready to go to church with him. But he wasn't sure he could hide it for long.

The next afternoon Nick brought sandwiches and after we ate, we discussed the wedding. I lounged on one end of the sofa, he at the other. "How many bridesmaids do you want? What colors do you like? Do you want a reception? A dinner and a dance?" Nick's questions came at me like seeds from dandelions blowing on the wind.

"Wow! I have a lot to think about. I guess I can get some bridal magazines for ideas. I could stop at a book store sometime."

"Sure. We can get whatever you have your pretty mind set to. Within reason of course."

"Speaking of weddings, and stuff. Where will we live? Will you move into my house? Or?"

"If you'll have me. I love this house. Do you want to sit on the swing?"

I nodded and we sat in the cool shade of the porch. Nick continued, "It will be fun to add to the garden, attach the garage, decorate a nursery, and—"

"A nursery! Can we just get married first?"

He gave me a wide grin. "Of course. Just checking to see if you were listening. This is kind of exciting, isn't it?"

"Definitely. I can't wait to tell my friends." After a few minutes of swinging in silence, I said, "I hope my parents take it well." I sighed.

Nick put his hand on my knee and squeezed. "I'm sorry about that," he offered, his voice soft and husky. He knew about the rift I had with my family. A warmth swelled inside me again as Nick gave me a bear hug.

"It isn't your fault. They'll get over it." There was another thing I was wondering. Thinking about ordering a gown, I wondered if I could still wear a white one. How did one know?

"Nick, should I wear a white gown or some other color?"

He stopped pumping the swing with his foot and twisted to face me and picked up my hands. "You can wear whatever color you desire. It could be pink or polka-dotted for all I care. Why do you ask?"

I didn't answer, looking away towards the street. Silence filled the air and my face flushed.

"Oh..." he didn't finish. He dropped my hands and slid closer, putting his arms around me, leaning me towards his chest. "Nat, Nat," he whispered. Then he pulled my chin up so I had to look at him. My eyes slowly met his. I could see nothing but compassion in his eyes.

He kissed me before saying, "You can definitely wear a white gown. You are as pure as fresh mountain air and nothing anyone says will ever change that." His voice was just above a whisper. "You are my true love, now and forever.

Don't give it another thought." He gently pulled my head to his shoulder, kissing my hair.

Relieved, I snuggled into Nick's shoulder and hugged him tight. I didn't ever want to let go. His shoulder was strong, his body completely healed. His musky aftershave teased my nose. We sat there a long time, neither of us saying a word. A perfect peace settled on me and I felt like the luckiest girl alive. A year ago, I was not a Christian, had few friends, kept a dark secret and never thought I would get married. This Jesus I was slowly getting to know, was more wonderful and more awesome than I ever thought possible.

Felix jumped on the swing. "Oh, Felix! Your timing stinks!" I cried.

Nick laughed. "Is he getting jealous?"

"I don't know. I hadn't thought about it, but maybe." I looked between Nick and Felix.

"Felix, you're going to have to get used to another man around here. In a few months, he'll be the boss."

Felix yawned, a big wide yawn that said, "Yeah, whatever," in kitty language.

"He'll get used to it. I know I will. And I think I'll like it very much." I leaned back again and we snuggled, enjoying the peace.

After Nick left, I washed the lemonade and lunch dishes. Then I took a deep breath and picked up the phone.

"Hi, Ashton, it's Natalie."

"How are you?"

"Fine. Just fine. I'm engaged to Nick, the guy I told you about earlier."

"Congratulations! I'm happy for you. He a good guy?"

"In every way. How about you and Mandy?"

"Working on it."

I grinned. "You chicken?"

"No. She wants to finish her degree first next spring. I don't want to add to the stress. But we're getting serious. I've already talked to her dad."

"Oh." I hadn't thought of Nick talking to my dad.

"You still there?"

"Yeah, just thinking."

"Mom and dad want to you to come home soon for a visit. They want to talk with you about stuff."

"I'll think about it."

"It would be in your best interest. They've changed."

"How?"

"It would be better if you hear it from them."

I let that go, not sure what Ashton meant. We talked for a few minutes more and hung up.

The next day, since Nick wasn't working this summer, we drove to the book store. Nick walked around the car and opened my door. "Allow me, Mrs. Norton, to be."

"Certainly, future Mr. Norton." I laughed. We strolled into the store, arm in arm. Once inside, I headed to the magazine section. Nick wandered to the car section. I picked up several titles and sat down at a nearby table. The first magazine I glanced through displayed beautiful expensive gowns, fancy flowers and useless china. In the second, I saw limousines, sharp tuxes, more fancy flowers and more useless china. Maybe looking at these magazines wasn't such a good idea after all. With the addition of both our budgets, we couldn't afford a single item in these magazines. Not that I cared. I was quite content with my life and happy with the added bonus of a loving husband to be.

Nick brought over a couple books and sat next to me. "Any luck?"

I laughed. "Not with these. These magazines are for the rich and famous. Neither of us qualify for either. So they're not going to be much help."

"We'll find help somewhere. But I'll help you with whatever you need. I don't expect you to do all the work. And we'll have to talk with Pastor Collins about premarital counseling."

"Definitely. I need all the help I can get, considering."

Nick brought his arm up around my shoulder and squeezed. "Oh, honey, don't worry about that. I know it's hard, but don't let it get you down. Any problem that comes up, we'll face together."

I gave him a hug and closed the magazines. "I'll try not to worry. I can't make any guarantees."

"That's all I can ask." He kissed me on the forehead before moving away.

I laid my magazines on the table and pointed to his stack. "What are you looking at?"

"Picture books of fast cars."

"Oh. I'm going to look at writing books and see if there are any I can review. I'll be back in a few minutes."

"Take your time. I'll just be drooling."

There were several new writing books out so I started a teetering stack at my feet. Some were on dialogue, memoir writing, self-contained writing workshops, column writing and one on words for the word lover. I qualified for sure. I took the stack back to the table.

"Do you want anything from the café?" Nick asked, eying my pile.

"An ice tea would be nice."

"Two teas coming up."

I perused all the books and decided to get the workshop one and the memoir one. I sipped my tea, barely able to absorb what happened this weekend. I kept looking at my ring and grinning from ear to ear. Nick watched me, chuckling at every grin. He put his book down and put his hand over mine and squeezed. "I love you, too," he said.

I grinned. I got up and returned the books I wouldn't be buying. I sat down next to Nick again. "Do you still love me?"

"More than ever."

We sat reading for a while longer and left for home, me a few dollars poorer. Nick had put his books back. He said they were just for fun, not for buying.

"How long is your Christmas break? Or your spring break?"

"Christmas break is usually ten to twelve days, depending on the day of the week Christmas falls on. And spring break is usually five days."

I took out a calendar from my purse. "Well, Christmas this year is on a Thursday."

"Hmm. Maybe we have off that whole week and the next then. I'll have to call Scott next week. I haven't seen next year's school calendar yet. Where do you want to honeymoon?" Nick turned us south.

"Anywhere, as long as it's with you."

"Ditto. Are you thinking about getting married during Christmas break?"

"Maybe. I'm not sure about honeymooning that time of year. What do you think?" I watched the scenery whiz by, eyeing begonias, roses and lilacs in full bloom.

"I don't know. Only one way to find out, I guess. We could try going to Hawaii. How does that sound?"

"Romantic!"

"Perhaps we could get married the Saturday before Christmas, and honeymoon right after. Our families could come here and spend an early Christmas if we get it all worked out. That way, I wouldn't have to take any extra time off, not that it would matter. How does that sound?"

"That might work. I'll order a simple gown and get Mrs. John and Mrs. White to help me with the decorations and the reception. You and I can look at wedding invitations at the print shop in town. For that matter, we can look at cakes at the local bakery, too."

"That sounds right up my alley." I swatted his arm. "Very funny." We made more plans as we drove closer to home. The prospect of not living in my house by myself anymore was wonderful. I didn't think Felix would mind either. I could hardly wait! We pulled in front of my house and walked up to the door. I unlocked it and when I turned back around, Nick pulled me closer for a sweet, lingering kiss. A warm, cozy feeling started at my lips and traveled down to the soles of my feet.

"Good night, my dear," Nick whispered. "And happy birthday weekend."

"It was, thanks to you. Good night." I went inside and watched him pull away. I slid off my shoes, and plopped on the sofa, looking at my ring. Felix wandered in and jumped on my lap. I petted him for quite a while, soaking in the weekend's events.

****

The following Sunday I put on a navy skirt and a red pullover sweater. I was excited to tell people at church about our engagement. I felt so much better after getting over mono. I picked up my Bible and ran down stairs. I fed Felix and ate some granola and fresh strawberries. Then I brushed my teeth and waited for Nick. He gave me a wide grin when he saw me. "You look as gorgeous as ever."

I blushed. "Thanks. You don't look so bad yourself."

We were at the church in no time. "Are you ready to get mauled?" he asked after opening the door for me.

"I guess so. And you?"

He grinned. "Let's get this abuse over with." He took my hand and we walked into the sanctuary. The first person we saw was Pastor Collins, walking toward us. "Hi, Pastor."

"Good morning, how are you two?"

"Great! Natalie and I are engaged."

Pastor Collin's face lit up. "Congratulations! How exciting. When did this take place?" He looked from Nick to me and winked.

"On my birthday, a week ago."

"I'm so glad for you two. Have you set a date?"

"We're thinking about over the Christmas break if the church is available."

"I have a minute before the second service starts; let's go check the calendar in my office."

We turned and followed him back down the hallway past the lobby and into the office area.

He opened a big calendar to December and looked down the row of Saturdays while we stood at his desk. "Every Saturday is clear, except for the first for program practice. What time are you thinking?"

We looked at each other and shrugged.

"Morning," I said.

"Afternoon," Nick said.

We laughed. "I'll just pencil in 'wedding' for now on the Saturday before Christmas, and you let me know the time after you figure that out. How does that sound?"

"Fine. Thank you. We also need to discuss counseling. Will you have time before or after tonight's service to talk about that for a few minutes?"

"Sure. We can probably do it beforehand if you come by a few minutes early."

"Thanks, we'll see you later."

"Congratulations. I know lots of people will be happy for you."

Nick nodded.

We returned to the sanctuary and sat down. "What time do you want to get married?" Nick asked me. Classes were still going on so not too many people were in the sanctuary yet.

"I guess it doesn't matter, really. It depends on whether we have cake and punch or a lunch or dinner. What would you prefer?"

"If you really want to know, I prefer short and simple. I don't like crowds much, you know."

I nodded. "How about we have a simple ceremony in the morning, with a brunch after?"

"My dear, that sounds perfect. Then we can leave late afternoon for our honeymoon and other things."

"Other things?" I teased.

"Yeah, you know..." He looked away, shrugging his shoulders.

"No, not really, could you expand on 'other things'?" Of course I knew, but I wanted him to squirm a little.

"Good morning, you two." We looked up to see Mrs. John. Nick escaped that one. We both stood up.

"Hi, Mrs. John. Look," I held out my hand.

"Oh, it's beautiful! Congratulations!" She leaned over to hug me. "How exciting. Did this happen last night, by chance?"

"On my birthday. We wanted to wait until I felt better to let people know."

She nodded. "We could see it coming, and we're so happy for you." It was time for church to start, so Mrs. John left to sit down by her husband. I saw her whisper in his ear, and then he turned to give me a big grin. I smiled back.

Pastor's sermon was on love, based on a chapter in First Corinthians. The subject was timely, so I listened hard.

After the service, we talked with Mrs. White and the Johns. We told them the date and that we had lots to discuss. I asked the ladies if they would help me with some of the details and they both readily agreed.

Nick and I drove to the café in town and picked up sandwiches and salads for lunch and took it to my house. We still had so much to discuss. While I set the table and got everything unwrapped, Nick poured our tea. He was becoming quite handy around here. I walked into the kitchen and watched him for a minute without him noticing. I took in his tanned skin that set off his navy shirt. Dark colors suited him. How did I get so lucky?

We sat down and Nick asked me if I wanted to pray. I looked at him, startled. It never occurred to me to pray out loud before. I prayed silently often now, but never out loud. It made me a little nervous, but I nodded.

"Dear God, thank you so much for loving us. Thank you for Nick and our upcoming wedding. Please help us make wedding plans and bless this food to our bodies. Amen."

"Amen." He squeezed my hand. "Let's dig in. All that congratulatory stuff made me hungry."

"Anything makes you hungry."

"What's your point?"

After shaking my head, I took a bite of salad. We discussed the time of the wedding first. We decided ten in the morning. We would serve a light brunch of bagels, a variety of quiches, sliced ham and cheese, fresh fruit, and cake and punch. I made a list of things to do and when. This Saturday we would order the invitations. Mrs. John told me this morning her niece works in a bridal shop in O'Fallon and she would take me one afternoon this week. After ordering invitations, we would go to the bakery and see their cakes. Mrs. White offered to make us one if we didn't find what we liked. She used to own a home-based bakery years ago.

We made progress on the list of things to do. We split the list up for things we could do separately and made plans for the items to do together on Saturday. Then we cleaned up our lunch mess and sat on the front porch with lemonade.

"Since you made your confession a while ago, about knowing I was the right one, I have a confession of my own."

Nick set his lemonade on the arm of the swing. "Oh, really? Do tell."

"I didn't want to go out with you at first. Not only because of my past, but because you were religious."

"Why? What did you think I was like?" Nick turned toward me with an intense gaze.

My face flushed before I could go on.

"Let me guess—a stick-in-the-mud with too many rules who didn't know how to have fun?"

My embarrassment deepened, if that were possible. I looked away, out into the yard where the flowers swayed in the breeze.

After a minute of silence, he asked, "Am I like that?"

I brought my eyes back around to look at his still serious face, my cheeks still warm. "No," I whispered.

"Mr. and Mrs. John?"

"Heavens no," I said louder.

"Mrs. White?"

"She's a dear!"

"So?"

I held my tongue. And then followed that brief silence with, "So forgive me for being a stereotypically narrow minded Generation X-er!"

"Alright." Nick nodded and took my hand. He kissed my fingertips, one by one. "Anything else?"

I shook my head. Nope, that was enough.

"That's all you're going to say?"

He took my hand, looked at me only with love and simply said, "Today is a new day."

I grinned. Indeed it was.

Chapter 17

Over the last several months, my daughter had been on my mind. Now that I was free of the shackles that once bound me, I had a new perspective and wanted to let her know why I gave her up and that I loved her even though she lived with another family.

I still had the business card from the attorney who handled the adoption. It was around here somewhere.

I wrote a typed letter to the adoptive attorney explaining what I wanted to do. I had no idea if the adoptive parents would let me write to her, but I enclosed a separate handwritten letter to her. She was still so young, only, five, so I wrote in simple words telling her I loved her.

I sent the letter shortly after Nick and I got engaged, not knowing if I would ever hear from her. I could only hope and pray she would write me and forgive me. In the meantime, at least I had wedding plans and writing projects to keep me busy.

I had met with Pastor Collins a couple times since my birthday and felt I was on the right road to recovery. Knowing it wasn't my fault and that I had forgiven the perpetrator, I put the trauma out of my mind. With my mind and heart carefree now, I relished making our wedding plans.

I was so thankful for all my new friends and a church family where I'm slowly fitting in. Nick and I had been going to Sunday school together, making new friends our age. Though the Three Musketeers (a tight group of girls who hung out together and were jealous of me) were still a little chilly toward us, they're slowly coming around. The trio had taken their time getting over the news that "their" Nick was engaged to an outsider. Then they turned their attention to a new single guy in the Air Force who recently moved to the area and started coming to our class. Poor Steve. I knew he came from Germany, but that was about it. If only he knew what he was getting into.

Once the Trio had realized Nick was going to marry me, they sort of accepted it and started allowing me into their circle by inviting me to their get togethers and jewelry parties. I was still cautious, and didn't totally trust them yet, but time would tell.

One July Sunday afternoon, Nick and I had a wonderful picnic lunch of cheese, grapes, French bread and sparkling grape juice. It was a beautiful day, the sun warm on our faces, the ground soft under our blanket. Sparrows chirped and monarchs flitted around. Carnations, baby's breath, irises, roses in yellow and pink, purple lilacs and pale prairie grasses surrounded us, their scents drifting on the breeze.

We discussed wedding plans and looked at brochures on Hawaii Nick picked up last week.

"Which island should we visit?" I asked before taking a sip of my juice.

"Maui might be a good one. Later this week, I'll research the web and see what we can find. How does that sound?"

"Sounds nice."

Nick dropped the brochures on the blanket. "Nat, what are you thinking about?" He took my hand and turned my chin toward him. He knew me so well.

I swallowed hard. "Lots of things. I spoke with my brother which went well. He says my parents would like me to come home for a visit. They want to tell me something."

"That could be good. Are you going to go?"

"I guess, just haven't decided when. I guess a few days at home can't be that bad, can it?"

"I doubt it. I'll pray for you."

I took a deep breath. "I also wrote to the lawyer who took care of my adoption and enclosed a letter for my daughter. I don't know if she'll ever write back but I felt I had to explain."

Nick rubbed my shoulder. "Oh, Nat. I didn't know. I hope you hear from her. I'm sure she'll understand someday if not now."

"It's only been a few weeks, but I can't stop thinking about her. I don't know what she looks like or what she likes. If she's into Barbie or Cinderella or eats her vegetables or likes to dance or watch movies. There's so much I want to know."

I put my head on his shoulder and we sat there quietly, watching the sun slowly sink.

****

I decided to go home the last week of July to get the visit with my parents behind me. I didn't want to dwell on it and thought I would deal with it head on. I wasn't sure what mom and dad wanted to chat about, and if it wasn't good news, I wanted to know and get over it and back to Illinois and to Nick as soon as possible.

Nick drove me to the airport on the morning of my departure. I had a short flight, but it took longer to get through security. Oh, the times we live in these days. Stupid terrorists.

I was nervous and just wanted the whole trip to be over with. "I love you and I'll pray for you the whole time. I'll miss you horribly, Nat. Come back, safe."

"Believe me; I'm not staying any longer than necessary. I'll see you in a few days. Do you have my arrival information?"

"Yep. In my wallet. I'll be here early. Call me tonight, ok?"

"I will. Make Felix be good."

"I won't let him get the best of me." He kissed me and I went through the gate. I turned and watched him walk away, suddenly feeling very lonely.

The flight was quick and smooth. The plane was full, but I didn't need to talk to anyone as my seatmates plugged into their devices as soon as possible. I tried reading, but couldn't concentrate and stared out the window behind the wing most of the way.

Ashton was already at the airport. We exchanged bear hugs. "How are you?" he asked. "You look great."

"I'm fine, and I'm very happy. I just hope this trip doesn't ruin everything." I sighed.

"Don't worry. I don't think it's bad news. Nothing I've heard about anyway." We walked side by side in silence. He led the way to his Ford pickup. He threw my bag in the back, worrying me a little.

I hopped in, getting queasy by the second. I haven't been home in years. The streets and neighborhoods haven't changed much except the cars were different and the trees taller. It's funny how I moved from one metro area to another that were both part of a larger community. Hudson, Wisconsin, is considered part of the Minneapolis/St. Paul metro area even though the St. Croix River runs along between Minnesota and

Wisconsin, just like the Mississippi River is between Missouri and Illinois. Mascoutah and surrounding areas are considered part of the St. Louis Metro Area. Maybe subconsciously, that's how I found my house, and wanted the similarities of my home town of living in a small community, but being near a large metropolitan area.

"You still writing?" Ashton's question pulled me from my thoughts.

I nodded. "I'm working on another novel. My editor wants the book by the end of the year, so I've been working hard on it. And working on wedding plans and other things."

"That's good. Mom and dad have copies of your books on the living room table."

That was startling. "Really?"

"Yeah. You'll have to give them a second chance, Natalie."

"More like the other way around," I muttered.

"Just don't go in with guns drawn, ok?"

****

I took the phone out to the patio, moved the chaise lounge to some shade and enjoyed another glass of fresh ice cold lemonade.

"Hi, Nick. I miss you," I said.

"I miss you too, honey. How's it going?"

"Great. Much better than I expected. I'll explain in person later. Would you call your parents and see if they want to meet my parents? They're going to fly down and see my house and everything."

"Sure, they wouldn't miss it and they can stay with Uncle Norton."

"Nick, that would be great. My parents can stay with me. Maybe we can grill like we did with the older folks."

"Sounds good. Are you sure you're ok?"

"Yes. I'm just overwhelmed. I can't wait to see you."

"Me, too. Call me tomorrow?"

"Absolutely."

"Love you."

"Me too."

****

The rest of my visit home was busy with wedding plans and soon we were at the air port.

I spotted Nick right away. I pointed him out to my mom. "You mean that gorgeous guy in the red polo and tan shorts? That's your Nick? Your photo doesn't do him justice."

I nodded. "Wow, Natalie. He's handsome. Is that a scar on his cheek?" she whispered as we got closer. I nodded again. "I'll explain later."

"Hi, Nick." I gave him a quick hug, and then introduced him to my parents. "This is my mom Carol, and my dad Steve."

"Nice to meet you, Mr. and Mrs. Alexander."

"And manners, too." Mom smiled at me.

"Nice to meet you, Son. I think we have a discussion in our near future, I hear," dad said to Nick.

Nick rubbed his jaw and ran his hand through his hair. "Yes, sir."

My dad laughed. "I won't hit too hard," he joked.

Nick relaxed, taking my bag. "Have a good flight?"

"Yes, not too much turbulence this time," my mom said.

"Good. The car's this way. I think it will be a tight squeeze, but we'll manage." We meandered through the crowds, not able to converse until we got to the parking lot.

"A Mustang?" my dad asked, surprised. "I haven't been in one of these in years."

I looked at my dad. "I've never seen you in one."

"It was before you and Ashton came along, sweetie. Boy, she was smooth. Remember, Carol?"

"Do I. Dark blue, with cream interior. Your dad wouldn't let me wear heels in the car. I had to take them off, so I wouldn't tear up the floor."

"Dad! Is that true?" I stood with my hand on my hip.

"Of course it was. Nick?" My dad appealed to Nick, of all things.

"I agree, sir. But Natalie doesn't wear heels. Otherwise..." Nick shrugged his shoulders like it would be a normal occurrence had I ever worn heels. He ducked behind the trunk or I would've swatted him.

I looked at him, shocked. "Nick! You aren't serious!"

"Of course I am, dear." His tone said, work with me here.

I got his message. "I admit he is particular about keeping it clean and all that. As a matter of fact, I wasn't sure the first time I sat in it if he had just washed it and cleaned the interior or if he was a neat freak."

By now we were settled in the car, my dad in the front and mom and I in the back. "Have you ever had anyone sit back here?" I asked.

"Just mom."

I nodded. Didn't look like anyone was ever back here. Not a speck of dust or lint anywhere.

We made small talk on the way to my house and dad and Nick brought in our bags. "Hi, Felix!" I scooped him up and gave him a big hug.

"Hey," Nick complained. "I didn't even get that kind of hug," he said, pouting.

"Oh, well come here, then." We hugged a long time, until I heard my dad clear his throat.

"Nick, Son, let's go out to the porch."

"Yes, sir." He gave me a worried look.

I just smiled. "I'll bring some tea out in a minute. I'll give mom the quarter tour."

She and I went to the kitchen. "Natalie, this is a remarkable house. How do you afford it?"

"Don't worry, Mom. It was a steal. The son wanted to get rid of it so he could go back to Colorado or California, wherever he was from. His dad had owned it, but died."

"I see. You've got it done up nicely." She rubbed her hand on the staircase banister.

"Thanks. Have a seat at the island and I'll get the tea started."

"So, has Nick always had that scar? It looks like it was pretty bad at one time." Mom settled at the island, her elbows resting her hands under her chin.

"Oh, man, you got that right." I explained the accident and how long he'd been in the hospital. She already knew how we met and fell in love.

"Natalie, I'm so happy for you. I'm so relieved you're able to forgive and move on. I'm so happy for you and Nick, too."

"I'm very happy now and like my new life. I'm only regretting one thing now."

"What's that?"

"That I might not get in touch with the girl I gave up."

"Oh?"

"I wrote to her through the lawyer, but haven't heard anything yet."

"I'm so sorry, Natalie. I feel so bad I didn't support you when you needed it the most." She hugged me tight. "It's in the past now, Mom. Things are going well."

I sat down, wondering how it was going out on the porch. Mom elbowed me. "They're fine."

I nodded.

"They're probably talking car stuff."

"I never knew dad had a Mustang."

Mom set her glass down. "Yep, he loved that car. But it wasn't really a family car, so he traded it in. I think he's always regretted it, though. But we couldn't afford to keep it and the new one, too. Back then most families only had one car."

"That's kind of sad in a way."

"It is, but it was a sacrifice he had to make, and I know he would do it again if he had to. You've got a great father."

"I know." I got up and poured tea for the guys. "I'll be right back."

I took the glasses to the front door, hearing snatches of their conversation. I waited for a lull.

"...yes, she did. We're working through it."

"...treat her right, like a princess."

"Yes, sir..."

I bumped the door with my elbow, announcing my arrival. "Fresh ice tea, anyone?"

"Thanks, Natalie," dad took a glass.

"Thanks, dear," Nick said, taking a glass. His face was flushed.

"Everything good out here?"

"Yep."

"I guess so," Nick answered, cautiously.

"Actually we're having a great conversation, Natalie. Nick sounds like a good guy."

"I think so." I winked at him and went back to mom in the kitchen.

"Should I rescue Nick from your father?"

I laughed. "I think so. He looks a little embarrassed."

"All right, I'll ask them to come in soon." She sipped her tea.

I fed Felix and refreshed our tea.

"Oh, I might as well go get them." She slid off the stool and took off like a soldier on a mission. A few minutes later, they all came back in. We made plans for our barbeque and Nick went home to wait for his parents who were coming late this afternoon. We would all meet here at six.

Dad walked outside and surveyed the house and the garage. Mom went to lie down and I unpacked and flipped through the mail. Nothing from my little girl yet. I didn't know if I would ever hear from her or not. I still held out hope.

The evening went well, with both sets of parents getting along. Nick and I were relieved. We stayed up late and then Nick and his parents left.

The next day, we had brunch at my house. Nick's parents brought bagels and pastries from a bakery. Mom and Mrs. Norton cut up fruit and made scrambled eggs. I got out plates and forks and we filled our plates, taking them to the dining room. I noticed some flowers that weren't there earlier. I would peek at the card later.

We made definite wedding plans, filling in our parents with the decisions we'd already made. This afternoon the Johns and Mrs. White were coming over for dessert. I already had the chocolate zucchini cake in the oven. Nick was excited.

Before everyone else came over, Nick and I excused ourselves to take a walk. "I need a break from the crowd, how about you?" I took his hand and we headed down the middle of the street.

"I agree. But it's great to see our parents getting along so well."

"I know. It is nice. How did yesterday go with my dad?"

Nick grinned. "It was fine. A little awkward at first, but ok. We talked about Mustangs before the serious stuff. I think he was as nervous as I was."

I nodded. We walked down the street in companionable silence. This evening ought to be fun with our friends and parents. I was looking forward to it.

When we got back to the house my dad called to Nick, "Hey, you think we guys could go for a spin?"

Nick grinned. "I know just the place. Come on Dad," Nick grabbed his keys and the three of them left for who knows where.

The three of us ladies sliced tomatoes, chopped onions and tore lettuce for the burgers. We discussed wedding details like the food and cake. Nick's mom looked very happy. "You know, Natalie, you're doing us a favor." She was shredding lettuce on a platter.

"Oh?"

"You know how stubborn Nick can be." She stopped shredding and looked at me.

"Yeah, I know." I grinned. "Guess I have to keep rocky road ice cream in the freezer, huh?"

She smiled. "Definitely that and a whole lot more. He doesn't like crowds, so I'm surprised he didn't mention eloping."

"I know. That's why we're going with short and simple. But he's never seemed like it would bother him. He's always assumed we would have a normal wedding."

"I'm glad. I don't want you to be deprived. He's our only child now, and though we spoiled him some, we were hoping he would find the right person to round him out. You two seem a perfect fit for each other." She wiped her hands on a dishtowel and gave me a hug.

"Thanks. I really do love him and he's been so sweet about everything."

Later that evening there was much laughter and commotion as we celebrated our engagement, made wedding plans and got to know one another better.

****

The rest of the summer flew by. I had my book to finish and wedding plans filled my free time. Nick started going through his household goods at his place and bringing some of it to my house. We tasted cake, ordered invitations, and met with Mrs. White a couple times. She was going to be our wedding coordinator.

Nick had to go back to work after a long break. School started right after Labor Day, but teachers had to go back a week before to get their classrooms set up. I helped him arrange the desks the way he wanted them (in six neat rows of six); hung up posters listing the parts of speech, how to outline and one with a list of the classics. It was fun imagining him up front, with the class full. It was no wonder why he was popular with the young girls in his classes. He said he tried not to let it get to his head. I swatted him on the arm after that comment.

I spent most of September to finish my book so I would have time for rewrites before the wedding. My mom flew down again and she and I went to register at Target and Kohl's. Between the stuff Nick and I both had, we mostly needed matching stuff. He had a nice stereo and television but I had better furniture since I was an antique buff. Nick and I went hunting one weekend for more living room furniture so we could have guests sit somewhere other than the floor. We found a set of wing chairs and two end tables made of oak.

Nick and I flew to my parent's house for Thanksgiving and wrapped up more of the wedding details. We hoped the weather would cooperate. While we were home, neighbors and family friends gave me a personal shower. It was a lot of fun and I received some nice things that Nick was sure to enjoy as well. I sent those thank you notes right after getting back home.

The church was giving Nick and me a couple's shower the last weekend of November. It was fun setting new things in place at my house. I didn't want to use any new sheets or towels until after Nick moved in. I did wash everything though and put it away in the proper place.

****

The day of our wedding on December 19th was cloudy and cold. But it didn't matter to me. I was ready for my wedding day and to walk down the aisle on my daddy's arm and meet my husband at the other end. My brother was an usher and he brought his girlfriend, who seemed nice.

Mrs. White and Mrs. John and Ellie, had all been a big help. Ellie was between jobs and had severance pay, so came to help me for a week before the wedding. We ordered much of our wedding paraphernalia locally as the economy hadn't been all that great. The cake, invitations, flowers and decorations all came from local businesses on Main Street. And of course the church was in town, too.

The church choir and orchestra were part of the ceremony as well. Most of the church attended, having known Nick for years. Several of his teacher friends were there and a few of his students, sworn to secrecy. Ellie was my maid of honor, and Luke was one of our groomsmen. He brought a girl, who he met in St. Charles. I was happy for him.

It was too cold to throw rice or birdseed outside, so we skipped that. We took off for the limo, waving goodbye to all our family and friends. It had been a perfect day.

****

Nick and I had a wonderful time on our honeymoon in Hawaii. We enjoyed fresh pineapple and mangoes and each other's company. The best part was we didn't have to say goodbye at the end of the day. The warm sunshine, trees, flowers, and luscious landscape were beautiful. It was back to reality though when we landed back at Lambert International Airport in St. Louis amidst swirling snow. We retrieved our baggage and headed across the river.

Mrs. John had taken care of the house and Felix for us. I hoped he'd been a good boy. It looked like snow had fallen while we were gone. Our porch and sidewalk were already cleared when we pulled up. The gravel drive needed no shoveling.

"Well, dear, welcome home. Let me carry you through the door."

"Nick!"

"Come on, now, Nat. A guy's gotta do what a guy's gotta do."

He leaned over and swiped a hand under my knees and away we went up the sidewalk. He'd already unlocked the door and taken one load of bags in.

I held onto his neck for dear life. He kissed me before putting me down. "Home, sweet, home."

Felix was sleeping on the sofa. "Hey, there, buddy. How are you?" I scooped him up and gave him a squeeze. He started purring. "I missed you, little guy. I hope you were good for Mrs. John." I let him go and took two bags upstairs. Felix tried to trip me on the stairs. "Well, I can see things haven't changed much," I laughed.

Nick made a fire after we finished unpacking. We read through the mail, taking turns reading wedding cards. "Here's a card from Indiana, do you know anybody there?"

"Not that I know of. Who's it from?"

He handed me the envelope. I opened it and a folded picture dropped out of a card. I unfolded the picture and saw a drawing of flowers and a sun. It had a message in the bottom right corner, "From Emily." I dropped the picture and grabbed the card. Tears ran down my cheeks as I read the short inscription. "Natalie, at first I didn't want Emily to know you wrote to her. But then, I thought that wasn't fair to either of you. My husband and I discussed it and though we feel she's young yet, she's very sensitive and intelligent. I've sent you Emily's kindergarten photo and a picture she drew recently. Thank you for letting us hear from you. Emily loves to eat Mexican and Chinese. She has a dog named Puddles and loves to read. We will save your letter and give it to Emily in a few years when she can decide how or when to meet you."

Nick wiped my cheeks and took the card, reading it. He set it on the coffee table and sat next to me on the sofa. He pulled me over to his shoulder. We sat there for a long time, neither one speaking.

The final burden was lifted from me and I felt so at peace with my life, God, and my new husband. I also knew that life wasn't always easy but now God was with me. One of the few Bible verses I knew so far from the book of Jeremiah had become a fast favorite: "For I know the plans I have for you, declares the Lord, plans to prosper you and not to harm you...." Jeremiah 17:9. (NIV)

I was finally home.

Please visit *michelleconnellwrites.net* for updates about her other books.

Made in the USA
Lexington, KY
07 February 2016